DEAD FLAGS

ANDREW RAYMOND

 HUNTERHILL
BOOKS

ALSO BY ANDREW RAYMOND

1

Washington, D.C. – 7.42am

You didn't rise to FSB Station Chief in Washington, D.C. without having some significant tradecraft. Grigory Vanyev had been given the most prestigious of spy jobs by Moscow for a reason. Like knowing when he had a tail.

He was in his Chrysler 300 saloon, cruising through the leafy suburbs of the district of Georgetown that had come to be his home for the last six years – the many overhanging trees turning autumnal browns, deep pinks and dark, plummy reds. But Vanyev's thoughts were not on the postcard scenes around him. They were on the white SUV behind.

There were many within the Russian intelligence services who believed that the D.C. Station Chief job, operating in the heart of American political power, was an ironically safe position. The Americans knew who Vanyev was, just as the Kremlin knew who the CIA Station Chief was in their own backyard. As had happened with the Cold War nuclear threat, the stakes were so high in D.C. and Moscow that a stalemate was the safest solution for all. The Americans knew that Russia would always have some kind of espionage presence in the capital, and vice versa. What mattered was getting the job done without being impeded. Neither side played games when it came to station chiefs. The risk of provocation was too high. Vanyev wasn't harassed or routinely pulled over by D.C. police, or his car searched, for the same reason the Russian ambassador was left alone.

Which was why Vanyev knew, if he had a tail in D.C., it wasn't the Americans. And if it wasn't the Americans, who was it?

The white SUV had followed Vanyev as he looped the block. The first time could have been accidental. Twice, a coincidence. But the third time removed all doubt.

He called the embassy and explained the situation to the head of the internal security team, Antonov. 'They want me to know,' Vanyev said. 'They're not even trying to hide.'

'Drive normally,' Antonov replied. 'I'll have the Americans get D.C. police on it to pull them over.'

'You don't think it's actually them, do you?'

Antonov said, 'The Americans wouldn't be so foolish. Give me the plate number.'

Vanyev didn't have to check the rear-view mirror to rhyme it off. At fifty-five years old, and decades into his career, such behaviour was part of his natural body rhythms, like breathing, or moving his arms when he walked. Waiting longer than expected for a response from Antonov, Vanyev asked, 'Is something wrong?'

Antonov muttered, 'Stupid Yanks. It *is* them. It's a Homeland Security plate. What the hell are they thinking?'

Vanyev's face tensed. 'Get me the ambassador. Now!'

Moscow, Russia – same time

Eight hours ahead, Russia time, Jack Colby was on foot along Ulitsa Mantulinskaya, heading for the United States embassy near the banks of the Moskva River. The sun was out and it was bitterly cold. Colby left a fleeting trail of mist tumbling over his shoulder as he upped his pace as subtly as he dared.

'I'm telling you,' he explained to his internal security chief, who was ensconced in the embassy, 'the car's passed me three times now.'

After giving him the plate, Colby was given the confirmation he feared most.

'It's a Russian team, Jack,' he was told.

'Impossible,' replied Colby. 'Check it again.'

'I *have*, Jack. It's them.'

In less than a few minutes, Colby had gone from feeling as safe as he did back home in Arizona, to feeling the ornate buildings closing in around him. He became acutely aware of how hard his heart was beating. His palms clammy beneath his gloves. He realised how out of practice he was. That it might be true what the younger agents had been saying about him: he'd gone soft in his old age.

Colby eyed the familiar landmark of the Kudrinskaya Square building, one of several Stalinist skyscrapers that towered over the city – the one closest to the U.S. embassy. He was no more than ten minutes' walk away. For all that it mattered, he might as well have been in Siberia.

Hearing the engine rev behind him, ready to make another pass, Colby wondered if this would be when they took their chance. Were the Russians really going to black bag the CIA Station Chief in Moscow? He couldn't believe they would be so reckless. He also wasn't going to wait around to find out.

As the engine grew louder, Colby veered off the pavement into Presnenskiya Park. It would take them at least a minute to regroup and find him among the labyrinth of walkways and alleys.

Colby gave his location over the phone, not realising how tightly he was gripping it. The phone connection felt like a life-support machine in the circumstances, but any sense of safety it provided was an illusion. Any team reckless enough to be tailing him would have no fear in attempting a daylight grab. In the park, he had at least given himself a fighting chance. On the pavement next to the fast-flowing traffic, he had been a sitting duck.

'Why would they do this?' Colby wondered aloud, trying to make sense of the irrational.' He broke off, hearing murmurs in the background on the phone. 'What's going on?'

Colby's security chief hurried into the embassy security suite. He surveyed the dismal information in front of him. 'Sir… We've got a, eh… D.C. has got word to us about an ongoing situation. The Russians are saying they have a man being tailed there.'

'Is that what this is about?' asked Colby, checking his blind spots, assessing any figures walking his way. 'Tell D.C. to back the hell off. They're going to get me killed.'

'It's not us, Jack! We're not that stupid.'

Then Colby spotted them.

In his position he had four different walkways to choose from. Each had a guy stalking towards him, hands in jacket pockets, and they all had eyes for Colby.

Colby said into the phone, 'I'm in Presnenskiya Park. Send someone, for the love of God. There's a whole damn team here.'

He lowered the phone from his ear. The time for talking was over. Now it was time to run.

Washington, D.C.

Vanyev was through with being polite. The D.C. police were nowhere, and his tail was now right up behind him. As Vanyev stopped at an intersection, the SUV nudged him.

At first, just enough to rock Vanyev's car. Then a little more, a little harder.

As the SUV backed up for a harder shove, Vanyev had no choice. They were coming for him.

There was a steady flow of traffic in front of him, but he floored the gas anyway, swinging out into it. A storm of horns blared as the drivers nearest Vanyev had to take evasive action, putting themselves into harm's way.

'Antonov, this is real! They tried to barge me...' Vanyev exclaimed. His engine revving through gears, he said, 'That's it. I'm heading for the embassy.'

Antonov thought that Vanyev was overreacting, his years in the capital turning the old dog soft. Only Vanyev knew the seriousness of his situation.

He could feel sweat accumulating under his arms. He was too panicked to be aware of his breathing, which was heavy and erratic. What the hell were the Americans playing at, he wondered. The repercussions would have to wait. For now, he needed to get to the only place where he could be truly safe.

But if you can't lose your tail, safe houses are no good. He needed to get to official Russian territory.

Moscow

Colby could feel the U.S. embassy's presence beyond the park walls, so tantalisingly close. Now that he was running as fast as he could, he regretted not putting more hours in on the gym treadmill. He was swift for his age, but he knew he couldn't sustain the speed for long.

He charged past the long line of chess matches taking place on the dozen bespoke concrete blocks that lined the avenue. Only a few old men looked up from their positions, the others too locked into their games with concentration.

When the four men in dark jackets came haring past seconds later, almost everyone took notice. Assuming it was gang-related, no one was going to intervene.

Colby thought about ditching his briefcase. He never walked with any officially classified documents, but he knew that there were still plenty inside that would be valuable to enemies of America. Having run in one direction, he realised that he had lost his bearings on where the park exit was. And now the four men were closing in around him.

Colby's phone line was still open to the embassy, the security chief hearing Colby's negotiations.

They were in a quiet part of the park. There was a large chessboard on the paving slabs, complete with human-size wooden chess pieces, and no one else around.

The men said nothing, slowing to a walking pace. They wanted to get closer, to make sure the job was done right.

Colby backed onto the large chessboard. He told the men in Russian, 'Whatever you want, you're not going to get it.'

One of them emerged as the leader, taking out a Glock pistol.

Colby sensed that it wasn't just for show. He backed up against one of the chess pieces standing on the black and white square, ready for a new game. A pawn. It fell over under Colby's weight.

He showed them his palms in surrender, dropping the phone and his briefcase. 'Don't do anything that can't be—'

He was cut off by the *thwift* of a suppressed bullet piercing his forehead. Then Colby collapsed to the ground as if his knee and hip joints had turned to jelly. The white pawn piece rolled back and forth next to him.

Washington, D.C.

The Russian embassy looked like an old Soviet building dropped into the lush surroundings of Wisconsin Avenue in downtown Georgetown. Morning commuter traffic was heavy – not that it was slowing Vanyev down. He swooped and swerved through any available gap. If there were none, he forced one open. Both front wings of his car were now heavily scraped. He didn't have a choice. Whoever was in the white SUV wasn't messing around.

If Vanyev was being aggressive in his attempt to escape, the men in the SUV were driving with total abandon, crashing into anyone who slowed them down.

Their progress was violent and loud, and got the attention of an idling police car which swiftly set off in pursuit. The siren and lights, and the sight of two speeding cars, prompted commuters ahead to get out of the way. Which wasn't necessarily good for Vanyev. It meant that he could go much faster, spearing through the clearing traffic – but it also meant that his pursuers had a much clearer road ahead. Whoever was driving the SUV was a lot more talented in a high-speed pursuit than Vanyev, whose reflexes and reactions had turned rusty after years behind a desk and attending embassy functions three nights a week.

He had to flick onto the wrong side of the road to continue finding a clear path, but the SUV was all over the back end of the Chrysler, barging and bashing, knocking Vanyev all over the road like a dodgem.

Still on the phone to Antonov at the embassy, Vanyev yelled,

'Get me the hell out of here! I can't hold these guys off much longer...'

He was right.

Vanyev gritted his teeth on the approach to the Wisconsin Avenue and Massachusetts Avenue intersection. Racing past the Washington National Cathedral on his left, Vanyev said a quick prayer, forcing himself to keep his foot on the gas.

It was in God's hands now.

Then God spoke in the form of a black armoured truck coming from Vanyev's left, T-boning the back end of the car. There was a crash of crunching metal as the Chrysler did a complete three-sixty at the centre of the intersection, bringing all the surrounding traffic to a stop.

The SUV pulled up safely behind. The man in the front passenger seat climbed out, holding a Vigilance Rifles M20 submachine gun. The American driver of the armoured truck told the shooter on the radio, 'He's all yours.'

The shooter unloaded a stream of automatic gunfire at Vanyev, who was cowering in his seat, trying to hide.

Vanyev knew that the car had bulletproof glass but had ducked for cover anyway, worried that the glass might have fractured or weakened in the crash. It hadn't. It was holding firm.

The shooter paused, speaking into his shoulder mic, 'Plan B.'

The others got out of the car. Each had their own M20, and unleashed a barrage of bullets at the car. The chassis was pounded with pockmarks; the windows with dull thuds. They couldn't break the car's defences.

Vanyev saw his opportunity and slipped the car into reverse. Still cowering at steering wheel height, he slammed the gas pedal, sending the car ploughing into one of the shooters, pinning him against the front of an abandoned car.

When Vanyev tried to accelerate away, though, the wheels

spun impotently in the air. The impact had lifted the back of the Chrysler up in the air, and its rear-wheel drive was now useless.

While Vanyev was a sitting duck, the leader of the team took advantage of one end of the car being in midair, tossing a grenade under it.

Vanyev prayed again. The explosion rocked the car from side to side, but the blast-resistant underside held.

The impact also broke Vanyev free from the grip of the car behind. His foot still on the floor, the Chrysler's wheels landed on the ground – tyres still spinning – before launching him off down Wisconsin Avenue again.

The shooters hurried back to the SUV, but it was the armoured truck that was in prime position now. Dazed and terrified, Vanyev couldn't navigate the road ahead with any speed as traffic bound for Dupont Circle and Downtown came to a standstill on both sides. The only way through was to mount the pavement, blasting his horn at the terrified pedestrians who scuttled out of the way.

He was now just a few hundred metres from the embassy, the big white box of a building obscured behind the many trees that lined the road.

Vanyev was so busy concentrating on reaching the embassy entrance, he didn't notice the steel tow line draped loosely across the road, tethered to a pickup truck on one side, and a lamppost on the other. As Vanyev accelerated towards it, the operator of the pickup truck reeled the tow line in, pulling it taught, lifting it a wheel's height off the ground.

As the front end of the Chrysler absorbed the full tension of the steel line, Vanyev felt the momentum of the car rock violently from the front to the back.

Vanyev felt the disorientation of being turned upside down as the back end flipped over. The car landed on the roof with a dull thud and, finally, smashed glass.

The pickup detached the line and sped away, ahead of the SUV arriving at the scene.

Russian Embassy security had already been on full alert. Now, recognising their Station Chief's car isolated in the middle of the road, and armed men rushing towards it to finish Vanyev off, the guards didn't hesitate in running towards the fray.

The moment they stepped off embassy grounds, their director shouted in their ears that they couldn't fire. They were no longer officially on Russian soil.

One guard didn't care. He'd take the rap. After all, this was America. There weren't many activities more celebrated than the act of firing a gun. And he had racked up plenty of hours at nearby shooting ranges.

He took out the point man of the group with a single head shot. He didn't stop running as he took aim at the next target.

Down went number two.

The rest of the Russian guards' colleagues joined in. They had permission now that the first shots had been fired. Not helping at this point was moot.

As the rest of the attacking team turned their attentions to the fast-moving Russians – swarming the road with polished tactical awareness, taking cover behind parked cars, sneaking shots whenever they could – the leader concentrated on Vanyev.

Vanyev was upside down, too hurt to move. He could see his beloved embassy building, so close. Its architecture a glimpse of home.

The leader crouched down.

All Vanyev could do was plead. 'Why?'

The leader took aim. 'Why not?' He fired two shots into

Vanyev's head, then called on the others to retreat. There were police sirens everywhere, getting nearer.

On both sides of the armoured truck an attacker pulled on a long canvas sheet that had been covering the livery underneath, now revealed the logo of the D.C. police. Another man ripped off a plastic box on the roof, revealing police lights.

Once they were all inside, the truck took off. Lights flashing, siren wailing.

Bright, loud, and invisible in the chaos.

Moscow

The shooter stepped in quickly to ensure the job was done, firing another two into the head and two in the chest.

When he was satisfied that Colby was dead, he and the others retreated, each going their separate ways. Swapping out hats, turning reversible jackets inside out – fading away.

Colby lay sprawled on the chessboard, surrounded by pawns. His blood seeped out across the squares. Onto white then black, then white again.

MI6 headquarters, London

At the European Division communications desk, alerts were pinging up for major cities all across the map on the video wall.

Moscow. Paris. Rome. Berlin. Amsterdam. Kraków. Athens. Tallinn…

As the full extent of the situation gathered pace, an analyst shouted across the room to a colleague, clutching a phone, 'I've got CIA on the line. The FSB in D.C. were just hit, and their man in Moscow had called in a tail…' The Israelis, the French, and the Germans were all on the phone too. 'It's not just embassies. I've got a Mossad substation in Cairo, and the Saudi General Intelligence in Istanbul have all flagged attacks.' The analyst didn't know how else to say it. 'Someone's hitting every major intelligence agency.'

The junior director in charge stared at the video wall in disbelief. 'Embassies are one thing. But how do they know about all these substations? These are classified locations.'

'Whoever it is, they're on the inside. With us.'

The director told his assistant, 'Get upstairs. Tell them we need to go into lockdown. And check that Thames House are seeing this too. We need to shutter every embassy in London and every MI6 substation. We don't know what this is yet.'

The director told an operator behind, 'Get her.' Reacting to their half a second of hesitation, the director bellowed, 'The Chief! Get her now!'

'What should I tell her, sir?' they replied.

The director surveyed the plethora of red icons still popping up on the map: highlighting each confirmation of an attack. 'Tell her that the entire intelligence community is under attack from the inside.'

2

Grant squirmed in bed as he saw the knife flash towards him. His legs kicked out under the covers, an involuntary reflex from the smell of cigarettes on Martin Haslitt's breath. Grant's body stiffened as he strangled the final breaths from Haslitt's body.

It felt so real, but a part of Grant tried to remind him it was just a dream. The same dream he'd been having for the past week. Replayed in exactly the same way each time, like a chapter of a Blu-ray movie stuck on repeat.

Each night, the scene played out as it had in Édith Lagrange's apartment in Lyon. Rogue MI6 operative Martin Haslitt slashing at Grant with a knife, so hard that it knocked Haslitt off balance. Struggling to regain his footing, Grant pulled his forearm up around Haslitt's neck. Then he squeezed.

He pulled Haslitt backwards, gaining leverage. In desperation, sensing death bearing down upon him, Haslitt kicked at the ground, his heels dragging down Grant's shins. Each kick brought a fresh wave of pain, opening up the wounds ever deeper, but Grant didn't let go. He didn't have a choice. He had already lost a lot of blood in the fight. He was on the verge of passing out. To let go against an operative of Haslitt's quality would have been suicide. Grant kept squeezing until Haslitt went limp.

It was over.

Grant had killed him. His first kill.

Then Grant heard Henry Marlow's voice – taken from his audio diary:

"I walked into that room one man, and left it a totally different one. I knew I would never be the same again."

That was always the point that Grant woke up. The duvet kicked off. For a moment, he flailed around, expecting to feel a dead body next to him. Then he reoriented himself to his surroundings. The wind battering the cottage. After sitting up for a few seconds, Grant got out of bed and went to the kitchen. If it was before three, he would try to get back to sleep again. If it was later, as it was tonight, he stayed up.

By the time the sun rose, Grant was well on his way to completing his morning workout on the beach, performed – regardless of how cold it was – in neoprene wetsuit bottoms and nothing else.

It might have been peak summer, but that didn't mean very much in the Hebrides. The weather that morning had been rough, with rain and wind hammering the Isle of Skye's northern Trotternish peninsula. Rain pounded down on Grant as he swam his two-mile loop, fighting the incoming currents from the Atlantic Ocean. The rain was so hard that each drop splashed up from the surface of the water, dousing him from above and below, filling his gasping mouth with salty sea water each time he pulled his head up for another breath.

Once he was ashore and clear of the water's edge, he dropped to his front to start Navy SEAL burpees. If there was a harder, more draining bodyweight exercise, Grant didn't know of it. A normal burpee required squatting down in a crouch, hands on the ground, then kicking your feet back. From there you transitioned into a push-up, jump back to the starting crouch position, then jump up. A Navy SEAL burpee took it even further by adding in an extra three push-ups between the jumps, as well as extra kicks on each leg.

Grant wouldn't leave the beach until he had performed one hundred of them.

Once they were done, his triceps and pecs burned like he'd knocked out ten sets of a heavy barbell in a gym. Like Navy SEALS, Grant didn't always have access to a gym, but that wasn't going to stop him staying strong. It wasn't so much the physical conditioning – though that would always be valuable in the field. It was about keeping a commitment to himself, that each day he would do something that was painful or unpleasant, that he didn't want to do. The way Grant saw it, his swimming and Navy SEALs routine was callousing his mind. Against the elements. Against life. He knew better than most that life didn't always give you what you wanted, and you had to be prepared for that. To arm yourself against it.

This was Grant's way of preparing. It was also a way of forgetting. About what had happened in Paris. The Congo. And everything else with Henry Marlow.

Half a mile off coast, a small fishing boat was bobbing through the rough water. The small shirtless figure of Grant was just about visible through the smear of rain, knocking out the final reps of his workout. The fishermen chuckled to themselves at the sight. One of them remarked, 'I thought *we* were mad.'

As Grant climbed back up through the towering dunes to reach his cottage, he looked down at his hands which were red raw from the cold and wet. Then he flexed his elbow. He could still feel the pressure of Haslitt's neck pressed into the crook of his forearm. Like an amputee's phantom limb.

By afternoon, the rain had passed, though the wind remained. Almost ever-present on Skye regardless of the season. There were many cemeteries on the island, but Grant was visiting one of the smallest. Where his mother and father were buried. Alasdair and Mairi Grant. The cemetery overlooked Tulm Bay, a sharp wind gusting across the lush buttercup-filled grass.

Grant wondered what his parents would have thought of what he had become. The man he now was: a killer. There was no going back. No erasing it. No escaping it.

The serenity of the moment was broken by the sound of a car approaching. A Ford Focus. A city car.

Grant knew who it was before the driver even got out.

His handler from MI6 headquarters, Leo Winston, juxta-posed against the wild backdrop in his smart suit.

Grant was in a loose black t-shirt, buffeted in the wind, pulled taught against the density of his muscular physique – tall and broad like a rugby player; lean and wide like a swimmer. His hair was short and unfussy. His face several days unshaven.

He took one look at the blue MI6 file Winston was holding and braced himself for what was to come. It was the light blue shade of an Albion file.

Winston showed him a screenshot from a substation CCTV, showing a man fleeing one of the many assassination scenes.

Grant knew the face well.

Congolese arms dealer and all-round psychopath Charles Joseph. Except Charles Joseph was meant to be dead.

Winston explained, 'We've got a problem.'

3

MI6 headquarters, London

Grant had made the journey in Winston's car, a basic Ford Focus from the agency pool with 'dead plates'. If a police camera logged the car for speeding or any other offence, when it came to running the plate through the computer, the officer would be informed that the plate code "GBX6" couldn't be processed. A plane would have been much faster, but Winston always avoided public transport where possible, especially when carrying classified documents. It also gave the pair time to talk. About Olivia Christie reopening Albion, and what would be expected of Grant. But he was more interested in talking about Henry Marlow.

'He lied,' Grant said, the first words out of his mouth for nearly twenty miles. 'In the audio diary Marlow left. He lied about Charles Joseph being dead, then reported to MI6 that his mission to kill him was complete. Whatever this is, it's been coming for a long time.'

Winston said, 'CIA and everyone else have been begging for a shot at him. But we need him as close to us as possible. However Joseph is involved in this, Marlow must know about it.'

Grant turned to him. 'I want a shot at him.'

Winston scoffed. 'Grant, we've had our interrogation team on him around the clock since you brought him in. With respect, if he's not breaking for professionals, he's not breaking anytime soon for you.'

'We need a lead.'

Winston kept his eyes fixed on the road ahead. 'That's what we're going to discuss. Next steps.'

'With who?' asked Grant.

'Alex Simeon. Imogen Swann's replacement. The new director of the Anticorruption and Internal Affairs department.'

'That didn't take long.'

'We couldn't afford to. The longer the position was left empty, the more attention it drew to the fact that the Hannibals were being run by a corrupt director. Treasonous, if you're feeling less generous. The Foreign Office aren't exactly ones for irony, so the entire department's been gutted by Simeon. While we're on the subject, I would strongly advise not to get tangled up with him.'

'He's difficult?' asked Grant.

Winston flashed his eyebrows up. 'In training, he grassed on his own instructor for marking his preliminary exam too leniently. He makes HMRC look like a bunch of Hare Krishnas.'

Before their briefing with Olivia Christie, Winston took Grant to the sixth floor that was home to the Anticorruption and Internal Affairs department. MI6 had two and a half thousand employees placed across six continents, with massive variance in how closely their activities were monitored. That meant that there were many officers, agents, and analysts operating with impunity and out of the watchful gaze of the Hannibals. No one really knew how the name first came about, but the inference was clear to anyone new to the agency: get caught making one mistake, or fail to follow protocol or procedure and they would bite your face off.

When the lift doors opened, Grant was surprised by the drastic changes to the familiar geography of the department. Gone were the open-plan booths and the formerly clear partitions between the director's office and the rest of the department. Now the partitions had been blacked out, including Simeon's window. Now the department was completely hidden from view to anyone behind a solid black wall.

'I like what he's done with the place,' Grant quipped. 'For secrecy, or is he only hiring vampires? Human Resources might have something to say about that.'

The only Hannibal in sight was Simeon's secretary, who leaned forward at her desk. She was an intense-looking young woman brought by Simeon from his previous Hannibal posting in Paris. 'Good morning, Mr Winston,' she said, consulting the day's diary. 'Mr Simeon is about to leave for a meeting.'

'I know,' replied Winston, neglecting to tell her it was his meeting. 'I'm trying to catch him before we go in.' He thought better of telling her that he had brought Grant there in the hope of extinguishing any enmity between him and Simeon before getting in a room with the Chief of MI6. It was an optimistic move.

The secretary pursed her lips, waiting for Grant to introduce himself.

He didn't.

Simeon rushed out of his office holding a large briefcase, the kind that a doctor was more likely to carry. Inside it was a chronologically arranged stack of files and papers that he had prepared the night before. He said curtly, 'Leo,' then he looked Grant up and down. 'And this I assume must be Duncan Grant. I wasn't expecting a welcome party.' He wore a grey roll neck under a grey suit, an outfit style that was known as his signature. He had six other subtle variations of it hanging in a wardrobe at home. His hair was diligently side parted, and he wore clear, thick-framed glasses, behind which were a pair of deeply probing eyes.

Grant was no stranger to strong eye contact, but Simeon had a way of tilting his head as a person spoke to follow the pattern and direction of their gaze – and to ensure the person knew that he was monitoring it closely. It made every conversation with the man tense and claustrophobic. It was also a move that suggested scepticism of whatever he was hearing.

Winston said, 'We were on our way to the briefing. I thought it might be an idea for you and Grant to get acquainted considering…' He trailed off tactfully, purposely.

Simeon didn't beat about the bush taking up the subject. 'Considering my predecessor had her secretary murdered and tried to do the same to Mr Grant here?' He held out his hand.

Grant took it and gripped it. He was pleasantly surprised at Simeon's strength, and gave the barest hint of a smirk.

'Is something amusing?' asked Simeon, confident that he had comfortably matched Grant's grip.

Grant had smirked because he knew from Simeon's hand that he wore gloves when he lifted weights. Something unthinkable to Grant. He knew because Simeon's hand was strong and he had a wide back. Which meant that Simeon did heavy deadlifts in the gym – surely the most brutal free-weight exercise. It fried every major muscle group. But the knurled grips on Olympic bars were especially cruel to the skin on your hands, and Simeon didn't have any calluses. Which meant that he must wear gloves in the gym. It was a minor thing. But to Grant, it told him a lot.

Endeavouring to answer his own question, Simeon said, 'Is it the new décor?'

Grant said, 'It's not the only thing that's changed around here.'

'True.'

Winston weighed in, 'There's not been any indication that anyone other than Imogen Swann was dirty. Even as a precaution, don't you think replacing every single Hannibal agent is a bit overkill?'

That wasn't how Grant would have characterised it. Highly suspect sprang to mind.

Simeon replied, 'I don't need employees. I need acolytes.'

Winston added, 'I hear that you've brought in scanners for checking your agents' vitals. To monitor for signs of illicit activity.'

'If I have my way, they'll be rolled out to every office and desk in the agency. Imagine if the FBI could have checked Robert Hanssen's pulse when he was copying classified documents for the Russians.' Noticing Grant's look of disdain, Simeon asked, 'You disagree?'

Grant replied, 'I think if a guy like Robert Hanssen was wired up to an ECG his heart wouldn't have gone above eighty-five. He was selling secrets within five years of starting at the Bureau. Guys like him that can rationalise their crimes will never give themselves away physiologically. He passed dozens of polygraphs in his time.'

'If I didn't know any better, Duncan, I'd say you weren't a fan of what we're doing.'

'I'm not. I don't like how you and your people are the only

ones working behind blacked-out windows, evading any oversight.'

'Right, because you don't work in the shadows, do you?'

'Your department's accountable only to yourselves. Your predecessor nearly killed my handler here. A man with more guts than any Hannibal I've ever met.'

'You don't think we have guts?'

Winston made a show of checking his watch, then got between the pair of them. 'Okay, we'd better get upstairs…'

Grant stayed meditatively calm as he went on, 'You might have guts. But I don't trust your department. That secrecy that you love so much is what made it possible for Imogen Swann to hide her crimes for so long.'

Simeon said, 'All I want, Grant, is to clean up this agency. Starting with my own department. Maybe Leo can fill you in, but I know more than either of you combined what the cost of corruption within MI6 is. If you don't believe me, you can ask Henry Marlow downstairs. My wife was sent to capture him in Tijuana. Like so many others before her, she never returned. Marlow killed her. I have nothing to hide, Duncan, because everything I ever cared about before has already been taken from me. I go to church every Sunday morning. I drink tea, never coffee. I go to bed by half-past ten every night, and I have literally never found anything in my adult life amusing. This job, this calling of mine, is my life. I'm cleaner than a surgeon's knife, and I won't rest until this entire agency is likewise. You have your mission and I have mine. But I'll tell you this now: for what I want – what I *need* – I will not let you or this ridiculous Albion project get in my way.'

Grant was taken aback at Simeon's intensity. For a moment, he thought that Simeon might actually shed a tear. Whatever he believed in, wherever it came from, Simeon believed it from the ground up, deep inside his bones. As they made their way towards the lifts, Grant retorted, 'Consider the feeling mutual.' He paused. 'Winston tells me you have a lead. What do you know that I don't?'

Simeon adjusted his jacket sleeves prissily as he got into the lift. 'We don't have nearly enough time for all the things that I know and you don't.'

4

As the briefing was going to involve a discussion of Albion operations, it was too sensitive for a standard conference room. Instead, they were using what was commonly referred to as a 'skiff' because of its acronym of SCIF. But also referred to as 'the Tank' on the tenth floor.

A Sensitive Compartmented Information Facility was a secure room that guarded against electronic surveillance, making any sort of audio, visual, or electrical penetration of the room impossible.

For a newcomer like Grant, it looked like someone had left a shipping container inside one of the conference rooms. It had, in fact, been built from scratch inside the room, piece by piece, by List X contractors – those with 'Secret' or above security clearance to work on government contracts that involved, among other things, classified blueprints. Behind the regular doors at the front of the container was a newly constructed steel door with a combination lock and five-spoke entry handle.

The inside of the Tank didn't look like much, but the most

impressive technology within it was hidden in the walls. Paranoia over the interception of electromagnetic waves had gathered pace in recent years within the agency – a method of remotely stealing data. It might have sounded paranoid and outlandish, but the agency's fears weren't completely unfounded. Several embassies had reported data breaches from outside their own buildings in recent years. And when it came to Albion, Olivia Christie, Chief of MI6, wouldn't take any chances. To safeguard against data interception, the Tank utilised NSA-approved TEMPEST standards. Electronic devices leak electromagnetic waves whenever they perform rudimentary tasks like switching bits from ones to zeroes, or move electron beams around to make images on a screen. If an adversary intercepted those signals, they could theoretically stitch together the content of classified information passing through or being stored on a computer. The Tank made such breaches impossible.

Christie was already inside, sitting at a desk at the far end of the SCIF. 'Come in,' she said. 'Make yourselves comfortable. As much as one can in this thing.' She removed her glasses wearily, having spent an uncomfortable amount of time with unpleasant reading in front of her.

Winston's deputy, Miles Archer, stood as the others entered, showing deference to their seniority – not to mention his engrained social awkwardness. He exchanged nods with Grant, both pleased to see each other again, though under regrettably grim circumstances.

Before everyone's backsides had touched their seats, Christie said, 'Twenty-four hours ago, the entire global intelligence community was attacked. Including our man in Berlin, Bob Gower. What are we going to do about it?'

After scrolling through her briefing notes, she flashed up an image of a podgy, middle-aged man exiting an MI6 substation with his hands in his pockets. 'Charles Joseph. Mid-forties, maybe early fifties. No one knows with any certainty. Even nationality is unconfirmed. Possibly Rwandan. Most likely Congolese. He started out in the Congolese military as a child soldier. One of the few to avoid getting strung out on heroin or crack or getting shot before his teens. By twenty-one, he was a general and became infatuated with guns. And money. At the time, weapons were flooding in from everywhere, funded largely by the West, of course. Joseph segued out of the army and into private enter-prise, selling arms all across western and central Africa. I don't know if any of you apart from Duncan have been there lately, but there is a hell of a lot of guns. We can thank Charles Joseph for that. He did business with the West, and for a while he was a friend and ally. Until he decided to go for the biggest payday of all and run for President. Everyone knew what a madman like Joseph in power would mean for the region, so we decided to put a stop to it. That meant sending Henry Marlow – our finest Albion operative – to kill him. And he reported to us that he did. We know now that, for some reason, Marlow didn't go through with it. Instead, it seems to have been the catalyst for some sort of sordid alliance. The moment our most lethal assassin turned against us.'

Seeking clarification, Simeon said, 'During which time, Marlow was still operational as an Albion?'

Grant replied, 'If Joseph was the catalyst, Imogen Swann's Kadir Rashid mission was the nail in the coffin.'

'It should never have been sanctioned,' said Christie. 'Imogen tried to cover it up by having Marlow killed, but he escaped. Then he went dark. Until a month ago.'

'So where has Charles Joseph been all this time?' asked Simeon. 'With Marlow? Plotting all this?'

Grant shook his head. 'Marlow had been hiding out at

Joseph's compound in the Congo, but I didn't see any evidence that Joseph had been there too.'

Winston got to his feet to examine the locations of the assassinations highlighted on the video wall. 'Joseph must be the driving force behind all this. What does he want?'

Christie knew that it wasn't the right answer but said it anyway to see if anyone would counter it. 'To cripple the intelligence network, to soften us up for a bigger attack somewhere down the line.'

Unafraid to think out loud, Grant offered, 'He wants anarchy. To create chaos and disrupt intelligence-gathering.'

'It doesn't add up, though, does it,' said Simeon. 'Taking out fifteen station chiefs from multiple agencies around the world requires vast resources and planning. What's the benefit? It's like risking your life to give your enemies a paper cut.'

Winston remarked, 'I'm sure fifteen families will be heartened to learn that their relatives died of a mere paper cut.'

'You know what I mean…'

Christie cut in. 'What we don't know doesn't matter. What does, is that this is a first strike against the international intelligence community.'

Winston kept examining the world map on the wall. 'What would the next target be?'

There was a long pause as everyone waited for Christie to answer.

She said, 'They've taken out the leaders of the groups and agencies in the shadows. Maybe they'll go after the ones in the light next. Langley. Lubyanka. Us. We need to find Charles Joseph. Before he strikes again.'

'I think I should talk to Marlow,' said Grant, ever suspicious of his formidable adversary.

'We've been over that, Duncan,' Winston reminded him.

'I understand. But Marlow and I have…' He hesitated to use the phrase.

Simeon didn't. 'A special bond?'

'Call it what you will,' said Grant, 'but I'm the only person he's talked to at all so far.'

Christie said, 'I'm open to it, but not until we've drafted something more concrete. What about these other operatives helping Joseph? He didn't do all this on his own.'

Miles had been up most of the night collating intel on the suspects' identities. And he didn't bring good news. 'There isn't a lot to go on so far. Most of the attacks were snipers, masked gangs ambushing in traffic, car bombs…The few suspects that didn't get away were shot at the scene. It's chaos across the board, frankly, and it's going to take some time to figure out what agency has who. If any. What we do know is a lot of this gang must have had access to restricted areas in embassies or substations ahead of time, or found out where targets were going to be at certain times of day. We believe that's how they found the FSB chief in Washington, and the CIA's chief in Moscow.'

'How big a crew does Joseph have in his pocket?' asked Christie. Before the words had left her mouth, she knew from Miles's expression that the answer was what she feared most. 'We don't know,' she said.

'We don't,' he confirmed. 'Estimates so far are anywhere from fifty to one hundred.'

'The question is why those fifteen station chiefs?' said Winston.

Simeon said, 'They hit the FSB in Washington and CIA in Moscow, Leo. They obviously wanted the big fish.'

'Sure, they got some. But I checked the itineraries of our most senior station chiefs. There were far easier targets elsewhere. Our station chief in Madrid was on the golf course. Nicholas

Warrington in Paris was shoe shopping.' Winston stabbed a finger on his briefing notes, the first page of which showed the faces of the victims. 'No, they wanted these fifteen in particular.'

For the first time, Christie looked noticeably anxious.

It was a brief moment, but Winston knew her better than anyone else at the table. He saw the way she kept her eyes on her notes that she knew something more.

Christie said, 'There were vulnerabilities in their detail, and they all paid the price. It was about sending a message.'

'What's the message?' asked Winston.

'That there's no one they can't get to.'

Grant suggested, 'We could do with a list of anyone else in the agency who's currently under disciplinary suspension or pending investigation. Anyone that could be a candidate for involvement in future attacks.'

Simeon said dismissively, 'Already being assembled.' He turned to Christie. 'And forgive me, ma'am, but we have a lot of people under investigation and no spare bodies to watch them around the clock or monitor every phone call or email they make. Especially people that we have trained – very well – in how to cover their tracks. They've already softened us up. The next attack is not a case of if. It's when.' Feeling the wind in his sails now, Simeon kept on. 'I'd like to get it on record–'

Christie gestured at the cramped space they were sitting in. 'There's no stenographer in here, Alex. Speak your mind.'

He took a beat, knowing that he was about to make enemies of most of the room – including Christie herself. 'The Albion programme is a remnant of a bygone age. It could arguably be the reason we're in this mess to begin with. Henry Marlow? He was a ticking time bomb, and we armed him and sent him out into the world. I say this with all due respect to Duncan, and to Leo…'

Grant spoke over him, 'You confer respect not through tone but by content, Director.'

Simeon carried on as if Grant had said nothing. 'I think this should be an Anticorruption operation...' – he raised his voice to be heard over Grant and Winston's barracking – '...led by me out of my office. It's the only way to be sure. All my guys are clean.'

'How do you know?' asked Winston.

Simeon pursed his lips.

Winston said, 'Should I repeat the question?'

'My guys are clean,' said Simeon. 'The Albion programme, on the other hand...'

Grant couldn't help but wade in. 'Yeah, and if my grandmother had wheels she would have been a bike. We're not in this mess because of Albion. We're in this mess because Albion was mishandled by Imogen Swann – *your old boss* – as she mishandled Henry Marlow. Hannibal's over*sight* amounts to over*reach*. It's too much power for one department to act unilaterally and in secret.'

'Oh yes, you'd rather have that power yourself, Grant, with a gun and legal sanction to commit murder.'

Redirecting to Christie, Winston said, 'Ma'am, if ever we needed Albion, this is it. With one man, we cut down any possibility of interference in the investigation. Why would we risk bringing in the Hannibals?'

Christie leaned forward and clasped her hands together. 'Alex. Tell them.'

Simeon opened up his briefcase and took out a file with a colour-coded tab. 'As part of my departmental clean-up, I went through Imogen Swann's hard drives personally. Line by line. Task by task.' He slid a copy of the code he'd found towards Grant and Winston.

'This is a transmission from a black flag sent to Imogen

Swann's computer six months ago. A transmission that went unanswered.'

'A black flag?' asked Grant.

Winston told him, 'Black flags are assigned to agents' personnel files for when they go on deep cover. Everything about them is erased. Tech support buries any online presence of theirs – you'd have to go through thousands of pages of search results before you found anything on them. Not to mention birth certificates, tax records, banking details. Entire lives disappear. The only person who can get them in or out is their handler.'

'What if the handler dies?'

Simeon fielded that one. 'We have automation set up through our department. If anything ever happens to a handler, their file comes over to us and we bring the agent in. The transmission you're looking at came into Imogen's "Eyes Only" drive. STRAP Two clearance required to open it.'

'I don't understand,' said Grant, scanning the page, 'this is just numbers and coordinates.'

Simeon said, 'The coordinates of every embassy and substation that was hit yesterday.' He paused to let it sink in.

Winston asked, 'You're saying one of our agents knew about this attack six months ago?'

'And Imogen Swann buried it, yes.'

'That doesn't make sense,' said Grant. 'Swann wanted Marlow dead. She wasn't working with him. Why would she hide information that would help locate him?'

Christie said, 'Right now, we have no idea.'

'Who's the black flag?' asked Winston.

'We don't know.'

'Haven't they tried to come in?'

'Where to? Here? An embassy? Their entire life was erased.

They don't exist, Leo. That agent's been out in the cold for at least as long as that transmission. Its location is all we have.'

'From six months ago,' Winston emphasised.

'It's all we have,' said Christie. 'Grant, I'm sending you and a Hannibal team there. Alex is the only person who can verify this agent's identity, if they're still there, or if they're even still alive. Whoever they are, they knew this attack was coming. If they knew about that, they might know what's coming next. We need to find them.'

Playing devil's advocate, Winston said, 'Or it could be a trap. If they're not on the inside with Marlow or Joseph, how did they know about the attacks?'

Christie said, 'We don't have time to waste waiting for Marlow to speak. The interrogators can do that. There's only one way of finding out if this source is a friendly or not, and that's boots on the ground. Grant, you'll lead them.'

Grant looked at the sent-transmission coordinates, baffled. 'Where is this?'

Simeon told him, 'It might be summer, but I hope you brought some warm clothes with you.'

5

The archipelago of Svalbard lies halfway between Norway and the North Pole. It had been used as a base by whalers and miners, until the League of Nations signed sovereignty of the island to Norway in 1920 when it was first populated. A stipulation of the treaty was that Svalbard would be a visa-free zone, meaning anyone was free to live and work there. For a long time, only some hardy Norwegians and Russians took the trouble to sail there. Now, many more nationalities had set up home as word of its existence spread across the internet. It attracted lost, lonely types. Off-gridders. People seeking isolation. Svalbard was the place you go when you don't belong elsewhere. In short: it was Duncan Grant's kind of place.

Because of its northerly latitude, the island was bathed in – or blasted by, depending on your perspective – constant daylight for four months of the year. For four other months, it was almost constantly dark. The sun never rising above the horizon, which meant people rarely left their homes. There weren't many places in the world where it wouldn't raise eyebrows to not leave your house for four months of a year. Making it an ideal spot for someone looking to lay low.

Like a drifter. Or a disavowed deep-cover intelligence officer.

Svalbard was mostly mountainous, covered in snow and ice year-round. Scattered houses dotted the landscape roughly following the only road, which snaked through the tundra. Taking in the intimidating sight of sweeping glaciers from the comfort of his aeroplane seat, Grant wondered what had to happen in someone's life to seek out such a place. It was a place where you could forget and be forgotten.

The plane from Oslo landed at close to midnight, the sun still comfortably above the horizon. Its light weak, pale, and thin. The airport was little more than a single runway, a tower, and a hangar. Upgrading the airport to international standards was too costly for the Norwegian government to approve, so only flights from Norway could legally land there, keeping the operation on the ground small and manageable, even at peak season as it was currently.

Winston and Simeon were holed up in the plush and warm Hotel Continental back in Oslo, eagerly awaiting the findings of the four-man group. Grant and the three Hannibals accompanying him fitted in with the other tourists onboard the commercial flight. Given the extreme climate, everyone was dressed in similarly heavy-duty winter gear, rushing to zip up 800-fill down insulated jackets, and get on woolly hats and gloves before exiting the plane. They were clothes more commonly found on Himalayan climbing expeditions.

The men's cover was as a geological surveying group, which allowed them to smuggle in their surveillance and tracking technologies in the reinforced luggage favoured by Arctic researchers and climate scientists. Weapons were arranged through the agency's unofficial Russian connections. The Russians were treated by the Norwegians as co-founders of the island, and were allowed to run air and shipping traffic as they saw fit. Their kit and ammunition were already waiting for them in a white Range Rover parked at the airport.

Grant sat in the back seat, surrounded by Simeon's best field operatives.

In the front seat, Simeon's point man, Murphy, monitored a tracker showing their proximity (or lack thereof) to the computer that had sent the black flag transmission.

'Looks like it's coming from Longyearbyen,' said Murphy.

Grant asked, 'What are the chances of anyone being there?' He already had a firm opinion on the matter. He just thought it would be interesting to know what the others were thinking on the matter.

'Zero,' said Barnes, Murphy's deputy.

Cunningham, the fourth man and driver, concurred.

Murphy said, 'If Swann really left them in the wind, Svalbard is as good a place as any to hide out. New faces can go unnoticed in a place like this.' Murphy eyed Grant in the rearview mirror. 'What do you think, Albion?'

Grant pushed his lips out with a nod. 'Two and a half thousand people, fifty different nationalities. No visas, no questions asked. You don't want to be outdoors for more than an hour. Nowhere else to go. Probably long since out of resources. Yeah, they're still here.'

Murphy said, 'The sound carries out here, so we need to go in quiet. We better hope they're in Longyearbyen where the housing is densely packed, otherwise they'll see and hear us from a mile away. If they have time for quick prep, that means possible resistance and interference.'

Interference. The term amused Grant. It came about because thick-necked field operatives like Barnes and Cunningham felt like idiots saying 'booby-trap'.

Grant emphasised, 'If Charles Joseph himself is sitting in there strapped to a suicide belt, I want us to have anticipated it.'

Murphy's deputy exchanged a withering look with his colleague, unseen by Grant. The message was clear: *pipe down, rookie. We've got this.*

It might have been Grant's operation, but the Hannibals would be running the show out there.

Murphy was tracking a unique electromagnetic signal from the black flag agent's phone or laptop – whatever they had used to send the transmission six months ago. The pulse was weak, gradually closing in on an ever-shrinking radius. When they reached the tiny 'capital' of Longyearbyen – the northernmost settlement in the world with a population over 1000 – it appeared that the signal might still be located somewhere within the confines of the tiny town. It had a spectral quality to it. A ghost town, with no one in sight. As if everyone had been frozen to death in their beds. There was no other traffic. Just a few polar bears prowling the outskirts of the town.

'Shit,' Murphy said, eyes on the scanner. 'Keep going,' he told Cunningham. 'It looks like they're out by the old mining settlement.'

The men in the back conducted final checks of their weapons, then eyed the approach to a solitary log house built at the base of a hillside. High above were the decaying remnants of the old Russian mining operation that had been abandoned decades earlier. Flanking the location was impossible without first scaling a treacherously steep hill. Only one way in, and one way out.

There were no lights on inside, and no vehicles parked outside. But a steady stream of smoke spewed from the chimney.

'We'll do a sweep first,' said Grant, as the car pulled up off the main road.

They swapped out their commercially available jackets for combat jackets finished in snow camouflage.

All four men had their Sig P320 XCompact pistols out as they quickly approached the building on foot. They spread out, making themselves harder targets from a distance.

There was silence all around.

When they reached the house, they swept the outer perimeter, looking for signs of life, using only hand signals to communicate with each other. The P320 had an oversized trigger guard, making it a more comfortable hold while wearing gloves, which was essential where they were: the hillside was in shadow, dropping the temperature below freezing. An almost-flat trigger freed up extra room compared to a regular curved trigger, giving the men total freedom of movement of their trigger fingers.

When they reconvened at the front of the house, staying out of eyelines from the windows, they agreed that there were no obvious signs of life inside.

Grant flicked his head in the front door's direction. He made a fist, then pumped it straight up and down to signal a breach. They were going in.

6

Grant gestured that he wanted to take the front with Murphy, leaving Barnes at the back, and Cunningham outside to surveil the perimeter for anyone approaching. But Murphy overruled him. He wanted as much back-up inside as possible. It was a decision based on making his men feel safer, rather than what was operationally sound.

Grant couldn't argue with him on the issue. They had to remain as close to silent as possible. In any case, Grant was outnumbered by Hannibals who were never going to contradict Murphy's orders.

So when Grant and Murphy entered silently through the unlocked front door, and the other two headed for the back, no one saw a figure cloaked in M05 snow camouflage rising slightly in their front-lying position, taking aim at the house with her rifle that was covered in McNett snow-camo wrap, making it almost totally white. The shooter pulled back the hood of her Ghillie suit, ready to step out of it to make a speedy approach to the house. Then she stopped.

Two Volvo XC90 off-roaders raced along the main road towards the long driveway, both coming from opposite sides, both cars at capacity.

The shooter pulled her hood back down over her head, becoming part of the landscape again.

A team of five emerged from behind the abandoned mining buildings at the top of the hill, dressed head to toe in snow camo, rifles poised.

Grant and Murphy, already inside, froze in the empty hallway at the sound of the two cars. Grant made a brisk rotation of his hand in mid-air, to which Murphy agreed. Sweep the house first to make sure it was clear. They soon met Barnes and Cunningham in the sparsely furnished living room, the remains of a fire burning out.

'They didn't leave long ago,' said Barnes.

Grant crouched down, registering the figures working their way down the hillside through deep snow. 'That's the least of our worries. We've got incoming at the back.' He took cover beside the living room window, ready for the imminent ambush, but Murphy and the others were busy rummaging through a pile of hard drives and an encrypted laptop left on the floor beside a mug of cold tea. 'What are you doing?' Grant whispered aggressively.

Barnes and Cunningham kept on checking the drives while Murphy joined Grant on the opposite side of the window.

'The mission,' Murphy replied.

Grant said, 'The mission is the man. Not data.'

'No, that's *your* mission.'

Grant shook his head. 'You can save all the data you want, but if we don't get cover at the back of this house, *none* of us are getting out of here alive.'

'We're not saving it,' Murphy snapped, 'we're deleting it.'

Grant knocked the back of his head against the wall and shut his eyes for a second, trying to think of a plan. He sneaked a look out the window and his heart sank a little more.

Whoever they were outside, they were well drilled. They had exited the vehicles and were moving in fast in an organised formation. Definitely professionals.

The man behind the point man squeezed his arm to give the all-clear to press forward. Their hand signals were sharp and direct. No one said a thing. Moving almost silently through the snow.

Two shooters at the back fired several rounds at the house, shattering the living room window.

Barnes and Cunningham covered their heads, fearing an all-out assault had begun. Grant waved them towards the wall. 'It's covering fire,' he whispered as the air turned silent once again. 'They'll breach the front next time. Get out of there!'

Cunningham looked at the laptop screen helplessly as the timer for file deletion ticked down too slowly. The hard drives were large, over two terabytes each, and needed plugged in at the wall. He couldn't move. When he tried to cut off the process early, Murphy gestured for him to stay put.

'No. Confirm when it's complete.'

At the back of the house, the window of the door was broken with a single jab of a rifle butt.

Grant could feel the house surrounded. It was only a matter of time now. He saw that the front door was about to be breached, and directed Barnes to expect it.

The moment the front door crashed open, Barnes was in position. He took the first man down with two chest shots, but the next man followed in so quickly he couldn't readjust in time. A single shot pierced Barnes's forehead. His body went limp, his head dropping.

Cunningham might have intervened if the completion of the hard drive erasing hadn't distracted him.

Seeing the next tragedy about to unfold, Grant ducked under the window, moving to a spot where he could return fire and protect Cunningham. He let off three shots in quick succession, taking out a shooter who had Cunningham otherwise locked in.

Murphy speed-crawled to Barnes while shots rang out from all angles, so rapid and so loud it was impossible to tell where they were coming from. It was automatic fire this time. They had started with stealth. Now they were opting for brute force. They had the bodies, and they certainly had the ammunition.

Murphy let go of Barnes after checking for a pulse. He was gone. Murphy lunged forward, shutting the living room door that led to the kitchen at the rear.

Grant broke off the remaining glass around the edges of the living room window to fire back. He knew they had to take out the enemy before they could get inside and press home their numerical advantage.

The men at the rear filed in, the living room now surrounded.

Someone in the kitchen stepped on a creaking floorboard.

Instinctively, Grant fired towards the closed kitchen door at chest height, then heard the thud of a body hitting the floor.

Outside at the front, more shots rang out. But farther back than the others. A deeper sound. More bass.

Rifle shots.

The men from the cars were no longer rushing in. They were turning toward an unseen sniper hiding in the snow, who had picked off three of their guys with head shots before they even knew what was happening.

Grant and Murphy took turns to fire out of the living room window while the men had their backs turned. The attackers were fish in a barrel now.

Grant reloaded while Murphy fired, and vice versa. Between heavy breaths, Grant told him, 'Someone's helping.'

But it wasn't much good to Cunningham, who was fending off the rear on his own. 'A little help here!' he called out, returning fire through the kitchen door that was shattering from a hail of high-calibre bullets piercing it relentlessly.

Grant hurried over to force them back with defensive fire, but by the time he got there he was out of bullets. There was no time to reload. As soon as he looked up, he saw a Beretta pistol coming out from behind the door frame. Grant knew from his "Kill School" training that if he tried to disarm the shooter by grabbing the pistol near the rear at the hammer, that was where the shooter had the most leverage, the most strength. But grabbing the pistol at the end of the barrel? That was simple biomechanics. No matter how tight the shooter's grip, it couldn't trump Grant's leverage.

It happened almost as soon as Grant saw the gun. He grabbed the barrel with both hands and forced it straight down. The gun came tumbling out of the shooter's hands and dropped to the floor. Still with no time to reload, now it was about hand-to-hand combat. Grant pulled a metallic keychain off his belt, nothing more than a short arrow shape. But when used optimally, it could inflict stunning amounts of pain and help to overwhelm an enemy. Even lethally, if used correctly.

Grant's hours and hours of rehearsing the moves in the Vauxhall Cross gym paid off. His muscle memory was fluid, his limbs ready, his mind nimble, ready to respond. He wielded the keychain and plunged the pointed end directly into the outer join of the attacker's elbow. Feeling like his arm was breaking, the attacker threw himself forward in response to the blinding pain, trying to break free. Exactly as Grant had intended. He now had total control of his opponent, who had involuntarily offered his back to Grant. He plunged the arrow into the man's ear, sending him straight to the ground. He felt something pop inside his head. It was his left ear drum.

He quivered and shook on the ground for several seconds, then went limp.

Grant retracted the keychain, now covered in blood, and reloaded his weapon. He waved frantically at Cunningham. 'Push it over!' he shouted.

Cunningham, who had been taking cover behind the couch to duck constant gunfire, followed Grant's call. He flipped the couch the moment the gunshots relented, turning it up longways to block off the door, forcing the men at the rear to divert around the front outside.

They skirted the exterior wall, slowing when they saw the dead bodies of their colleagues littering the driveway. One shooter peeked out from around the corner of the wall, trying to get some idea of what they were dealing with.

That tiny glimpse from two hundred yards away was all the sniper needed.

Blood geysered out of the back of the man's head, prompting a hasty retreat by his partner to the back of the house. There, he rushed straight into Grant who took him down with a head- then a chest shot. Once he was on the ground, Grant fired twice more into his chest to make sure.

Murphy and Cunningham, not wanting to take their chances with the sniper out front, followed Grant out the back.

Murphy hovered near the area that the sniper could reach. Assessing the blood spatter, Grant stopped him from going any further.

He said, 'We can't assume they're on our side. Not yet.'

The sniper stood up fully from her position, stepping out of her thick Ghillie suit, still in snow camo, but now in a much lighter anorak that allowed greater mobility.

All the attackers down, she left her suit and rifle on the ground and took out her sidearm. 'Identify yourselves,' she shouted, marching towards the house, taking aim and ready to fire at anyone that moved or failed to follow her instructions.

Grant called out, 'MI6! Albion.'

The sniper kept marching forward. She was English. Late thirties. 'Albion was closed years ago,' she called back.

'It's reopened. My name's Grant. I'm with a Hannibal extraction team. We're here to take you in.'

'Bullshit,' she replied, taking cover behind one of the Volvos. 'You're here to finish me off.'

'Imogen Swann's dead. She buried your transmission. We only just found out. You were right about the station chiefs. The fifteen.'

There was silence on the other side of the house.

Murphy made a move, readying his pistol. 'Sod this…'

Grant swiped his arm away before Murphy could pull the trigger. 'The hell are you doing?' he whispered. 'We're here to get information.'

The sniper called out, 'Okay. I'm coming out.'

Grant edged along the wall, keeping low. When he saw the sniper standing in open ground, holding out her sidearm to demonstrate compliance, he made a show of doing the same. 'We're here to take you in. You're safe now.'

She tossed her gun on the ground and exhaled heavily as she leaned on her knees, like it was a breath she'd been holding in for years.

Only now that Grant could see her eyes, and the ravaged look on her face, did he feel sure that the attack was over.

She stood against the bonnet of the Volvo, letting it take

her weight as she peeled off her white balaclava, revealing matted, tied-up red hair. She closed her eyes and looked up, clouds moving across overhead, draining light from the night sky.

While Grant holstered his weapon, Murphy sent Cunningham back in to retrieve the hard drives in the living room.

Grant asked her, 'Who are you?'

Opening her eyes, she said, 'My name's Gretchen. I'm a deep-cover Hannibal.'

Murphy steamed in without any empathy for what she might have gone through in the past six months. 'We need to get you out of here. We can debrief in the car–'

Grant held him back. 'The chief isn't here, Murphy. You can impress her with your report.'

He stabbed a finger in the direction of the house. 'Hey, I've got a dead agent in there because of her and I want to know what he died for, Grant, so back the hell up!'

Reasserting his position, dominating Murphy's personal space, Grant told him, 'What he died for? He died for a damn hard drive, that's what. You compromised this mission by prioritising data over human life. I look forward to hearing your boss explain that one away to C.'

Murphy had nothing to say to that.

Grant concluded, 'We get these bodies inside until mop-up gets here. Then we clear out to Oslo as planned. Got it?'

Gretchen started shaking her head. It hadn't been a breath of relief from her before. It was anger. She yelled, 'You stupid bloody…' She wheeled around, gesticulating to the sky. 'I was out! I was bloody *out*! I was safe. You idiots are on this island less than an hour, and a whole platoon of assassins shows up at my door.'

'How do you know how long we've been here?' asked Murphy.

'What I know that you don't, shit Rambo, could just about cover Greenland. You think it's a coincidence those guys were suited up, huh?'

'Like you?' asked Grant. 'Those guys were in position long before we got here.'

Gretchen ploughed on, 'First you leave me out in the cold, then when I find somewhere safe you burn me.'

'Excuse us for saving your life,' said Murphy.

'I think you'll find it was the other way around,' she countered.

'Enough,' Grant said. 'Murphy, get Cunningham out here to help us get these bodies in. Those gunshots will have been heard a mile away.'

'It's the middle of the night,' said Gretchen. 'No one's coming.'

Grant started dragging a body towards the front door of the house. 'Yeah, because when these guys have failed to call in thirty minutes from now, no one's going to send back-up.'

Realising he was right, Murphy and Gretchen set to work.

Grant stared at the anonymous face of the dead body he was dragging. His gloves stained with the man's blood. Once he laid him down in the hallway, Grant took off his gloves to inspect his hands, turning them over. Removing the gloves took with them any trace of the killing he'd had to carry out to survive. His hands were clean. Not a hint of a tremble. It unsettled him. He'd put down five guys. One of them up close and personal. He wasn't sure what he should have been feeling. Calm and composed was a good sign for being an Albion. What it meant for Duncan Grant, though, was still unclear to him.

7

Grant, Gretchen, Murphy, and Cunningham made it back to Oslo, Norway, by the next morning. MI6 had sent in a mop-up team to contain the scene around Gretchen's former house as soon as possible, allowing the four survivors to leave for a debriefing with Leo Winston and Alex Simeon. Both of whom had plenty of questions they wanted answered.

So, too, did Murphy, now that they were out of public spaces. In the people carrier taking them from Oslo Airport to the agency safe house, Murphy eyed Gretchen with disdain as she slept on the seats behind.

He shook his head. 'I'm glad she's feeling so relaxed about what went down out there. I want to know how she knew we were coming.'

Grant said, 'Let her sleep.'

'She was already hiding in the snow when we arrived, Grant.'

Grant had his own questions, but he wasn't in the mood to pick a fight. Whatever Simeon had told Murphy about the importance of deleting Gretchen's hard drives, Grant doubted it would have been the truth. He was better off saving his energy for Simeon. 'I get it,' Grant said. 'Save it for the debrief. I know I am.'

Murphy turned away from her. 'I don't know how she can sleep.'

Grant had been wondering the same thing. Only an operative that had been in some pretty hairy situations could sleep so easily and so soon after an intense gunfight.

Gretchen's eyes rolled and flickered in a restless REM sleep.

Grant wondered what sort of things she was seeing. He guessed, though, that it was considerably more than what he had in his career so far.

They pulled up on the corner of an intersection where trams were crossing in Oslo's upmarket, traditional district of Torshov. The summer air was gently cool, a world away from the freezing temperatures of Svalbard.

The safe house was a cavernous old apartment on the third floor of a block owned entirely – several steps down the line – by a shell company financed through an MI6 slush fund. It was always staffed but rarely used as a base for actual operations. When the call came through from Vauxhall Cross before dawn to the night watchman that four operatives, two directors, and the Chief would be coming in later that morning, he thought he was being pranked.

All the windows were blacked-out, impervious to natural light, which kept the apartment always on the cold side. Even in summer. Budget cuts had meant that the heating was kept off except for wintertime, when it was so cold that the pipes would crack otherwise.

Simeon and Winston were ready in the large stately study

that was lit by a couple of lamps on a console. Simeon paced by the window, holding his hand out to a pinprick of sunlight that came in through a tiny scratch in the blackout paint. It was no threat to the integrity of the room, but its presence irritated him.

Winston perched on the armrest of a leather couch, arms folded. He stood up when Gretchen entered, offering her the couch.

Simeon eyeballed her as he made for the hall to talk to Murphy.

'How are you holding up?' asked Winston.

Gretchen looked up at him. 'You're the first person to ask.'

Grant followed Simeon into the hall. When he and Murphy saw Grant approaching, they broke up their little huddle. Murphy stepped in front of his director to absorb the brunt of Grant's wrath.

'What the hell was that?' Grant seethed.

Simeon pushed Murphy out of the way, not wanting to appear emasculated. 'You've got your job to do, Grant, and I've got mine.'

'Not when your job jeopardises mine.'

'The mission was always about information.'

Grant's tone quickly escalated from testy to volcanic. 'That was a deep-cover agent out there who needed us, and she ended up saving us because *your* crew was too busy trying to delete hard drives! Your point man was all for shooting her.'

Simeon met Grant's anger head on, but restrained his volume. He pointed towards the study. 'Right now, we don't know *who* that is in there.'

'What was on the drives?' asked Grant.

'You should talk to Christie.'

'Something about you, or the department?'

'Talk to Christie, Grant! There's no point asking me the rules of chess when you're sitting at a draughts board.'

'What the hell is that supposed to mean?'

Winston thundered into the hall like a harassed parent trying to separate warring siblings. 'If you lot are quite finished, we've got a lot to talk about. The Chief's on her way in. I don't know about you, but I'd like to have some answers for her by the time she gets here.'

Grant grabbed a bottle of water for Gretchen, making no attempt to avoid bumping shoulders with Murphy on his way past.

Simeon told his point man, 'You'd better wait downstairs.'

Gretchen was exhausted to the point that sitting upright was an effort, but she was eager to explain what had happened to her. And what she had to say would shake Grant, Winston, and Simeon to their cores.

She had been a model intelligence officer ever since being recruited out of the London School of Economics, where she had graduated in Political Science. Her brilliant mind should have made her a career analyst, but her agility, strength, and quick reflexes made her a fearsome field operative. She proved herself invaluable to every department who was lucky enough to get her, the most recent being Anticorruption and Internal Affairs under the direction of Imogen Swann.

Gretchen explained, 'I wanted to be a Hannibal to do some good. Having been out in the field, I knew the damage that rogue operatives could do. So when Director Swann brought the Henry Marlow assignment to me, I put my entire life on the line to bring him in. I went through his old field reports, and something didn't add up about his apparent assassination of Charles Joseph. The

DNA evidence to confirm Joseph's identity looked like someone had tampered with it in the lab. It got me thinking that the way to find Marlow was actually to find Charles Joseph.'

Grant could see why she'd come to the conclusion. 'He might have been a warlord and an arms dealer, but he didn't have tradecraft in the art of disappearing like Marlow.'

'And I'm sure that's why I was able to find him.'

Winston's eyes widened. 'You found him? Where?'

'Qatar. I'd heard he was hiring ex-operatives from intelligence agencies. Over the last two years, Joseph's been building a private army of disavowed agents. The worst of the worst. Disavowed agents fired for all manner of illegal activities. Bribery, corruption, or just flat-out murder.'

'The scum of the earth,' Simeon suggested.

'You could say that,' Gretchen replied, maintaining a detached manner about the concept. 'There's a lot of temptation out in the field for operatives. They're investigating drug dealers. Arms dealers. Mercenaries. They built the entire architecture of their operations around black-market cash. It's not a world of spreadsheets and accountability. It's a world of skimming a little off the top here or there because no one's watching. Every man for himself. Little by little, those skims become entire stacks. Agents are making ten times their salaries in a month. It's the wild west out there. And Charles Joseph is paying them better than anyone else can.'

Winston said, 'I don't understand how he got in this position. He was an arms dealer with a nice little operation in Congo. In central Africa, he was a dime a dozen. Whatever changed has to be connected to Henry Marlow.'

'That was always the question for me,' said Gretchen. 'Once I had confirmation that Joseph was alive, I did everything I could to find Marlow. But I couldn't get near him or anyone who had seen him. I wanted the collar on my record…' She took a deep breath, replaying in her mind the moment that changed her life. 'So I suggested to Director Swann that I go on deep cover.'

'How deep?' asked Grant.

'*All* the way,' said Gretchen. 'I knew Joseph had sources everywhere. If I was going to infiltrate his operation, it had to look real. Swann certified me as disavowed. A black flag. I wasn't just out of MI6. My entire past life was over. Birth certificates, tax records, everything. I reported directly – and only – to Swann. And it worked. Joseph took me in. He never trusted anyone new with direct operations, but I extracted plenty of useful information from his foot soldiers, the guys who had been around for over a year. Hardened guys who would shoot their own grandmothers if it meant turning a profit of untraceable cash. I kept expecting to hear about operational blowback but it never came. At first, I thought they were holding off so that I wasn't compromised. It didn't add up. I was feeding Swann everything the agency needed to intercept, or at least gain a foothold on where he was going to be. Nothing was ever acted on. Swann strung me along, telling me it was all about finding Marlow, and that if we lost Charles Joseph, all paths to Marlow would be lost forever. So I bedded in, ever deeper. For eighteen months, I was a different person. It gets so that you forget who you really are. It was like I couldn't even dream for myself anymore. Eventually, little by little, I got closer to Joseph, but I never got a location on Marlow.'

Increasingly sceptical, Grant asked, 'You ever get inside Joseph's Congolese compound?'

Gretchen replied, 'I couldn't get near it. It was only ever open to Joseph's most trusted operatives. I held on, knowing that my disavowed status would hold up, and they would bring me in closer. It was just a matter of time. That was when I found out about the station chiefs hit. There was a list of fifteen targets that Joseph was going to take down. Synchronised attacks. It was the only way. Using disavowed and corrupt insiders, he could get all the information necessary to strike in such a way that was impossible to counter or predict. If everyone fell at the same time, no one could initiate lockdowns, or scramble other senior officials to safety.'

Simeon loomed over her, arms folded, always happiest when playing the role of bad-cop. 'What did you do to stop it?'

'I only had access to Swann through encrypted messaging channels. She never answered.'

'What about a burner? There's not a street market in the world where you can't buy a mobile phone.'

'I tried, and again Swann never answered.'

'What not try an embassy? You had a credible threat.'

'I was disavowed! They would have arrested me on the spot and sent me ping-ponging around black sites for the next year. It would have been months before I even received a hint of habeas corpus and spoke to a lawyer or got so much as a phone call. By then it would be far too late.'

All eyes fell on Simeon to get his appraisal. He couldn't deny the likelihood of Gretchen's account.

She continued, 'I was a ghost. The only thing I could do was keep sending transmissions and hope that eventually someone else would find them and act on them.'

'What about direct contact?' asked Winston.

'With Swann?' She scoffed. 'That worked well. I risked my life to break cover and travel to London to door-step her at her home. She apologised, trying to make out that there was a mole in the department, and that she couldn't respond. She assured me that my intel was making its way through the proper channels, and the station chiefs would be secured. I told her I wanted to come. She said fine. We met that same night at a safe house in the docklands. But she tried to black bag me using a couple of field operatives that I knew were dirty. I barely got out of there alive. That was when I started running. I thought I had found safety in Svalbard. Until your operation burned me.'

If Gretchen had satisfied Simeon even moderately, he didn't show it. He reasserted a powerful stance in front of her. 'An operation that you seemed to be plenty prepared for. How did you know we were coming?'

She remained leaning forward on her knees to show that she wouldn't cower in his presence. 'At an airport with only one or two flights a day, it's not hard to keep track of who's coming and going. I'm friends with a baggage handler there. I asked him to look out for any groups of British men who arrived with a lot of luggage and looked like they could handle themselves.'

Simeon asked, 'What were you paying him?'

'I wasn't.'

'So you were sleeping with him.'

Gretchen gave him a withering, pitying look. 'It says a lot about your perspective of human nature that you think the only two currencies in this world are money or sex.'

'They certainly are in Anticorruption.'

'The baggage handler and I just talked. We went fishing together. Climbed the mountains. We were friends. Day one of "Kill School" isn't how to fire a gun.' She turned to Grant, offering him the chance to answer.

He quoted from his lead instructor, 'An established relationship is more powerful than any other ammunition.'

Simeon pressed on, 'And your past as a spy never came up?'

'That was one of the principal reasons we were friends. We never spoke about the past. I know this might be a foreign concept to someone like you, Director. But in Svalbard, we looked out for each other. People end up there for all sorts of reasons: relationships, personal problems, being hung out to dry by the agency you've dedicated your life to…whatever it might be. I didn't know if your team was there on Imogen Swann's orders or not, so I took precautions and bedded in. And lucky for your crew that I did.'

The study door flew open and in stepped Olivia Christie. She was slightly flushed from what had been a sustained state of disturbed panic since leaving London.

When she laid eyes on Gretchen, she said, 'I swore I wouldn't believe it until I saw it for myself. Gretchen Winter.'

Gretchen stood up, pushing her hair back as she did so. 'Ma'am.'

'How much have you told them?' she asked.

'As little as they need to know.'

'Told us what?' asked Winston.

Gretchen added, 'I don't know their clearance levels. Frankly, until you walked in the door, I couldn't be sure who any of these men were. But I didn't have much of a choice. If they wanted me dead, they would have finished me off in Svalbard.'

Winston asked Christie, 'What's going on?'

She answered, 'Before Gretchen here joined Anticorruption and Internal Affairs, she was an Albion operative.'

A lot of what Grant had seen from her so far now made a lot more sense. Her tradecraft. Surveillance. Weaponry prowess. Tactical knowledge. Making a peaceful home in a wild and extreme environment.

Christie told Gretchen, 'It's alright. You're safe now.'

8

Christie knew that she had some explaining to do before she lost the confidence of everyone in the room. 'When Henry Marlow disappeared after the Kadir Rashid situation that Imogen mishandled so horribly, I had Anticorruption open up all of Marlow's case files to check we hadn't missed anything. Gretchen here found that DNA evidence taken by Marlow relating to Joseph had been tampered with, so I sent her to investigate the possibility that Charles Joseph was still alive.'

Gretchen asked, 'What happened to my transmissions and reports to you, Chief?'

Christie shook her head. 'I never received any, Gretchen. Everything went through Imogen. It was supposed to keep the mission more secure.'

Grant edged forward in his seat. He wasn't the only one with a bone to pick with Christie. He said, 'When I was hunting Marlow you gave me an Albion file that told me Charles Joseph was dead.'

Winston grew nervous, praying that Grant wouldn't overstep

the mark and lose his temper at the Chief. He needn't have worried.

Grant kept his composure. 'Having the information that Marlow never killed Joseph could have changed everything. I went to Joseph's compound, ma'am. He could have been there.'

Christie took the blame without complaint. 'I know. But we didn't have complete confirmation that Joseph really was alive. We had *doubt*. We also had a highly classified agent on deep cover, and I couldn't jeopardise her mission. You should know that Leo didn't know a thing about it. It was my call. If I thought you couldn't handle whatever might have been waiting in the Congo I would never have allowed Leo to send you. The only apology I owe is to Gretchen, for sending her in to investigate Joseph's whereabouts on Imogen Swann's watch.'

Gretchen asked, 'When it became clear what Swann had been up to, didn't you check to see if I needed brought in?'

'When your file was transferred to Internal Affairs there was no record that you were still active. Imogen had deleted all of your check-ins.' Christie sighed. 'I assumed you were dead.'

Winston suggested, 'That's the problem with having agents answerable to one handler alone. I still don't understand why Imogen buried Gretchen's reports. She wanted to kill Marlow before he could talk to anyone like Duncan, and reveal the truth about the Rashid hit. She should have been first in line to try and find him.'

Christie answered, 'What you should really be asking your-selves is who else Joseph has under his command.' She held up her phone, which was showing confirmation of lab analyses that had just come through from Miles Archer. 'Miles has been briefing me on the IDs of those dead operatives in Svalbard. The mop-up team pulled blood, fingerprints, and retinal scans. Randall in forensics has confirmed that they check out. A mixture of Mossad, CIA, and the Finnish Defence Forces. All of them disavowed and fired on corruption charges.'

Gretchen said, 'That fits with everything I've seen inside his operation. Ruthless operatives with a history of corruption and crime, all highly motivated.'

Keen to figure out the next steps, Winston asked, 'What does Joseph want, Gretchen?'

'From what I observed, the only thing that drives him is destroying his enemies. He's seen more in his lifetime than we could ever imagine. And his list of grievances seems to be long.'

Simeon remarked, 'Let me get out my tiny violin for the heartbroken arms dealer and terrorist.'

His recent memories of the Congo all too fresh in his mind, Grant replied, 'You've got no idea what you're talking about. If a child is raised in hell, don't be surprised if he turns out to be the Devil.'

'I'm sorry, I thought this was MI6, not the Samaritans.'

Gretchen said, 'It's too easy to dismiss Joseph as a madman. He's so much worse than that. Madmen don't act with calculation. He's reckless, but he's not impulsive. He knows exactly what he wants, and he'll go through a hundred people to get just one. That's the difference between him and Marlow. If Marlow is a laser-guided missile, Joseph is a cluster bomb. Marlow won't kill more than he needs because it's not operationally efficient.'

Grant nodded. 'Killing more than you need jeopardises the wider mission.'

'Exactly,' said Gretchen. 'Charles Joseph doesn't have that discipline. He has a plan, but he's indiscriminate. That's why he and Marlow joining forces is the nightmare scenario. When you combine what makes them unique? You get the best of both and the worst of both.'

Thinking back to the pictures taken at Joseph's old

compound, Simeon insisted, 'He's a madman. They both are.' He wandered towards the window. He took out a short piece of black tape that he'd removed from the edge of a secretary's folder in the reception area and used it to cover the tiny sliver of light coming through. He pushed his lips out in satisfaction once it was done.

Gretchen could see that Simeon wasn't getting her point. 'It's alright to be scared of him, Director.'

'I'm not scared,' he retorted.

'You should be,' she countered. 'It's understandable to fear what you don't understand. We believe we're on the side of good, and that it's implacable. He wants to prove that we're not.'

Eager for tangibles, Grant asked, 'How?'

'I fear that if we don't find him, we'll only find out once it's too late.' She looked at the worried faces surrounding her. 'I know some of you are sitting here wondering if Charles Joseph turned me.' She shook her head. 'It's not me you should be worried about.'

Simeon, pacing in the background, halted. 'What's that supposed to mean?'

'Within an hour of arriving on one of the most isolated islands in the world, your guys had twice as many enemy opera- tives on their tail. No one has resources like that just hanging around a place like Svalbard by chance. A plane flight is three hours. They knew in advance where you were going to be, and how many of you to expect.' She scanned the faces around the room. 'You've got a leak.'

Having come to the same conclusion, Christie leaned down to whisper in Winston's ear. 'A word. Outside.' She said to Grant, 'You too.'

9

The apartment was gloomy no matter where you went, particularly the main hall which was far from any windows. Appropriate mood-lighting for what Christie had to tell Winston and Grant.

To lead in to it, she started with something procedural. 'Grant, I want you and Gretchen to work together to find Charles Joseph. There's a lot you can learn from her. I also rather selfishly want two Albions for the price of one on this. We've only seen the first step so far.'

'The first step in what?' asked Grant.

'Tragic as it is, assassination victims can always be replaced. There must be more on the way.'

'Then what does he do next?'

Winston folded his arms tightly, bracing himself for what he had to ask. 'Ma'am, you're C for a good reason. There are things you need to know that we don't. I understand that. It's the job. But you can't tell me with your political and operational experience that you don't know what the link is between all of those station chiefs.'

Christie backed away, needing some physical room to collect
her thoughts. 'In two thousand and one, the FBI and CIA failed
to share information about a couple of Arab men learning to fly
planes down in Florida, but who had curiously little interest in
learning how to land safely. Richard Clarke at CIA had already
warned that something, quote, spectacular, was likely going to
take place that year. But none of the information about what was
going on at flight schools in Florida reached him or the White
House. A flight school in Minnesota alerted the FBI about a man
named Zacarias Moussaoui who had been asking suspicious
questions about security measures around commercial cockpits,
but FBI headquarters refused a search warrant on Moussaoui's
laptop citing lack of probable cause. It almost seems quaint
nowadays to see how reluctant the Americans were to inconve-
nience a man with known links to Pakistani military training
camps. But everyone was too scared to share information because
they didn't want anyone knowing that they got their intel from
tapping phones or paying informants. Not to mention the petty
competition between agencies to get credit for arrests. The Americans' failures could have been anyone's. Ours. The Germans.
The French. So we combined our efforts. Even the Russians were
onboard. We formed a network that we called the Fifteen Flags,
running black ops in the hope of avoiding the next nine eleven.
You two know as well as I do, the next one will probably be
chemical or nuclear. And if even one of us takes our eye off the
ball, we all lose. The station chiefs that were assassinated were all
the most senior directors in the Fifteen Flags network. I had
enlisted Bob Gower in Berlin to represent us. A few months ago,
it would have been my head on the block. Poor sod. I think
Charles Joseph is trying to dismantle the network.'

Winston ventured, 'If the network is broken then someone
stands a better chance of getting another bigger attack through.'

'The sort of attack that I see in my worst nightmares,' said Christie. 'Marlow and Joseph have been working on this for years. Frankly, if you're not thinking of nine eleven or worse, you're not nearly scared as you should be.'

Grant took a deep breath to steady himself. 'First the network…'

'Then he goes after us,' said Winston. 'Then probably CIA. All the other dominoes would fall after that. Leaving them free to attack at will.'

Christie said solemnly, 'I told Simeon to prioritise deleting Gretchen's hard drives. I couldn't be sure what sort of intelligence was on them. The network has been compromised enough as it is. I couldn't risk having any further intelligence falling into the wrong hands.'

Grant wished that she could have just trusted him with the information in the first place, but he had a job to do now. And he didn't want Christie giving away his Albion role now that Gretchen was back in play. So he held his tongue. 'I understand, ma'am,' he said.

She said, 'There's something else. About Gretchen.' She hesitated. 'We might need to send her back to Joseph.'

Grant couldn't hide his surprise. 'After six months away? Ma'am, wouldn't that look very suspicious to him?'

'I want you focussed on the job, Grant. Leave concerns about appearance to me. But when the times comes, I might need you to sell it to her. For that to work, you'll need to establish trust with her. Albion to Albion.'

'Ma'am,' Grant said affirmatively, even if he didn't like the sound of it.

When he returned to the study, he couldn't look Gretchen in the eye. She'd risked her life on deep cover for the agency. Now that she'd survived everything that had been thrown at her,

Christie was already preparing to throw her back to the wolves. By Grant's reckoning, it was an act of desperation. The sort of recklessness that got operatives killed.

Once they were alone in the hall, Christie asked Winston, 'You know him better than I do, Leo. What's his temperature on this Gretchen situation?'

'Grant might work best alone, ma'am, but he wouldn't turn down any chance to defeat Henry Marlow once and for all. A former Albion might be just what he needs.'

Christie said, 'Get your man ready, Leo. He's got the fight of his life ahead of him.'

Miles Archer, who had crept to the periphery of the hall, knocked gently on the wooden wall.

Christie shot around. 'What is it?'

Miles cleared his throat, then took two attempts to start his sentence. 'I'm just off the phone with London, ma'am. Apparently Henry Marlow wants to talk.'

'The negotiators are already on site. What are they waiting for?'

Miles replied, 'He says he'll only talk to Grant.'

10

On the Bombardier Global 7500 private jet on the way back to London, Grant sat on his own, a couple of seats to himself. Gretchen had done likewise, while Christie, Winston, and Simeon sat together near the front. Grant stared out the window at the ongoing white expanse of cloud below, gaming out every scenario he could think of for the Marlow meeting. Was it just for Marlow to lord it over him, that even in MI6's temporary custody he could rewrite the established world order with Charles Joseph?

Grant's concentration was broken by the sudden appearance of Gretchen. She held back slightly in the aisle. 'Is this seat taken?'

Grant looked over his shoulder. 'Looks like it.'

She sat down with a smile. 'You're the new Albion, then.'

'So they tell me.'

'How long?'

Grant checked his watch. 'About thirty-seven hours.' The worst thing he could do, he thought, was try to convince her how trustworthy he was. How good he was at his job. Thirty-seven hours in, there was no proof he could point to. No experience she could pull from. He knew that it was going to take some time.

She leaned closer to him, lowering her voice. 'They're going to send me back in.'

'To Joseph?'

'Christie doesn't have a choice.'

'I'm supposed to be the one to sell it to you.'

'Go on, then. What's your pitch?'

'Honestly?' He paused. 'I'd think about walking away.'

'Walking away?'

Grant said, 'You've survived more than most of us can imagine. The longer you go on, the more your odds diminish.'

'If that's the case, why aren't you walking away?' she asked.

Grant showed her his watch. 'Because I've only been doing the job thirty-seven hours.'

She smiled and titled her head, as if appraising him. She liked that he didn't try to put up a macho false front. A lot of other operatives would try to justify their role to someone like her – a veteran of the same position as Grant. He was happy to let his actions prove who he was. Though she'd already had a minor glimpse of how he handled himself in a field-combat situation.

'I know what's on the line for you, Gretchen,' he said. 'I want you to know I won't treat that recklessly. I won't let you down.'

She paused before a confused expression broke across her face. 'The only thing I fear more than betrayal, Grant, is loyalty. Loyalty is what got me in this mess to begin with. It for damn sure isn't going to get me out.' She smiled at his cagey silence. 'Are you really so green that you think loyalty will protect you? You realise that what they did to me wasn't personal.'

'I know it could have just as easily been me. I'm not naïve, Gretchen.'

'You could have fooled me.'

'In your shoes, I wouldn't trust me either. One thing I can promise you, though, is you'll always get the truth from me. That's something those guys up there can't guarantee.' He flicked his head toward Winston, Simeon, and Christie.

'Even your own handler?' asked Gretchen.

'I trust Leo not to send me into a situation without being fully informed. But if Marlow proves anything, it's that people like you and me will always be expendable.'

A hint of recognition flashed across Gretchen's face. 'You worry that what happened to him could just as easily happen to you.'

Grant said nothing.

'Then what happened to me must really be a trip,' she added. 'Marlow is easier to write off because his mind broke. But I did everything that Imogen Swann asked of me, and then some. That scares you.'

Grant tried to brave-face it. 'Imogen Swann was dirty. Leo isn't.'

'I don't think it's Leo you need to worry about.'

'What do you mean?'

'You really are naïve…Do you think that Olivia Christie knew nothing about Swann burying my reports and trans-missions?'

Now that she mentioned it, Grant craned his neck for a glance at Christie, who was on her feet at the front of the plane taking a phone call.

'You don't get it, do you,' said Gretchen. 'We're just blunt instruments to them. But you actually think they'll reward your loyalty. If you're a good little dog who behaves himself.'

Grant looked down at his hands, uncomfortable at the thought that she might be right.

She pulled her head back slightly, like a camera operator trying out a different lens. 'How *did* you end up being an Albion?'

'I kept saying yes to things. First SAS recruitment. Then when Leo recruited me. And now this.'

Gretchen settled her gaze as his internal life came into focus for her. She had him now. 'You keep saying yes to things so you can continue being anyone but yourself. Do you practise it in the mirror? I bet you do. Looking normal. Like someone who hasn't had their heart ripped out. That's the thing when you suffer a tragedy at a young age…' Registering his reaction, or lack of, she recalibrated. 'One parent dead? Both? I'm right, aren't I? It's hard to hide. Grief like that sticks to you like glue. You never lose it. All that's left is to bury it. You can't be yourself anymore, because that person is broken. So you have to become someone else. Anyone else. Maybe even join the SAS where all you are is a surname. There *is* no moving on because you can't change who you are. All you can change is what you are.'

'You've got me all figured out,' said Grant, stung from how accurate it all was. 'What you really want is to be a ghost. You were angrier that we found you than Imogen Swann selling you out. No one ever really knows who we are. Sure, if you put in ten-plus years of marriage you might break the surface level of things. You might even share your dreams and nightmares with them. But they never know what it truly feels like. You don't like me because you don't know yet if you can trust me. You see my loyalty to Leo and being an Albion as a point of being suspect.'

She stared at him with a deadened glare. 'You've been an Albion how many hours? When you've been deep cover for as long as I have, look me up. I just wanted to let you know that if I think, for even a second, that you're working me, I won't hesitate to put a bullet in your head.'

Grant accepted the premise with a nod. 'Normally it takes at least a few more hours before someone decides I deserve a bullet in the head. The flip side of that is whether I think for even a second that you're working me.'

'Let me guess,' she said. 'A bullet in the head?'

He shrugged. 'Then we understand each other.'

She got up to leave, but still had one remaining question. 'Tell me. Why does Marlow only want to talk to you?'

Grant replied, 'I'm sure you can read all about it when we get to Vauxhall Cross.'

At the front of the plane, Simeon was in quiet deliberation with Winston while Christie took another in a long queue of phone calls. Simeon stole a sharp glance towards Gretchen, who was returning to her seat three rows away from Grant. 'You think she can be trusted?' asked Simeon. 'She was abandoned by the agency. What if she wants revenge? Recruited to Joseph's cause and we've welcomed her back with open arms.'

Winston was next to sneak a look. 'I don't know that we should trust anyone right now. Not our own teams. Even each other.'

Simeon reached into his suit pocket and took out his wallet. He opened it up, revealing a photograph of a young woman the same age as he was. She was wearing a necklace made of oxidised silver, giving it a black patina. Dangling from a hoop were strands of sterling silver, which had two pearls set into them. 'I bought this for Anna for our first wedding anniversary. I knew it was supposed to be paper for your first, but it was right as soon as I saw it. She used to say the two pearls were us. This is what Henry Marlow took from me, Leo. My wife. My life.'

'I'm sorry, Alex,' said Winston. 'I can't imagine how...' He broke off. Unable to conjure any suitable words.

Simeon stared at the photo. 'I'm going to finish this, Leo. Whatever it takes. I need to know that Grant will do the same.'

Winston said, 'He will. We all will, Alex.'

11

The basement cells in MI6 headquarters were set up in a row in a large gymnasium-type room, with a high vaulted ceiling and no windows. The cells themselves were cubes of bulletproof and soundproof glass, separated by concrete dividers to avoid the possibility of communication between detainees on the rare occasion there was more than one being held.

Ordinarily, a suspect like Henry Marlow would have been handed over to the Met's Charing Cross Police Station. Now the go-to destination for the most high-profile criminals in organised crime or terrorism cases.

MI6 had no powers of arrest, only of detention, and Olivia Christie had gone cap in hand to the Home Secretary to detain Marlow for a further two weeks before he had to be handed over to the Met for official charges to be brought.

Grant was surprised to find two other inmates in the cells when he arrived. One a human trafficker who was awaiting pick-up from the CIA via the United States embassy. The other an American paedophile who had been snared at Heathrow Airport and apparently had incriminating evidence against a prominent British businessman.

When Grant approached their cells, both the men shuddered, fearing that Grant was there to interrogate them. It was with great relief that they watched him continue past to the cell at the very end.

The ceilings of the cells had microphones built into them, and could relay conversation through speakers set up outside. This was how MI6's interrogators had gone about interviewing Marlow since his capture by Duncan Grant weeks earlier. Although the term "interviewing" suggested a two-way conversation. Marlow had spent most of the time lying on his back with his eyes closed, occasionally announcing that he was 'bored', or humming Beethoven's 'Für Elise' for no other reason than to amuse himself at the thought of them spending hours afterwards dissecting the supposed symbolic meaning behind the gesture. He knew he was ten times smarter than anyone the agency could send to interrogate him anyway – unlike a gifted child who thinks they know more than their therapist, there truly was no one MI6 could send who was capable of unpeeling the layers of Henry Marlow. For that, Marlow had been waiting for Grant.

Marlow was dressed the same as when Grant had last seen him. White jumpsuit and white slip-on canvas shoes. The most striking change was that his head had been shaved close to the scalp.

He was sitting on the edge of what constituted his bed: a plain foam mattress sitting on top of a concrete block. A man in his position couldn't be trusted with items like pillow cases or bed sheets.

With little ceremony or body language that communicated the importance of the meeting, Grant sat down in the chair that had been set up for him.

Marlow spoke without looking up. 'I hope you didn't cut your holiday short on my account, Duncan.'

Grant had decided ahead of time that he wouldn't speak. Not until Marlow gave him something significant.

'You're not giving me the silent treatment, are you?' Marlow asked. 'I doubt very much that the army of professional negotiators outside would have advised that for our little play date. This is the first I've spoken to anyone since you were last here.' He paused and looked up, as if hearing something in the air. 'I can hear them already, jabbering in your ear about what to say in that radio earpiece of yours. It's terribly rude, Duncan. I invited you here so we could be left in peace. Take it out. It's demeaning to us both.'

Despite the protestations from the control booth in his ear, Grant whipped the earpiece out. There was nothing they could tell him that Marlow hadn't already anticipated or that he couldn't run rings around.

The radio now dangling from his collar, Grant said, 'They can still hear you from the microphones. You know these cells record every whisper. Every whimper in your sleep.'

'Whimper?' Marlow chuckled. 'How little you know me. That hurts. Here I was thinking we had so much in common. Me an Albion operative.' He turned his head to meet Grant's eyes. 'And now you too.'

Grant tried to give nothing away. Unfortunately for him, he was sitting across from a man who seemed to have an open window into Grant's soul.

'So it *is* true,' Marlow cooed, a smile growing. 'That's what they do, Duncan. If you do a job well enough, your reward is giving you a much more dangerous job next time. They reopened Albion. And you're the first one back.' He put a hand to his chest in mock pride. 'My little Duncan is all grown up. An Albion just like me. Are you sure you're ready for that?'

Not wanting to enter into his mind games, Grant asked sharply, 'What do you want?'

'I told you to come back to me when you were ready,' said Marlow. 'Are you ready now?'

'I know that Charles Joseph is alive.'

Marlow couldn't help himself from grinning. 'You swallowed those audio diaries of mine hook, line, and sinker, didn't you.'

Ignoring the barb, Grant said, 'Love the new haircut. Guantanamo chic?'

'So predictable of them. Take away the prisoner's dignity, etcetera. I suppose playing Slayer and Metallica at deafening levels isn't far off.'

Grant leaned forward in his chair. 'How far back did it go between you two?'

Marlow rose from the bed, meandering towards the glass. 'Oh, Duncan. Trying to play up to my vanity by imploring me to regale you with how clever I've been. It's fine with me. It just reflects so poorly on you.'

'It can't have been as simple as one madman discovering another. You're not that simple. You never have been. What did you see in him?'

Marlow replied, 'A way to win the fight once and for all. If MI6 had twenty men like him, the world would be a completely different place.'

'I don't doubt that,' said Grant. 'There would be bodies hanging from lampposts in every city. Rivers full of blood.'

'Maybe you should consider that sometimes the most humane thing is to let the world burn. And that's exactly what I'm going to do. That's what's so beautiful about it. I'm going to burn the entire system down.'

'Now you're quoting from your diaries. I thought that those were all fake.' Grant rose from his chair and approached the glass. 'You made up the stuff about Charles Joseph, but all the other stuff was real, wasn't it? About what it meant to be a killer. Those parts were real. You meant those words. I could hear it in your voice. You couldn't help but let a bit of your real self slip out. You had been a ghost for so long, the idea of being able to communicate with someone else even moderately on your level was irresistible.' Grant wagged his finger, sensing he was on to something. 'You couldn't resist speaking some truth to whoever was going to find the recordings. So someone would understand.'

Marlow showed no emotion. 'I did it as a courtesy. A warning, if you like. They don't care if you live or die, but I do. Look at us right now. They've sent you in here because they're so desperate for answers. They don't care about the repercussions.'

'Repercussions? That's big talk for a man standing behind bulletproof glass.'

'All you're thinking about is the present, Duncan. I'm talking about what happens a week from now.'

'What happens then?' asked Grant.

'The entire corrupt intelligence system will be destroyed. You don't realise, but it's already too late. And you could have prevented it. Your inability to take a life when nothing but vengeance is on the line will be your downfall, Duncan. It's your weakness: preserving life at all costs. No doubt you see it as an ironic virtue in an assassin. Killing only those you really have to. But you can never truly be an Albion until you've shed that old morality.'

'I don't need to be an anarchist like you to be an Albion. You can't stand the idea of someone having a purpose outside of vengeance. You think you can prove that underneath it all, we're all corrupt. Even me.'

'You actually doubt that? Now I'm questioning your intelligence, Duncan. Look at it out there. Entire nations are tearing each other apart. Cultural civil wars fracturing society one snarky tweet and Facebook post at a time. It's the same story the world over. Societies fragmenting. Frothing at the mouth to destroy each other. All they need is a little push. When Charles and I are done, when our work is complete, all that will be left is chaos. I knew whoever found those recordings would deserve a chance to get out. To get away before it starts. There's still time to join us.'

Grant shook his head. He had to admire Marlow's audacity. 'What do you want?'

Marlow said, 'Let me go. Or face the consequences.'

'You seem to have forgotten where you're standing.'

'And you seem to have forgotten what MI6 did to you. They were willing to let you die just to stop me.'

'That's the job. Imogen Swann was—'

Marlow interjected, 'A rotten apple, yes, yes. But what about Olivia Christie? She doesn't even trust you enough to give you basic information before you walked in here.'

'What basic information is that?' asked Grant.

Marlow smiled. 'That would be telling, Duncan. Isn't it fascinating, how little they trust you. How closely they hold their secrets. I wonder what else old Olivia hasn't told you or Leo. Maybe she has a reason for that. To keep you under control the way they did with me. Then one of these days, they'll send you on a job and you won't think to question the target. Then you'll face a choice. Do whatever they tell you, or face the consequences. Which is the same choice I'm giving you now.'

'And that choice is between what?' asked Grant.

Marlow answered, 'Me, or carnage.' He held a hand up to stop any interruption. 'Now think carefully before you answer this, Duncan. I'm giving you one last chance to walk away intact.

You go back to your little sheep farm or whatever, looking off enigmatically out to the sea. You put a fire on in the evening, knock back your fifth whisky of the night, trying to salve that ache in your soul before going to bed, alone. And you'll lie awake in bed staring at the ceiling, wondering what your life could have been like if you had just taken my generous offer of mercy and walked away. How much more you would have. Maybe a woman lying next to you. Perhaps Gretchen.' He paused. 'You're wondering how I know that, aren't you?'

Grant stared at him, rooted to the spot.

Marlow said, 'Did you know they sent her after me? Funny how she's the only one who ever got away. I wonder why that would be…'

Grant tried not to let the words affect him. He knew Marlow was trying to get into his head, to plant a seed of doubt.

'Did they tell you they all died?' asked Marlow. 'All the operatives they sent after me? Gretchen's a special one. She got closer than anyone else. Maybe a little too close. Have you been thinking about her? I'll bet you have. How she must understand what it's like out there in the field. Taking lives. All those faces without names…Do you see them in your sleep? I do. Sometimes, I still feel them in my fingers.' He nodded slowly. 'Yes… You know what I'm talking about.'

Grant paused, considering his options. Then he said, 'We're done here.'

Marlow raised his voice as Grant began to walk away. 'I'm disappointed but not surprised. You don't realise that accepting my offer is the smart thing to do. Instead, you're choosing the option that makes you feel better in the moment. A week from now you'll wish you could go back to this moment and choose differently…' He dropped to his knees, as if he was about to commence a prayer. A feeling of intense joy appeared to rise through him. 'Oh, I can't wait to see your face, Duncan. It's going to be quite something.'

Grant stopped and turned around. 'Today is the last day you'll see my face, Henry. If you don't give me something, you'll be locked up for the rest of your life.'

Marlow pouted in disagreement. 'Things change.'

Trying one last time, Grant asked, 'What happens in a week?'

'I take away everything in your life. What little remains in your insignificant little life.'

'You can't stand it,' said Grant. 'Someone having a higher purpose. Meaning. When all you crave is anarchy. Destruction. I caught you. I stopped you. Then I locked you up. And I'm going to do the same to Charles Joseph.'

Marlow, still on his knees, said with dead eyes, 'There's not much time to come to your senses, Duncan. Tick tock, tick tock, tick tock...'

12

SIX DAYS LATER

The Tank on the tenth floor had been repurposed and expanded as the Albion investigation room, now twice the size of the original mobile unit. Even so, it had a claustrophobic feel to it – not helped by the malfunctioning air-con unit that had turned the Tank into a mild sauna. Both Grant and Gretchen were down to short sleeves, and were consuming litres of water in there every day. Their discipline in sticking to the security protocols of the Tank kept the door closed at all times. They were using the Tank for a reason, and with the spectre of compromised officers within MI6 itself, neither Grant nor Gretchen was willing to compromise the mission for the sake of some short-term fresh air.

The discomfort of the Tank was compounded by the reams of intelligence that had accumulated on the white boards around the inner edges of the Tank. In the aftermath of the Fifteen Flags assassinations, information had streamed in from every corner of MI6, MI5, CIA, FBI, Mossad, Russia's FSB, the Australian Secret Intelligence Service, France's DGSE, Germany's BND... Even China's Ministry of State Security.

It had been a period of forced contemplation about who the real enemies were, despite some old grudges dying hard. When even the Russians and Chinese were pitching in to help, it was a simple case of desperate times, desperate measures.

There was almost too much information coming through. Too much for Grant and Gretchen to process themselves. Over the previous six days, they had been relying on Winston's former helpers in the European Task Force control room and elsewhere to filter the most vital intelligence their way. Knowing where to start was the issue.

Many of the operatives and agents involved in the synchronised attack had been captured or identified, confirming Gretchen's portrayal of Charles Joseph's private army of mercenaries. All previously disavowed agents who had taken to the black market to offer their services, and all with a personal stake in the success of their missions.

After the first three days, time ceased to matter very much to Grant and Gretchen. There was no natural light in the Tank, and no windows in the conference room outside it, which made it easy for days to turn into nights without either operative realising it. The regular cycles of the day became one long, drawn-out saga of artificial light, no exercise, and stale air. The lack of exercise particularly affected Grant, who often took breaks to perform bodyweight exercises in the conference room while Gretchen continued to work or took a twenty-minute nap on a bench. It wasn't that time ceased to matter. Time – or lack of it – was what was driving both of them to such extreme working patterns.

With each day that passed, Grant felt a creeping sense of dread as the clock ticked down.

Grant stood in front of a wall that had once been systematic and organised, now littered with overlapping sources and intel on Charles Joseph's whereabouts. Since Joseph's face had been captured on the CCTV of an MI6 substation in Nairobi on the day of the attack, no further images of him had been found. By anyone. Anywhere.

Hands on hips, evaluating the overwhelming quantity of information in front of them, and how little it added up to, he told Gretchen, 'It doesn't make sense.'

Waking up with a start, she lifted her head from the table where she had been napping, unnoticed by Grant. 'What doesn't?'

'He orchestrates this incredible attack that would have taken months of planning, and we still don't know where he was in all that time. We can't trace him back anywhere. Then, on the day of the attack, he allows his face to be captured, knowing that it will blow his cover. Why does he do that? He had nearly one hundred operatives at his disposal. He's been planning this thing without a single intelligence agency anywhere getting wise, and disappears again afterwards like it never happened.'

Gretchen had forced herself upright, although she had slept barely twenty-five minutes in the last thirty-six hours. 'Joseph was identified by over a dozen station staff. He was there.'

'What I mean is,' said Grant, 'why did he show himself when he didn't have to? He could have pulled this off without anyone finding out he was ever involved.'

'Unless he had to be there. Or he wanted to.' Gretchen pulled herself out from behind the desk to consult the official report on the Nairobi substation hit. 'The victim was Patrick Dembele.'

Grant found Dembele's picture on the wall and re-pinned it front and centre. From memory alone, Grant rhymed off, 'Fifty-seven years old. Born in London, his family moved to Kigali when he was nine years old. Distinguished military intelligence career with the Rwandan Defence Force. MI6 Station Chief in

Kenya for four years. Before that, Deputy Station Chief Kigali, Rwanda...'

Something Grant had said prompted Gretchen to hurry over to a filing cabinet that had filled up with disconcerting haste over the last six days, full of personnel files and detailed histories on each of the victims. The European Task Force, and their other continental equivalents downstairs, had prioritised investigating the lives of the most prominent victims. People like the CIA's man in Moscow, Jack Colby, or the FSB's man in Washington, Grigory Vanyev. Only Gretchen had paid much attention to victims like Patrick Dembele who weren't from the more prestigious agency arenas like Washington, D.C. and Moscow. Cutting Grant off and continuing to hunt through Dembele's files, she said, 'The Rwandan Defence Force wasn't always called that. At the time of the genocide from ninety to ninety-four, it was called the Rwandan Patriotic Front. When they won the war, they renamed it the RDF.' Gretchen found the page she was looking for. Dembele's MI6 background check. 'Dembele was a major player in the side that won the Rwandan civil war.'

Grant looked at her in confusion. 'What does that have to do with Joseph?'

Gretchen brought over the forensics report on Dembele's death. 'He died from three major stab wounds to the chest. How many other station chiefs were stabbed?'

Grant cleared away part of the white board that had listed all of the causes of death. 'Fifteen victims. We've got snipers, car bombs...Dembele is the only stabbing.'

'It's hard to stab someone,' Gretchen said. 'You can shoot someone whether you're terrified or feeling brave. But stabbing requires guts. Force. If it's not a self-defence situation, then you're probably looking at—'

'Anger,' said Grant.

Gretchen nodded. 'Rage. Joseph went there for a reason. I think he wanted to deliver the blows to Dembele personally. We need to explode this guy's life.'

'We already have.'

'We need to do it again!'

'We can't keep doing this, Gretchen. We're running out of time.'

'Well, what do you suggest? Get a nice ten hours of sleep and hope someone leaves us Joseph's location overnight?' She leaned on the open cabinet drawer then slammed it shut with a sigh. 'All we have is a vague warning from Marlow that something is coming in a completely vague time frame.'

'He's not giving us specifics because I don't think he knows. He can't say for sure. All he knows is that it's coming.'

'We don't know if any of it's real.'

'Trust me,' said Grant. 'If Marlow said it's coming, then it's coming.'

Her tone getting testier, Gretchen snapped, 'How do you know?'

'Because I've seen with my own eyes what he's capable of.'

'So have I, Duncan.'

'My point is, he's been ahead of us every step of the way to this point. He's sitting in a cell downstairs because he wanted it to happen. This isn't just for his own amusement.'

'Maybe it is!' Gretchen paused, considering their options. 'Look, I trust that you're the guy when it comes to Marlow around here these days. But if you're really sure that something worse is coming, then maybe we should discuss the possibility of letting Marlow go.' Anticipating his protests, she stepped towards him with her hand out. 'I know what you're thinking, but hear me out. We've had Marlow locked up in a high-security prison cell and he still managed to wipe out fifteen intelligence chiefs around the world. Isn't there an argument to be made for letting him go, and in doing so, letting him take us closer to Charles Joseph?'

Grant tried his best, but he couldn't get there in his head. 'I've been through too much to let him go, Gretchen. We have to get Joseph first.'

She gesticulated at the surrounding the walls. 'If you've got any ideas, I'm all ears...'

The buzzer for the Tank door went. After checking the video screen to see who was outside, Grant buzzed them in.

Winston recoiled as he entered – a wall of hot air hitting him. 'Dear god,' he complained, pulling his tie loose. 'It's like an old folk's home in here.'

'You should feel right at home,' said Grant with a smile.

Gretchen fetched a bottle of water from the fridge and tossed it to Winston. 'Air con's down.'

Winston held out the bottle in confusion. 'Call maintenance! They work twenty-four hours a day.'

'That's the problem,' said Grant wearily. 'So do we. We'd need to dismantle everything, including the intel on the wall, and vacate the Tank for at least six hours. We'd be out of commission for half a day, and we don't have half a day to lose right now.'

Winston asked, 'When was the last time either of you slept?'

Grant answered, 'Don't worry about it. What have you got?'

Winston handed over a computer analysis log. 'That's just in from CIA. They took it from Jack Colby's laptop. They found it in his office in the American embassy in Moscow.'

Not understanding any of it, Grant handed it to Gretchen who was more familiar with the format.

Winston said, 'The laptop bore traces of the DeathWeep malware programme.'

'That's not too surprising, is it?' said Gretchen. 'It infected about a million computers last year.'

'At some point it got onto Colby's personal laptop from his home wi-fi connection. So no, nothing too strange there. Where things start to deviate are some of the search terms used by the malware programme.'

'Search terms?' wondered Grant. 'I thought DeathWeep was about stealing credit card details and passwords.'

'It was. And it still is,' replied Winston, taking out his phone. 'When the malware gets onto a computer, it turns the hard drive into a slave. Normally, a pop-up appears demanding payment to release the hard drive from the malware's control. And a lot of people pay it because they're scared or they don't understand what's happening. The DeathWeep programme is so good, you can only look into it after the fact, but once it's gone, you can see all the places the scammer at the other end was looking. They might do a search for "password" or "credit card" to find something valuable. On Colby's laptop, it was a hack, alright, but for information. Not money.' Having called up forensics and all-round tech expert Randall on video chat, he asked him to elaborate. He placed his phone on the table for Grant and Gretchen to see. 'Go ahead, Randall,' said Winston.

He explained, 'More and more, we've been seeing Russia using malware hackers for espionage purposes. The industry of illegal hacking and crimeware and ransomware is rampant over there. They don't even call it the black market. They call it "free" market, because the directories where you can hire someone to steal credit-card information or passwords are as easy to access as buying something off eBay. The one stipulation the Russian government has always put on the trade is that none of the illegal activities rip off Russian citizens. Everyone else is fair game. And there are hackers, like Arkady Bogov, who are so talented, the

Kremlin realised they could be put to good use. Bogov has infected so many computers with DeathWeep, they've been getting him to search infected computers with terms like "Department of Homeland Security" to find compromising material. In return, they give hackers like him immunity from prosecution.'

Winston added, 'The FBI knows exactly where Bogov is, and has been for the last year. But they can't exactly carry out an unauthorised extraction on Russian soil.'

'Not likely,' said Gretchen. 'The Kremlin would consider that an act of war.'

Grant asked, 'What does this have to do with Jack Colby?'

Randall said, 'Our analysis of his logs shows that some of the search terms used by the DeathWeep virus included "official diary" and "schedule". Despite infecting the laptop for over a week, not a single credit-card detail was taken, even though Colby had saved two cards on his internet browser. Charles Joseph used Bogov's virus to find out where Colby was going to be, and when.'

Winston concluded, 'It's likely that's how they found out about a lot of their victims.'

'Okay,' said Grant. 'So we take Bogov. How do we get to him if he's in Russia?'

'He's not in Russia.' Winston handed him a surveillance photo. 'This was taken four hours ago. Apparently, a few times a year, Arkady Bogov can't help fleeing the cool embrace of the Motherland and hauls arse for a holiday.'

Gretchen leaned over Grant for a look. 'Where is he?'

Winston replied, 'Where I would go in the summer if I wasn't cooped up in here.'

The photo showed a man in his mid-twenties with bleached blonde hair, walking through the crowded Calle Elvira market street in Granada, with a young, pale woman on each arm. He had on leopard-print tracksuit bottoms, a huge gold chain, surfer-style sunglasses, and a baggy black t-shirt that said "SWAG LIVES MATTER."

Behind him, trailed two security guards who looked like they could handle themselves.

Winston said, 'Boys and girls, meet Arkady Bogov.'

13

There was no breeze in the air to blow the many Union Jacks hanging outside the gilded sign of The King's Arms – one of the few traditional pubs remaining in Westminster. As was often the case, the barman had not long called last orders. Winston preferred it that way: he was rarely, if ever, out of work on time to be earlier, and the quieter period around last orders allowed him to keep a close watch on any new or irregular faces.

Old habits die hard. As his mentor had once told him, old habits tend to keep you alive.

'Evening, Barry,' said Winston, resting his forearms on the bar.

'Leo,' he replied. 'How goes it?'

It didn't take much small talk before Winston disclosed that he was four years sober. Almost to the hour.

Barry commented, 'You know this isn't the place where you get a special medal for that kind of thing. Not that I've got a dog in the fight, you understand. This isn't my place, and truth be told, the margins are a little better on lemonade these days than it is lager.' He paused, just to check.

Winston said nothing.

'But you don't want lemonade, do you.' Barry started pulling a pint of bitter. 'It's like I always say, Leo...'

'A right waste of good bitter.' He gave a gentle smile as Barry placed the pint down. He took a moment to contemplate the simple drink in front of him. It was crazy to him that a little glass of innocuous brown liquid could have done him so much damage. Or, rather, had assisted in him doing so much damage to himself. So many people could have one glass then walk away. That's where the problems had kicked in for Winston, though. He couldn't understand anyone who wanted just one drink. How, he thought, could you not want to feel like this forever? Drunk. Wasted. Plastered. It was glorious and it was awful.

He had gone to meetings. He had worked through the steps. All twelve of them.

He had admitted he was powerless over alcohol. That much was clear to anyone who had known him in his drinking years.

He had taken a fearless moral inventory, that was for damn sure. It crushed his soul to think about the things he had done.

Those, and all the other steps, he had down. Except for number eight.

Made a list of all persons we had harmed, and became willing to make amends to them all.

He couldn't, hand on heart, say that he had done that. He had sent operatives into hairy situations and they hadn't always come back in one piece. It was number eight that made him think about China. And Olivia Christie.

She wasn't, as far as he knew, an alcoholic. The concept of making amends for past wrongs was probably not in her vocabulary.

It got even worse when he thought about step number six.

We were entirely ready to have God remove all these defects of character.

Winston had never been much of a believer. When it came to questions about the Big Guy in the Sky, he always thought agnosticism was the only position that really made sense. He couldn't imagine being so confident about something so mysterious.

But the idea that only God could remove or correct the defects in his character disturbed Winston. If he didn't really know God, how could he improve himself? Get stronger? Was he really in all this alone? Like in that damp, rotten prison cell in the basement of the Ministry of State Security in Beijing?

The decision to leave came suddenly.

The next time Barry turned around, Winston was gone, and his pint was still there. Untouched.

The further Winston got into Pimlico, the more he felt that he was being followed. It was a quiet part of the city at that time of night midweek, and he'd heard footsteps nearby, but seen nobody to pair them up with.

He started taking figure-of-eight loops through the streets of two-storey Georgian terraced houses. He didn't want to go home until he was absolutely sure he'd lost the tail. Still, the footsteps always seemed to be half a street away. The figure that went with them straying out of sight at the key moment.

Winston then made a mistake he hadn't made since his early days: he rounded a corner while looking over his shoulder. He walked straight into a man, six foot three, wide shoulders, and a chest that could bench press 150kg.

The sudden impact made his heart lurch. Then came the relief as he saw the face.

'Grant...bloody hell,' he wheezed.

'You said we should talk,' Grant replied.

Winston did another shoulder-check before setting off again, this time pulling Grant in the direction of his home on Cambridge Street.

Unseen in the shadows, half a street away, was the figure that had been following Winston. And following Duncan Grant too.

14

Winston's flat was smart, elegant, and – if he was honest with himself – too expensive for him, but he liked that it was a short walk to Vauxhall Cross and it meant that he didn't need a car of his own. It was a miniature version of Olivia Christie's much grander, stately townhouse in Cadogan Square, Knightsbridge.

Grant flashed his eyebrows up when he entered the flat, impressed with the place. He got the impression that Winston hadn't made up his mind what he wanted the place to be. Modern, but not too crisp or clinical. Classic and traditional without being too stuffy. Certainly nothing that could be described as bohemian. Winston had zero interest in expressing his personality through the interior décor of his flat.

He did a quick inventory of anything sitting out that he might not want Grant to see. He didn't like unexpected visits that didn't allow prior tidying up. As Grant's handler, he didn't want to be judged too harshly for having the latest Lee Child hardback face down on his coffee table instead of some sophisticated non-fiction. In his early twenties, Winston had stockpiled history books on the American Civil War and the Second World War and Hitler and Stalin and the American Presidents, planning a deep-dive of 'proper reading' once he was in his forties. Almost all of it remained unread on his bookshelves. At fifty years old now, he realised he'd got it all wrong. The time to read that stuff was early, not late. Now, he could barely entertain reading anything that didn't start with a sentence like "A shot rang out…"

Winston directed Grant to the only sofa in the living room, while he took the armchair. Strange, he thought, how often we end up giving away the chairs we usually sit in to our guests. 'I did a sweep this morning,' explained Winston.

Grant found it quaint, and a little endearing, that Winston thought someone might want to bug his home. 'The Cold War really screwed your generation up, didn't it?'

Winston replied, 'I'd like to think it taught us a thing or two, as well. Like background checks.' He opened up his briefcase and took out a manila folder.

Grant's pupils dilated as they registered the light blue colour of an Albion file. 'Gretchen?' he said.

'STRAP Two clearance or above,' said Winston. 'Unredacted. Everything that was ever written down. Or survived Imogen Swann's late-night shredding sessions.'

Grant hungrily skimmed the pages, getting more in ten seconds that he'd got in nearly a week in close quarters with Gretchen. 'What's the protein?' he asked.

'You two haven't talked much in the Tank?'

'We're two covert operatives who don't entirely trust each other, and don't know each other. It's not exactly been a Tennessee Williams play of gushing emotions in there.'

Winston chuckled. Not just at the observation, but that a guy as hard as Grant knew about Tennessee Williams. 'As far as the protein goes: she was good. Very good.'

Even in Grant's limited experience, he knew that "very" wasn't an adverb that Winston casually threw around.

He went on, 'She wouldn't have been an Albion otherwise. Imogen Swann wound her agents so tightly back then, a case like Marlow was only a matter of time. Gretchen, however, served her time with distinction then simply moved on. No burn-out, death, or scandal. Imogen Swann took her into the Hannibals when Marlow went AWOL and none of her other agents could get him back. Gretchen got much closer than a lot of others did, but not close enough for a kill shot.' Winston sniffed. 'You don't trust her.'

Grant said, 'I made that mistake last time with Édith Lagrange.'

'I only had two rules in the field: trust no one, and never get too close. You learned your lesson with the former. Don't make a mistake this time with the latter.'

'What makes you say that?'

'Because right now Gretchen Winter is the only other Albion you know who isn't Henry Marlow. It will give you an artificial sense of connection, and if she isn't on the straight and narrow, she'll play on it. Use it.'

Grant slowly flicked through the file, admiring Gretchen's achievements. And her commitment to preservation of life. There was no bravado. No showboating. Just a true professional. It was exactly the kind of Albion that Grant wanted to be. 'Clean as a whistle.'

'Yeah,' said Winston. 'Maybe a little too clean. If I was sending someone to derail you–' he pointed at the file '–that's who I'd send to do it.'

Grant took a moment to consider his handler's opinion. Was he getting Gretchen wrong? Grant thought. Had he been too quick to see the good in Gretchen as a tonic against his experiences with Marlow?

Winston, holding his cards to his chest, asked, 'Where is she on letting Marlow go?'

'She thinks we should consider it.'

'Even though he's given us no credible threat?'

Grant dropped the file on the table. 'You don't have to convince me. Over my dead body does Marlow get out of Vauxhall Cross. If what's coming is the price we pay for keeping him, then so be it.'

Winston nodded. 'We have to get Joseph.'

'And if we don't?'

He puffed. 'Depending on what we're facing...then the Chief might have to do the unthinkable. And I don't want to put an operative in the position I was with her many moons ago.'

Grant had heard rumours about Winston's past and something that happened in China. He'd also caught a glimpse one day, in the European Task Force control room, of a thick scar that stretched down Winston's forearm to his wrist. Rumours were, the two were related. Grant knew that if he couldn't ask now, sitting in Winston's living room late on a midweek night, there probably would never be a right time.

'Leo...' Grant began. 'How much do you trust Olivia Christie?'

Winston took a long breath. 'Let me guess: this is about China.'

'I hear things.'

Winston headed for the kitchen, pouring them both a tumbler of tap water. He had nothing else to offer for a drink. Not even tea or coffee. After handing Grant his drink, Winston returned to the armchair. 'I won't go into specifics. The basics are that Olivia and I were on deep cover in China. She was my handler. The mission went south in a hurry and we needed an extraction. It never came. Leaving us on the run for a few days, totally cut off. This was long before SIMs and burners. We had to flee our hotel in the middle of the night – at some point Olivia and I got separated. A red van pulled up at the end of this little market. I'll never forget it. These six guys streamed out of this thing, and another van cut off the lane behind me. I was trapped. I tell you, if you think China is hard now, it was worse back then. Once you were swallowed up in that prison system you never got out. Not without intervention from on high. So Olivia and I, before we travelled there, we swore to each other, if either of us got caught...' he paused, the weight of the decision still heavy on his shoulders, 'we would shoot the other.'

Grant looked at him in shock.

'It sounds extreme, I know,' said Winston, 'but we knew, if we were caught we were as good as dead anyway. The Chinese didn't waste resources locking up foreign spies for decades at a time. They just took you out to the countryside and shot you on the parade ground of some labour camp, then had the prisoners bury you in an unmarked grave. I remember thinking, when those guys came piling out of that van, how big they seemed. Tall and strong. I've always looked after myself, but I couldn't hold off six of them. Olivia had hidden in the doorway of a market stall. When they took me away, I kicked and wrestled with everything I had, fighting to give Olivia a clear shot. She had the gun in her hand, pointed at me. I yelled at her to pull the trigger. When I yelled, I'd never heard my voice like that. Such desperation. Knowing that in a few more seconds there would be no escape if she didn't take the shot. It's strange how we can fear pain more than death. But we often do.' Winston shrugged. 'Sometimes doing nothing can still be a violent act. I kept begging her to shoot me, but she couldn't do it. They dragged me backwards towards the van. They slid the door shut, and the lights went out.

Olivia managed to get away. I was locked up for weeks in solitary before they began to interrogate me.'

'The MSS?' asked Grant.

Winston nodded.

The Chinese Ministry of State Security. Civilian intelligence, state security, and secret police agency.

Winston said, 'They went to town on me. I don't really know for how long. They say that if you have a baby and it starts to choke, when the paramedics come they ask the parents how long the baby was choking for. Invariably they describe it as lasting twice as long as it actually was. That's what the stress does to you. Everything gets warped. I thought I had been held for about nine months to a year. When I was released, the woman from the British embassy told me it had been six months. I didn't believe her until she showed me a newspaper.'

'Six months,' said Grant in wonder. 'And you never broke.'

'Not there, I didn't. My interrogator and I didn't get on so well. The thing with the MSS, they're not really sticklers for the whole human rights thing. One day I woke up and found him standing over me with a big old butcher knife. Him and someone else held me down and gouged the blade up my arm. Bastards tried to suicide me off their block. It must have really pissed them off when I clotted faster than they thought. Or maybe they thought I'd stop fighting.'

'Didn't anyone try to get you back?' asked Grant.

'Olivia did what she could. But we had just caught a Chinese informant working for MI5 and Beijing knew about it. It was a quid pro quo, until we realised that the Chinese informant didn't have anything worth a damn and handed them back. Beijing eventually agreed to an exchange.'

Grant asked, 'You don't still wish that she'd taken the shot. Do you?'

Winston thought about it for a moment. 'I struggled for a long time about that when I got back. Drinking helped. Because I hated not being able to sleep. Booze was the only that guaranteed I could get to sleep. My nightmares didn't come when I was asleep. They came when I was awake.'

'Mine come at night,' said Grant.

'Do yourself a favour, Duncan. Never start drinking heavily. In this game, in no time at all, you'll find yourself in a nightmare you can't wake up from.'

'How do you deal with it now?'

'Olivia was the one who got me sober. Now, I do this thing sometimes...I go to the King's Arms and ask for a pint of bitter. But I don't drink it. I just stand there, staring at it. Staring it down. Like I'm telling it, "you don't control me anymore. Look how strong I am, to stand here and not even flinch. I can take it. There's nothing the world can throw at me that I can't take." Because I know what I've lived through. And if I can survive that cell – that interrogator – I can survive anything.'

'I should go.' Grant put his glass down on the table. Before he stood up, he said, 'There's one thing I don't understand...if Gretchen was sent after Marlow, why were we told that no one had ever come back from trying to kill Marlow?'

'That's a question that's been hounding me since I laid eyes on that blue file.'

Grant stood up, preparing to leave. 'I have an early flight.' He stopped in the hall. 'Leo...if it ever came to it...And I asked you to...'

Winston was adamant. 'I'd pull the trigger, Duncan.'

Outside, a sudden summer rain shower had broken out. The sort that catches everyone off guard when they're woefully under-dressed after a hot day.

At the end of Cambridge Street, looking at Grant walking unperturbed in the rain, stood Gretchen, holding the hood of her light rain jacket over her head. Once Grant had gone, she disappeared into the darkness from where she'd come.

Although she was within walking distance of her almost completely bare flat overlooking Hyde Park, Gretchen got on a night bus around Piccadilly, asking for a day ticket rather than a destination.

She sat downstairs, watching the rapidly gathering rain slosh by the kerbside. She never sat upstairs on double-decker buses. It was bad tradecraft. In a crisis, it left only one exit – the narrow stairway – that can easily be blocked. Downstairs had a wider exit, and windows that could be kicked out if necessary.

It wasn't long before the windows steamed up, and the bus filled up with twenty-, thirty-somethings returning home for the night, tipsy. One particular couple sat three rows in front of her and proceeded to kiss each other with a rare and disarming passion. Gretchen had registered their rolling luggage when they got on the bus. They seemed too hungry for each other to have been away travelling together. Gretchen wondered if they'd been on separate journeys and found each other by chance.

Whatever their situation, Gretchen couldn't remember what such passion felt like anymore. To be kissed. To be wanted that much. That fingers-digging-into-your-back kind of wanted. True desire where you lose yourself and forget that you're sitting on a bus where other people can see you.

Gretchen got out of her seat suddenly and rang the bell to get off. She was two stops early. It didn't matter. She just needed to be somewhere else.

15

Grant had never liked working with a partner. Not in training, and certainly not on his first Albion operation. He knew that he could learn plenty of things from Gretchen, and there were many positives to working as a pair. It was two sets of eyes, for a start, allowing for much greater coverage. But there were also negatives, as Grant was discovering, being surrounded by happy families and couples in Heathrow Airport, close to peak summertime. On your own as an operative, you can blend in because you don't have to talk to anyone, and your body language can be muted without giving anything away. Next to Gretchen, he felt awkward and mechanical. Out of sync with her.

As they made their way through the duty-free area, Gretchen paused, pretending to look at some perfume. 'You've got to loosen up,' she told him. 'You're too stiff.'

'I know,' he agreed.

'Here,' she said, taking his free hand and putting it around her waist. She showed him the perfume bottle. 'Look at the box, look at the obscenely expensive price, then look at me with a smile.'

He did so with a carefree and easy-going manner.

Gretchen playfully swatted his arm, then led them back to the walkway. 'There we go. Just another happy couple. Easy.'

Grant said, 'Or we could just take out our phones and ignore each other like everyone else seems to be.'

She took his hand. 'This way's better.'

Grant couldn't disagree.

The heat at Málaga Airport was jarring after the chill and rain in London. The heat only intensified on the hire-car drive to Granada, making their way deeper inland to Andalusia at the southern tip of Spain. They didn't see a single cloud in the ninety minutes it took to get there. The surrounding countryside was bone dry. Mile after mile of hillsides were covered in olive groves, the ground a pale red underneath the dots of greenery.

When they got close to Granada's city limits, they decided to take a drive-by of Bogov's modern, state-of-the-art villa on the outskirts of the city, on a rural vineyard far from prying eyes.

'Don't slow down too much,' Gretchen reminded him.

'I know, I've got it,' said Grant, craning his neck for a look at the front gate.

Gretchen readied a camera at her open window, keeping it as close to the bottom of the window frame as possible.

'All clear,' Grant confirmed, seeing no one around.

Gretchen held her finger on the top button, taking a stream of photos of the front of the villa.

Once they were safely away, Gretchen reviewed what they had.

'Okay,' she said. 'I've got a young female. Twenty-one to twenty-threeish. Might be younger. Blonde. Pale. Wafer thin. Could be Russian. Her colouring's not dark enough to be from around here. Security looks minimal.' She pinched the screen to zoom in on a security hut at the end of the driveway. 'Guard looks like he's sleeping.'

'Could be a different story inside, though,' countered Grant.

'No sign of Bogov. But I've got three supercars in the driveway. And one heavy coming out the front door in a dark suit and tie.'

The idea of wearing a suit in such heat made Grant recoil. 'Access isn't great,' he said, looking around. 'This is the only road in or out.'

Gretchen checked the rest of the photos. 'Unless we want to take him up and over a ten-foot hedge then across about ten miles of open countryside.' She then compared her photos with the drone images MI6 had assembled, showing the heat patterns of movement. 'It looks like most of the people inside are assembling at the back of the house.' She turned the photo, then considered the angle and approach of the afternoon sun. 'It will be more shaded out there. But unless Bogov is holed up with about seven other girlfriends at a time, he's got a lot more security in there than we know about.'

They were staying in Granada's Albaicín district, a World Heritage Site of mostly white *carmen* houses in a Medieval Moorish style, built onto a hillside overlooking the rest of the city. A labyrinthine and intricate network of narrow streets wound their way from near the top at San Nicolás, all the way down through Calle Elvira – the busiest street that formed the spine of

Albaicín – plunging towards the River Darro. The houses
sprawled across the hillside, the alleys packed with little shops and
cafés.

Grant and Gretchen had been in their tiny one-bedroom
apartment near the top of the hill for only ten minutes when
word from Vauxhall Cross reached them: Bogov was on the
move, and heading in their direction. GCHQ had picked up an
internet search for a Moroccan restaurant at the foot of Calle
Elvira, specifically checking their lunch menu and opening times.

Gretchen and Grant had to hustle to get there ahead of their
Russian target.

In the end, they made it with time to spare, after Bogov had
to stop by the side of the road to be sick. Relentless heat, lack of
water, and too much vodka made for a poor combination for
Bogov. He couldn't handle his booze, much as he liked to think
he could.

In his inebriated state, he had brought two of his girlfriends
with him, each sizing up the other with similar pity. An air of
'How did we end up stuck with this creep?' exchanged silently
between them as they took their seats outside under the shade of
a canopy. Bogov wore baggy shorts and a white button-up shirt
that he left hanging out, as if he'd been startled awake by a fire
alarm in the middle of the night. He wore surfer-style wrap-
around sunglasses and chain-smoked.

Gretchen and Grant, dressed in casual and unassuming
summer clothing, heard him before they laid eyes on him. His
hacking cough could be heard a good distance away, as well as
his barracking his security detail in obnoxious Russian. He
slouched in his chair, nursing the first in a long line of straight
vodkas throughout lunch.

His two security guards sat at the next table, wolfing down
chicken tagine from elaborately patterned dishes, eager to get

their protein in after a heavy weights session in Bogov's gym that morning – a gym that Bogov only entered to leer at his girlfriends doing yoga.

Gretchen grabbed Grant by the hand, as if overtaken by a sudden bout of affection. As she leaned in to kiss him on the cheek, she whispered an improvised plan to him.

Grant laid the groundwork by pointing at the upper floors above the restaurant building where the owners lived. Gretchen mentioned the architecture as Grant snapped away. As he lowered the camera, he kept his finger on the shutter button to catch pictures of the security team. Gretchen took up a position in front of the metal restaurant sign, playfully posing by jutting a hip out to the side.

Following the cue, Grant gestured for her to back up, and back up. Bringing the camera up to his eye, then imploring her to keep going.

The moment that Gretchen collided with the sign and knocked it over, Grant panned the camera towards Bogov, who didn't seem to register the subsequent loud clatter on the tiled ground.

Gretchen covered her mouth in fake shock, apologising to the waiter who hurried over to fix things.

'It's no problem,' he promised her. 'Maybe it's the...' He motioned at his face to indicate her sunglasses.

She and Grant left swiftly, trying to keep their backs to the Russians.

Once they were a safe distance away, Gretchen asked, 'How was it?'

'Like we thought,' said Grant. 'Lax. Sluggish reaction times. Each of them went in different directions. One lunged towards the noise, another flinched away for cover. But one of them made a move towards his inside jacket pocket.'

Gretchen wasn't intimidated. 'We knew they'd be carrying. What matters is that they're not the most adept at using whatever they're packing. What about Bogov? No one made a move towards their principal?'

'Nope. A guy like that, who can blame them.'

A contact across the city had tracked down the local cleaner who cleaned Bogov's villa. Considering how poorly Bogov paid them, and the trashed state the place was normally left in, the cleaner was only too happy to take €500 to relay what he had seen go on there. He also had overheard the previous day that Bogov was planning a visit to the traditional Arab bath house at the foot of the hill where the Alhambra palace was situated. It was an excellent opportunity to catch Bogov without his security detail, and might offer a chance at turning him if they cornered him and put the fear of God into him. Something that both Grant and Gretchen were capable of.

It would be risky. But they both thought it was worth it.

Once there, Bogov would be far too drunk to remember anyone's face from the restaurant incident, but his security wouldn't. Grant was certain that they had paid little attention, but if he and Gretchen appeared after Bogov arrived, it might prompt some suspicion.

They got showered and changed in good time and met each other in the first pool. It was the first time they had seen each other undressed to any degree. Until then, they had both been dressed for freezing temperatures, or in loose summer clothing.

Grant's thick legs easily filled out his shorts. His upper body in a classic V-taper of wide shoulders, rock-solid chest, and slim waist. Gretchen's gaze lingered a little longer than she knew it should have on his muscular look. He looked like he was wearing a plate of armour.

Gretchen wasn't the only one looking. Grant drank in her silhouette for as long as he thought he could get away with.

'No sign of him yet,' said Gretchen, edging into the water.

Grant refocussed. 'It was just old Spanish men in the changing rooms,' he said.

It was a surreal place to be on an espionage mission, quite at odds with the peaceful surroundings. There was no music. Just the gentle trickling of water in the various pools at different temperatures. The air was moist and warm and steamy, the scent of essential oils and sweet mint tea in the air.

Then a sharp voice cut through the calm atmosphere. The same voice they had heard back on Calle Elvira. But muffled.

Around the corner from the pool, through a glass wall, Grant could see that it was Bogov, blind drunk, arguing with the staff at the entrance. They had refused him entry on the grounds of being intoxicated. His security team had to pull him away.

When Grant returned to the pool, Gretchen asked, 'Did they make you?'

'No,' he replied, feeling like he couldn't return quite as close as he had been to her now that Bogov wouldn't be appearing. 'What should we do?' he asked, hoping for a particular answer.

She paused, thinking the same thing. 'We can't get changed and follow him on foot. We took a swing on this and we missed.'

Trying to be subtle, Grant suggested, 'He's going to Sacromonte tonight. Let him get home to sober up for a while, and we'll reload tonight.'

Gretchen tilted her head back into the water and shut her eyes. 'Sounds good,' she said.

Grant looked across as an older couple vacated a tiny well-like pool. 'It's the coldest one in the house,' he said. 'Fancy?'

'Why would I sit in a cold one?' she asked.

'That's what you do here. You go from hot to cold on a loop. Maybe drink some tea in between.' Seeing that she was unconvinced, he told her, 'It's invigorating. Or have you spent too long in front of warm fires, or wrapped up in insulated jackets?'

With a reluctant smile, she said, 'Alright.'

The pool was narrow but deep, designed for standing only and no more than two at a time.

Grant waded in first, used to the sudden shock of cold water from his ocean swims off the Skye coast. Holding out his hand to Gretchen, she held back when her foot first hit the water on the first step down.

'Just plunge in,' he said. 'It's the best way. Come on,' he urged her, 'before your body cools down from the last pool.'

Her mouth fell open as the water sloshed around her ankles, then quickly rose past her knees, then her waist. She was silent as she took in a long lungful of air, holding it until the water lapped up past her chest like it did with Grant.

'Nice isn't it,' he said.

'That's one word for it,' she groaned, then broke into a chuckle. For a moment, she lost her footing on the tiles below and fell into Grant.

He caught her by her forearms and held her up.

She could feel his natural strength. It was the first time she had felt truly safe in years.

Grant helped her upright again. The feeling of being almost in an embrace with someone was foreign and strange. He had forgotten that feeling.

They both had. And it had to remain unspoken between them.

They had a job to do. They understood that.

What they understood most, though, was that they were

standing next to the only other person who could possibly understand them.

Grant reminded himself to be a bloody professional.

As did Gretchen to herself.

They were also wondering the same thing: am I being worked here?

16

Visitors to Granada were always pointed in the direction of the Alhambra – and with good reason. Moorish poets described it as "a pearl set among emeralds", referring to the colour of the magnificent medieval palace against the backdrop of woods. But for those looking for tradition, beauty, and raw, unfiltered passion, it didn't get much more intense than witnessing zambra flamenco in the Sacromonte caves where there were several *cuevas* – the venues where flamenco was performed. Sacromonte was on the upper hillside of the historic quarter of the city, the main thoroughfare a twisting cobbled road overlooking a dangerous precipice to the river below.

Natural caves had been carved into the hillside down the centuries, doubling as homes for the performers and staff.

The *cueva* that Bogov had decided to visit was as traditional as it got in Granada. They performed zambra flamenco – an intense type unique to the region – in an intimate cave, where copper pots hung from the walls and ceiling, along with dozens and dozens of old photographs showing the evolution of the *cueva*. Hardly a thing had changed in a century. The dancers' outfits were mostly the same. The hairstyles. And, of course, the music.

Not that Arkady Bogov and his entourage cared much for the authentic atmosphere, except the one girlfriend he had brought with him. At her insistence, Bogov had grudgingly put on a smart shirt. Which he had left hanging out.

Grant and Gretchen were already in their seats that lined the edges of the long, narrow room where the performance took place. It was hot, intimate, and crowded. Barely enough space in the middle of the room for the performers.

Bogov was last to take his seat. He had sobered up since being ejected from the Arab bath house, but not by much.

There were a number of solo performances in the first half. Some with dancing, some without. The longer it went on, the more it looked like Bogov would leave early. He was practically asleep in his chair.

By the time the closing number came around, the temperature in the *cueva* had soared. The dancers were pouring sweat. They retreated to the margins of the room as a solo guitarist brought out an old wooden chair. The same that his father and grandfather before him had sat on for performances. To start, he plucked single, deep notes. Then his fingers moved nimbly down the guitar fretboard with stunning fluidity, plucking more and more notes. The ease of motion was matched only by the beauty of the plaintive chord progression he played with rapidly picking fingers.

The dexterity was impressive, but it wasn't simply a display of technical prowess. The expression on his face said everything about how deeply he felt each note.

After a brief pause, a second rhythm guitar joined in, along with handclaps from the female dancers, who punctuated off-beats with stamps of their feet, making their way back into the centre of the floor.

The crowd looked on in hushed awe at what they were hearing and seeing.

Grant only had moderate Spanish.

Gretchen was fluent, and offered to translate the singer's deep sense of longing and loss.

He nodded his approval.

'Softly, a furtive teardrop falls from her sparkling eyes,' she whispered. 'Many others have gone before me...and now I don't know which way to turn...'

Grant was listening to the music, his head turned slightly towards Gretchen. He couldn't look directly at her while she translated as she needed to be close to his ear. Instead, Grant stared at her hands in her lap.

Gretchen kept on, 'What more do I need than her...For a single moment, the beats of her beautiful heart are close to mine...Could my sighing bring her comfort...and whisper in sweet reply. Oh heaven, then I could die...No more I'd ask you... Then I could die.'

The singer didn't have a microphone, nor did he need one. Grant had never heard anything so thunderous and tender coming from the same voice at the same time. All without the use of a microphone.

Grant and Gretchen were as transfixed as everyone else in the room. Grant spotted at least two people with tears in their eyes.

The emotion crested, like a wave rising and rising, then finally breaking in a stunning crescendo.

Silence.

Then the clapping took over, and the dancers took the centre of the room, as the guitar played on without vocals. The dancers were every bit as intense as the singer, saying much without words.

As they neared the end of the piece, they encouraged random members of the audience to join them.

A female dancer reached for Grant's hand at the same time as a male dancer – both head to toe in black – reached for Gretchen's. There was no time to discuss the situation, but it was clear that most of the crowd were participating. By dancing, they actually fit in better. Bogov was one of the few who wasn't dancing, getting aggressive with his girlfriend who accepted the hand of a male dancer. She was only too keen to be in the hands of someone who had genuine passion for something beyond money.

Grant admitted in Spanish to his dancer that he didn't know what he was doing.

She told him that it didn't matter. She pointed to her heart. 'This is all that matters,' she told him.

After a minute with their respective partners, the flamenco dancers brought Grant and Gretchen together in the middle of the crowd, then released them to each other.

Grant pulled her close as the dancer had demonstrated. He wrapped his arm around Gretchen's waist, turning her slowly, seductively.

One thought crossed his mind: *if she is playing me, then damn is she good.*

They looked deep into each other's eyes, and for a moment they both genuinely forgot why they were there. Bogov was going nowhere. Too busy scowling at his girlfriend who was enjoying the dancer's smooth movement and kind smile.

Eventually, Bogov had seen enough. He lunged at the dancer from his chair, knocking it over and grabbing the man by the front of his shirt. Bogov pulled his fist back, but one of his guards stopped him before he could land an actual blow.

The other dancers piled in. The older ones were the angriest. Zambra flamenco was no place for anything other than passion and love. Violence and aggression had no place there. Fighting in the *cueva* was like fighting in someone else's living room.

Then, another back-up security team piled in who were very different from the sloppy amateurs Grant and Gretchen had documented earlier in the day. This crew were well-drilled and disciplined.

In a few seconds, they had their principal separated from the male dancer, and ushered him out of the *cueva*, keeping his head down as they were trained to in such situations.

The music had kept going, but most of the room had stopped dancing, retreating from the sudden violence. Gretchen, still held in close by Grant, looked up at him. 'He's going off the rails. We need to take him. Tonight. Or his team might get him back to Russia before he gets arrested.'

17

The cleaner that their contact had found mentioned one item that seemed to be of particular interest to Bogov. The only thing in the villa that they were absolutely, under no circumstances, to touch, or go near. Looking vaguely in its general direction was only barely tolerated.

The item was an Ormolu clock. Sometimes referred to as a 'death clock'.

It was an antique mantle clock, made with gilt brass, meticulously handcrafted with extraordinary detail thanks to the Ormolu process. The term came about from the process of applying ground gold-mercury amalgam to a bronze object. A process so dangerous that France outlawed them in 1830. And with good reason. Almost every gilder who made one of the clocks died from mercury poisoning – before anyone discovered there was any danger in handling the chemical with bare hands, or breathing it in for hours at a time in an enclosed room.

The phrase "mad as a hatter" came about from hat-makers who used mercury in a similar process. They absorbed the mercury into their skin and inhaled it, which made them delirious and lose their minds.

Nowadays, a genuine, original-period Death Clock could fetch upwards of £75,000. Often more at auction. The clocks had generated a cult following among young millionaires like Bogov who were seduced by the dramatic name, becoming the ultimate status symbols to leave in the background of Instagram photos in your home.

For a Moscow-slum kid like Bogov, the day he bought his Death Clock was the day he knew he had really made it. It was far more than just a status symbol to him. It was a source of power, and proof of his newfound wealth. The clock came with him everywhere he went. If he couldn't bring it, then he stayed at home too.

Bogov's cleaner couldn't say for sure what was inside the clock. It could have been an irrelevant family heirloom. Or something of vital importance. Either way, it was Grant and Gretchen's only lead, and they had to run it down.

If Bogov was taken out of the country, the Death Clock would go with him. And an extraction on Russian soil was not something that anyone wanted.

So Grant and Gretchen waited until nightfall, well past ten. He had lobbied for a quiet entry, which was fine with Gretchen. The drone thermal-heat maps, the sudden appearance of more capable guards at the *cueva*, painted a picture of an experienced crew working behind the scenes.

The duo moved silently along the grass verge next to the driveway, staying under the trees that lined the way. The first body they dropped was the guard at the security hut at the end of the driveway. Grant's gun made an almost silent "*pfft*" noise, as a poisoned dart landed right over the man's heart. Grant's commitment to using darts for the initial stages impressed Gretchen. Not just operationally, where it made total sense: leaving a lot of dead Russian bodies behind never helps in the long run. But from a moral perspective, it was the kind of consideration she hadn't heard from an operative in her line of work. Especially an Albion.

With the driveway guard on the deck, Grant checked the man's pockets for a keycard or something that might give them access to the main house. Gretchen covered the house, then felt Grant's hand on her back, signalling that it was time to move again.

A motion sensor caught them as they made their way gently but swiftly across the gravel, prompting a bright white light to turn on, illuminating them.

They were dressed fully in black, wearing light shoes for quiet navigation of the house, their tops slim-fit to prevent material flapping around or providing something to grab on to in a scrap.

Grant didn't break stride when the light came on. He readied the swipe card from the guard, using it to enter, causing a click from the lock that would have been completely inconsequential under any other circumstances.

Grant and Gretchen froze in the doorway, listening for any sign that they had been heard.

They had.

Gretchen heard it first, from Grant's left. A shoe landing on a tile. She reached behind Grant's head to throw it forward out of the way, then she fired the dart shot.

In the darkness under an archway, a heavy body fell forward into a shaft of light, landing with a thud.

Grant slowly exhaled, mouth closed. He holstered the dart gun and took out his Glock 17. His relieved expression said it all. *Time for bullets.*

Gretchen did likewise.

They hadn't bothered with suppressors or subsonic ammunition – both of which were far from silent. With so many people in the villa, if they needed to fire live rounds in the house, they would be waking some people up for sure, regardless of ammunition.

What little activity had taken place was already enough. The security team – the skilled ones – were assembling at the back of the house, where they had set up their station, monitoring an extensive bank of CCTV images.

Half-seen figures dashed from one room to another. A flurry of footsteps. Then silence again.

Gretchen pointed forward. They hadn't come all that way to retreat at the first sign of resistance.

No one wanted to be the first to fire as the muzzle flash in the darkness would give away their position. But then the lights in the front reception area came on above Grant and Gretchen, the unexpected flash piercing their vision for a moment as the gunfire started at the other end of the house.

The pair dived for cover behind a long marble console table. Grant upended it, requiring all of his strength to flip it onto its side to use as a temporary shield – his lugging heavy timber around on the beaches of Skye for a workout proving highly practical.

'Keep your head down,' said Gretchen, who shot a single round at the light above. It showered them both with bulb glass, but it put them back where they needed to be: in the dark.

'Go,' Grant said, eager to take advantage of the darkness again.

They played off each other beautifully. Fire then move. Fire then move. Covering each other to take up optimum positions, watching out for being flanked by anyone from the front of the house.

Bogov appeared at the top of the stairs in leopard-print boxer shorts, holding a submachine gun like he was Tony Montana in *Scarface*. He was as reckless as Montana in his firing, too. Unleashing a torrent of bullets in Grant and Gretchen's general direction. The only thing he succeeded in damaging was the value of his property.

While the Russians kept firing, Gretchen yelled at Grant, 'Take him!' indicating Bogov. 'I'll get what we came for.'

She could see it on the living-room mantlepiece. Perilously close to destruction. She had put down three bodies, Grant another two, so she knew that there were still sufficient enemy forces around.

Bogov was yelling in Russian from the top of the stairs, 'Kill them, boys!'

While Bogov reloaded, Grant took a peek around and fired a single shot through his knee. Bogov collapsed to the ground in agony, his leg flopping underneath him. Unable to take his drunken bodyweight, Bogov tumbled down the stairs, losing his submachine gun on the way. Grant dragged him onto his feet, holding a gun to his head. 'Tell them,' he told Bogov. 'Tell them I have a gun to your head!'

Bogov wanted the agony in his leg to stop. More than that, though, he wanted to survive. He begged and pleaded for his men to stop firing.

Grant kept Bogov between him and the other guards. 'Tell them to put down their weapons.'

Bogov relayed the message, then added a little something at the end.

Gretchen's Russian was patchy, but the feverish change of tone told her that Bogov was up to something. She got off two rounds apiece at the guards who had attempted to outdraw her. They were both too slow.

No one else fancied testing her further after that.

Gretchen beat a path for the clock.

'You stupid pig shits,' Bogov cried. 'You did all this for the clock? I have cash upstairs. You have no idea who you're stealing from!'

Grant held his forearm around Bogov's neck, dragging him towards the front door in preparation for an exit.

Gretchen grabbed the Death Clock and opened up the top, finding a steel-encased memory stick inside. 'We're good,' she called out, still careful as she backed towards the front door, never turning her body away.

It was sensible technique. The only problem was that she then didn't see the Russian hiding in Grant's blind spot under another archway.

Gretchen had a natural instinct to count the bodies on the ground versus how many were still standing. The quick maths of the situation told her they were still short a body. Then she heard Grant behind being disarmed by the guard.

Bogov threw himself to the ground, still wailing and thrashing his upper body around.

The guard had a pistol to Grant's temple. 'Drop the memory stick,' the guard demanded.

'Forget the memory stick,' spluttered Bogov. 'Shoot them both...'

Grant knew that he didn't have long to act. The gun was being held near the front of his temple, which meant that if he tried to break free by moving his head forwards, it brought more of his brain into play in a potential firing. Moving his head backwards would present a lesser risk. The *overall* risk still wasn't great, though. There aren't many people that will take any kind of odds with a gun to your head. The way Grant saw it, a gun to your head was the ideal time to try something risky. Otherwise it's game over.

Grant could almost see the barrel of the gun in his peripheral vision. That meant the guard was letting it drift further forward. Now was the time for action before he corrected it.

Grant threw his head backwards, then placed the web of one hand across the barrel of the guard's gun, and the web of his other hand against the rear. Before the guard could counter, Grant had pushed the gun up and out of the guard's hand, then redirected the weapon straight back at the guard's face.

The guard backed up quickly, almost falling over his heels. All he could see and taste was blood.

It would have been the simplest thing for Grant to fire a round into his chest. It would make their exit much easier. But the threat had been eliminated, and now Grant had Bogov back in his control, which curtailed any further action from the guards.

They all hated Bogov anyway. They weren't going to risk their lives for him, and certainly not for some memory stick.

Grant dragged Bogov across the front hallway, telling him, 'Take the Porsche keys. The Taycan outside.'

Bogov managed to follow his orders through the pain, reaching out a flailing hand towards the bowl that contained his various car keys. He grabbed at three, then tossed the two that he didn't require.

Gretchen threw the front door shut behind them, holstering her weapon as Grant threw her the key.

'You drive,' he said. 'I'm on crowd control.' Using Bogov as a shield for his front, Grant dragged him backwards towards the car.

'Please,' Bogov pleaded, grasping at his bloodied leg. 'I'll pay you anything…'

'Your money can't help you now,' Grant told him, hauling him towards the boot while Gretchen started up the engine.

Sensing that his time was running out, Bogov shook his head rapidly and grabbed a fistful of Grant's black t-shirt. 'Everything I know is on the memory stick…I don't know anything else… Please! Just shoot me. It will be ten times better than what they will do to me…'

Gretchen revved the engine. 'Got to go,' she said with concern.

Grant wrestled Bogov into the boot, tying his hands with wire cuffs.

Bogov's pleas continued, 'There's nowhere you can take me that is safe. Not even your own custody…'

Grant was about to shut the boot. Then he paused. 'Who are you so afraid of? The Kremlin?'

Bogov looked at Grant like he was mad. 'Charles Joseph! Who else?'

The Russians inside had regrouped, ready for one last attack. One of them had pointed out that the Kremlin wouldn't be best pleased at them losing one of their most valuable assets.

The front door flew open, along with a burst of gunfire from Bogov's submachine gun towards the car that was already racing away. The guard in charge redirected the line of fire away from the car at the last second. 'Arkady's in the boot, you idiot! Get back inside and call it in.'

18

The safe house was deep in the Andalusian hills, on the outskirts of the Sierra Nevada National Park. The night was electric with the sound of insects, the ground and plant life throbbing and alive. Bogov's muffled cries joined the chorus as Grant covered his mouth while he hauled him into the old farmhouse.

Gretchen took a long check of the panorama. They were in an ideal location at the top of the hill. A set of headlights would be visible from a mile away, and the sound of an engine obvious long before preventive and protective measures had to be taken.

The building might have been old, but it was technologically advanced from a security point of view. Cameras covered all access points, through the empty barn in the back, and on all windows which were kept shuttered – not uncommon in the area.

The inside was barren. The floor covered in broken tiling, every surface thick with dust. Grant took Bogov to the only functioning room in the place: the basement, which was behind an electronically locked steel door. Behind it was a bare-bones communications set-up, all encrypted and hooked up to Vauxhall Cross.

In a small cell was a metal bench, bolted into the concrete at the centre of the room, with metal hooks to attach a detainee's restraints. Grant locked Bogov in.

'What about his leg?' asked Gretchen out of earshot.

'He won't bleed out,' replied Grant.

'Are you sure about that?'

He thought for a moment.

Gretchen suggested, 'Let's patch him up. He'll be more willing to talk if he knows we don't want him to die.'

It made sense. Grant did it while Gretchen fetched them all bottles of water. She opened one for Bogov and tipped it into his gaping mouth. When she stopped pouring, he instinctively gulped for more.

Gretchen said, 'After you talk.'

'Please,' he cried, 'I'll tell what you want to know. Don't hurt me...'

Bogov had chosen a career at a computer keyboard precisely because he didn't want to end up at the violent end of criminal behaviour – he just wanted to get rich with as little effort and danger as possible. He was the very opposite of mind over matter when it came to pain. Just the thought of it turned his body stiff.

Grant asked, 'Where is Charles Joseph?'

'Please,' Bogov answered. 'I swear, I don't know.' His eyes were like saucers, desperate to communicate his truthfulness. 'I never even met him!'

'What do you do for him?' asked Gretchen, pulling up a chair alongside him.

'I write code to hack computers, that's all.'

Gretchen kicked at Bogov's shattered leg. The pain turned him rigid, locked in an agonised pose until the pain faded.

Grant didn't react, but inside he was surprised at how little the act of violence meant to Gretchen. Her expression was no different to when they were walking through Málaga Airport, or floating in the Arab bath house. He found it slightly chilling.

'I want more than that, Arkady,' said Gretchen.

Bogov looked to Grant in appeal.

'Don't look at me.' He pointed at Gretchen. 'She asked you a question.'

Bogov relented, nodding his head. 'Okay, okay, I'm sorry... When I wrote malware, I was approached by Kremlin official.' He shrugged. 'A spy. FSB or whatever. He said they wanted to hire me so they could use malware. In return, they would protect me from prosecution.'

'That was very generous of them,' said Grant.

'I never targeted Russians. That's why. It's the only no-no in the industry. You can sell your software products to Russians, but you cannot steal anything from Russians. I target international. Steal from Europeans. Americans. Asians. Whatever. Russians buy credit cards I steal. Passwords. But Kremlin...they want my malware because it is the best. *The New York Times* wrote an article about me. That's how good I am.'

Gretchen pulled her seat much closer, her face right beside Bogov's. 'Tell us about Charles Joseph, Arkady.'

'He hired me as private contractor on the side. Same deal as the Kremlin. I infect whatever computers they want with malware. Then when computer is under my control, I am free to go anywhere, find anything, steal anything. He gets access, I keep whatever I can make profit on.'

'Who has Joseph had you target recently?'

'There are hundreds each week. You cannot expect me—'

Gretchen kicked his leg again.

Bogov howled in agony. It was worse than the last time.

'Please!...I cannot remember names. I don't use names. All I use are locations and IP address.'

Grant moved in closer now. 'Then give us locations.'

As the pain receded, it seemed to spark a thought in him. 'The next one is in the Netherlands. The Hague.'

'How many? How many people, Arkady?'

Gretchen added, 'Give us a number and you get more water.'

Bogov answered, 'One. It's only one target. Someone Joseph is obsessed with. He has been hounding me to get my virus on his computer.'

Keeping his tone insistent without being overly aggressive, Grant demanded, 'Who is he? I need a name, Arkady.'

'He's a prosecutor at the International Criminal Court. An Italian. Roberto something.'

Gretchen headed straight for a computer on the MI6 network to get the full name.

'When will the attack happen?' demanded Grant.

'Soon. Very soon.' Bogov begged, 'Please, I swear I don't know exact time. I just get him access...Joseph is the one who does searches on their computers.' Gasping for breath and sweat stinging his eyes, he hung his head as if he was about to pass out. 'Everything is on the memory stick. Logs of what Joseph found are all on there.'

Gretchen tossed over a bottle of water to Grant, who gave him a drink.

His thirst quenched, and the immediate threat of further pain over, Bogov leaned to one side. Once the adrenaline of the attack, the getaway, and the interrogation, dissipated, he drifted into a chaotic, restless sleep. Half awake, half asleep. His brain couldn't take any more and was shutting down.

Grant locked the cell door while Gretchen found the name they needed.

'Roberto Mercatone,' she said. 'By the looks of his career he's spotlessly clean. Immaculate record with Italian prosecutors where he went after the Sicilian Mafia. A whole telephone directory of huge wins on government corruption.'

'Joseph wants him for *something*,' said Grant. He called up Randall on video link at Vauxhall Cross. Having proven himself invaluable in the Henry Marlow capture, Winston had lobbied Christie personally to have Randall taken on as part of the Albion team to crack their case before the week was out. Both were standing in the background, awaiting news of Grant and Gretchen's progress.

After explaining what they had, Randall emphasised that Grant shouldn't plug the memory stick into anything connected to the MI6 network.

'You've no idea what's on it,' he told him. 'It's probably best to exercise caution when handling a memory stick from the man who created the most infectious malware programme in history.'

'Thanks for that,' Grant said, as if he needed reminding. He took an air-gapped laptop from a locked metal cabinet and turned it on. It was not – and never had been – connected to the MI6 network, or any kind of wi-fi.

He shared his screen with Randall as he scrolled through the logs. 'I'm going to need a bit of direction here, Randall,' said Grant. 'It's like you're speaking Latin to me again.'

There was a part of Randall that was in awe of seeing the actual code of the DeathWeep virus. Like being shown the inner workings of a concert pianist's brain. He had spent much of his student days working through the night as a white hat hacker, finding vulnerabilities that people like Bogov looked to exploit for financial gain. The sole intent of white hats is to make the online world safer. On paper, Bogov was wicked. But when given a rare glimpse of his actual work, Randall couldn't help but be impressed. 'Remarkable…' he purred, then quickly parked his grudging admiration. 'Wait, go back.'

Grant scrolled up half a page.

'What's wrong?' asked Christie.

Randall was typing away frantically. Then stopped. He said, 'Ma'am, there was a search via the malware on Mercatone's computer. My Italian is a little rusty, but I do believe…' He paused to check online. 'The search term was "schedule" in Italian.' Randall dry gulped. 'Along with tomorrow's date.'

Grant broke away with Gretchen for a moment's private consultation. 'Joseph's already demonstrated a personal willingness to get involved. If Mercatone is going to be hit tomorrow, Joseph will be there. Bogov said himself that Joseph's been obsessed with one target. We find Mercatone, we find Joseph.'

Gretchen couldn't help wondering aloud, 'But why would Joseph be targeting the ICC? It's more of the same, like the Fifteen Flags attack. Assassinating a long line of individuals isn't going to shake anything up long term.'

Christie came into the camera's view. 'Grant, Gretchen, an extraction team will be with you in two hours to take possession of Bogov.'

'Okay,' said Grant. 'I can contact MIVD and AIVD…'

Dutch military intelligence, and their version of GCHQ and NSA. The Netherlands might not have had those agencies' reputation on the international stage, but the country's location and global transport links made it a crucial hub for intelligence regarding international crime.

Christie cut in, 'No, Grant. Hold off on that just now.'

In the background, Winston could be heard questioning why.

Grant and Gretchen were equally confused.

Christie asked Randall for the room. He was only too happy

to leave the Tank. He loved the toys and advanced software access, but he had no interest in agency politics.

Christie knew that the time had come to explain what she had been keeping secret since the Fifteen Flags attack. She had delayed and delayed, but now the operation could no longer bear the load of her secret.

She explained, 'We can't let the Dutch – or anyone else – know about Charles Joseph.'

'Why?' asked Grant.

She looked directly into the camera. She knew she owed Grant that much. She said, 'Because Joseph was an MI6 asset.'

19

Christie looked like someone unburdening herself of a great weight: ashamed of having kept it secret from her most trusted allies, and relieved to finally tell them. 'The conflict in the Congo was about as messy as they came. Everyone wanted a piece of it. We needed someone connected, someone influential, and someone who wasn't a complete psychopath. God knows this country hasn't chosen wisely in the past. It was before my time as chief, of course, but someone, somewhere, made the decision that Charles Joseph was our man in the Congo. And for a time, he played the part well. He kept us informed, removed the most dangerous elements from the region, and in return we paid him handsomely. We were bankrolling him in the hope that he would defeat the rebels who wanted to steal the coltan supplies that fuel most of the Congo's economy. And that every mobile phone in the world at the time needed. It was a play that anyone else in my position would have made. It's what we do. Form alliances. Protect the nation.'

'In return for this support,' said Grant, 'MI6 sent its most lethal assassin to kill him.'

'Joseph was taking our money and using it to hurt our allies in the region. He was playing both sides.'

'So we decided to have him killed.'

'He was an escalating threat.'

'To our ability to access coltan supplies, you mean.'

Behind Christie, Winston warned Grant to watch his tone.

Grant complained, 'Gretchen and I are risking our lives to save innocent people and protect the international intelligence network. At least I thought I was. We're actually running around covering up MI6's dirty secrets. That's why Simeon's men were so eager to delete Gretchen's hard drives, isn't it? To destroy any evidence that Joseph was our asset.'

Christie didn't bother to deny it. 'And what would happen to the country and our safety, Grant, if the international community found out Joseph was ours? An MI6 asset responsible for a devastating attack on our most secretive and powerful intelligence network? We'd never get another source or sniff of intel from anyone for the next decade. Our entire intelligence apparatus would be crippled for decades. It's easy to judge from your side of the screen. That I'll give you. But from my chair, some decisions are decidedly messier than anyone would like. Do I want you to stop Joseph by any means necessary? Of course. I also have an obligation to defend this country. If word about Joseph's history with us got out, attacks like the seventh of July and the Manchester arena bombings would be annual events.'

Gretchen stepped more into view beside Grant. 'Ma'am, I know that this is complicated, but I think the best thing that Grant and I can do is get back to the immediate threat. The important thing is that everyone wants to find Charles Joseph.'

This is our chance. We agree we can't let the Dutch find out he was our asset. So let's just get this done.'

Winston asked, 'Is there anything we know that would shed light on why Joseph would target a prosecutor for the ICC? We all know what sort of atrocities Joseph was committing in the Congolese jungle with his men, but the ICC doesn't have any open or pending investigations on him.'

'I'll get the Central African desk to investigate,' said Christie. 'Maybe now would be a good time to discuss moving Marlow. As a precaution. Until we have a clearer idea what's going on.'

Winston was shocked that she was even entertaining the notion.

Grant shook his head. 'Ma'am, Marlow wants us to move him. He warned me that we couldn't trust our own operatives. But all of Joseph's people that we have ID'd so far were already disavowed. Marlow wants us to think that Vauxhall Cross is unsafe, so we put him out in the open where Joseph and his crew can take him.'

Christie said, 'Alex Simeon agrees with that position, Grant. I asked him earlier. He thinks moving him would be a mistake.'

Winston chimed in, 'With Joseph's manpower, I couldn't swear we would hold them off, ma'am.'

Christie sniffed. 'What a bloody mess. Okay,' she told Grant and Gretchen. 'Let's deal with The Hague first. Find Mercatone, then find Joseph.'

Once the arrangements had been made, Gretchen went outside to the lower balcony for some fresh air. Seeking coolness, all she found was warm and sticky night air.

'Bogov's asleep in the cell,' she said. 'I checked on him.'

Bogov's condition was the last thing on Grant's mind. 'What the hell was that?' he pointed back inside.

'We've got a job to do, Duncan,' she answered. 'Not dredge up the past.'

'I don't understand why you don't care about the duplicity. It's our necks on the chopping block.'

'Duplicity? Duncan, I've had a decade of it. After a while, you stop caring.'

'Do the lies never end, Gretchen?' he asked. 'This isn't what I signed up for.'

She stepped towards him, laying a hand on his bare arm. 'Yes, it is. You want to be an Albion? This is the cost of doing business.'

His eyes searched across the dusty ground.

'You don't like the Mercatone job,' said Gretchen.

'Something's not right. It doesn't fit. If Marlow and Joseph have some great objective, why are they going after single targets? They're actually *regressing* in scale.'

Gretchen put her hands on her hips, worried at the prospect. 'Unless Roberto Mercatone is the start of something else.'

Bogov was passed out from the pain medication Gretchen had injected him with after bandaging his leg. He would be extracted before dawn when Grant and Gretchen left for the Netherlands.

There were two military cot beds in the basement at opposite sides of the room. Gretchen hadn't taken hers, choosing instead to keep watch from the first-floor balcony.

Grant had tried to get his head down for a few hours, but eventually abandoned the notion of rest. He couldn't sleep with Bogov in the same room, leaving security to Gretchen alone. He wished they were back in Granada. On the dance floor of the *cueva*, feeling her sweat rappelling down her back and through his fingers as he held her tight against him.

He then felt a sudden surge through his body, like an electrical pulse. He had fallen asleep and was dreaming.

When he sat up, he saw that the basement door was flapping open. Exhaustion and hunger had lowered his body temperature. He slipped out of the basement, not wanting to wake Bogov. He found Gretchen on the first-floor balcony, drinking a cup of coffee.

'Can't sleep or just being vigilant?' he asked.

'A little of both,' she replied.

'Is it can't sleep, or don't like sleeping?'

She paused. 'The latter.'

'I hear that.'

'Is this the part where we bond over our shared painful histories?'

Grant didn't know what to say.

She said, 'Sorry, that was meant to be a joke.'

'It's okay if it wasn't.' In Grant's mind, what felt like a minute passed, but was closer to ten seconds. Ten seconds can feel unimaginably long sometimes. 'For what it's worth, I don't think that we're the same.'

'For what it's worth, I think we are.' She drank a little more of her coffee until she hit the grainy bottom, then tossed the last dregs over the balcony into the bushes.

'Marlow said this thing to me. "Faces without names." That's what he sees. Is that what you see?'

'All the time. Hence the dislike of sleeping.'

'I know the names of the people I killed. Even in Svalbard. I had Miles dig out their files.'

'Give it a few more years.'

'I don't know that I want to.'

'You don't mean that,' she said.

'I thought being an Albion I could do some good. I'm two solo missions into my career, and my two primary targets were both paid by MI6 at one time or another. I had a corrupt Anti-Corruption director try to have me killed…' He threw his hands up in defeat. 'What are we doing out here, Gretchen? What are we fighting for? What are we really protecting?'

'I'm not the best person to ask that question.'

Grant paused. 'Why did you become an operative?'

She stared out at the countryside. In the darkness, it was peaceful and threatening at the same time. Everywhere was like that in the end, she realised. There was no escape. She exhaled as she stepped away from him, laying a hand on his shoulder as she passed. 'I don't remember.'

Before she left the landing, Grant found himself saying, 'Come to Skye with me someday.'

She stopped and raised her eyebrows in surprise.

'When this is all over,' he clarified. 'I think you'd like it.'

Her body language said she was considering it. 'You should know, Duncan. I won't make the nightmares go away. No one can. I've tried, believe—'

Embarrassed, he said, 'Forget I asked.' He checked his watch. 'You should get your head down. I'll take over here.'

Reluctant to go until the awkward air had cleared, she said, 'I didn't mean to be…'

He pursed his lips at her. 'It was my mistake.'

20

One major complication in the Hague operation for Grant and Gretchen was that they had to find and tail Roberto Mercatone, but they couldn't just extract him. The whole point of finding him was to wait for Charles Joseph to appear. The idea of using an innocent civilian – and a prosecutor for the International Criminal Court – was not something that sat comfortably with Winston or Christie. The only director who didn't seem to have a problem with it was Alex Simeon, who had joined Winston and Christie in the Tank for final preparations.

'We want to get Joseph,' Simeon argued. 'That's the mission. Mercatone isn't the job.'

Winston countered, 'That doesn't mean we leave him for Joseph like a lamb to the slaughter. We want to get Joseph, sure. But at *any* cost, Alex?'

'These people – Marlow, Joseph, all of his operatives – all of them are scum, Leo. They take everything we care about and they grind it under their shoe.'

'What if I suggested shooting an innocent civilian in the head in exchange for Joseph?'

'Hyperbole isn't what we need right now.'

'Then you agree that there are limits to what we should or shouldn't do. My limit, Alex, is allowing Joseph to slaughter Mercatone right under our noses. I won't permit it.'

Trying to stay neutral, Christie said, 'They both know what's at stake here. We need to trust them to finish the job.'

Mercatone kept a driver on payroll. The forty-five-minute drive from his residence on the outskirts of The Hague to the International Criminal Court headquarters – where he spent most of his working days – was valuable time for him to catch up on time-consuming phone calls and emails. The driver changed week to week, so when Duncan Grant pulled up outside Mercatone's house in his usual car – a Jaguar XF saloon – Mercatone didn't think anything of it.

In a neighbourhood of modern, sophisticated, carbon-neutral houses, Mercatone left his comfortable home to get into the back seat of his comfortable car, not knowing that his life was about to be turned upside down by a Scottish spy dressed in a driver's uniform-suit. Dylan van der Poel, dutiful employee of *Den Haag Bestuurder en Atoverhuur* – The Hague's premier private driver and car rental company – was currently tied up and gagged in his small apartment, where he would be found in a few hours' time after an anonymous phone call to his employers.

Grant couldn't speak Dutch, and his accent was clearly foreign. But like so many in the Netherlands – and within the UN, where English and French were the dominant languages, and it was impossible to hold high office within the organisation without fluency in both – Mercatone was able to give his destination in English.

It wasn't the destination that Grant and Gretchen had expected and planned for. Instead of being told to drive to the ICC's stunning glass headquarters on *Oude Waalsdorperweg*, Mercatone asked to be taken to Scheveningen Prison.

Apologising for not knowing it, Grant asked what it was.

'The detention unit,' replied Mercatone crisply. 'The United Nations Detention Unit.'

Grant had a radio earpiece picking up everything said and heard.

Back in the Tank at Vauxhall Cross, Miles Archer – flanked by Christie, Winston, Simeon, and a translator from MI6's endless pool of talent who was fluent in Italian, French, and Dutch – directed Grant on which way to go.

Five cars back, parked outside the house of one of Mercatone's neighbours, Gretchen started the engine of her BMW 5 Series saloon, which had plenty of grunt for fast pursuits, and space in the back if they happened to bring on any cargo.

Communication with MI6 from Grant was impossible. The Jaguar was a standard model, with no soundproof divider to stop Mercatone hearing. It did offer one advantage. One that Winston had anticipated.

During the journey to the detention unit, Mercatone took a phone call in Italian. His speech sounded sharp and aggressive. Grant took only occasional glances in the rear-view mirror, but it was clear that Mercatone was angry about something.

The call didn't last long. Mercatone pocketed his phone with evident frustration, then told Grant, 'The law is at once the most beautiful and vile system man has ever created.'

'Yes, sir,' Grant replied. He still hadn't been given any translation from the call.

He slowed as traffic came to a halt ahead. Speaking tangentially to Vauxhall Cross, but seemingly to Mercatone, Grant said, 'It's so frustrating when you don't know what's coming. No information.' He gesticulated at the dashboard, saying pointedly, 'Nothing on the radio.'

Winston told him, 'Patience, Grant. It's coming.'

Christie gave Winston an affirmative nod for thinking of the translator. 'Good prep,' she said.

'You never know what might be said that could be useful,' Winston replied. 'It's for Grant's benefit. I always tell him, every good op needs a contingency.'

The translator handed him the transcript of what she'd heard.

'Okay, Grant,' said Winston. 'He said that he's meeting a new lawyer for David Karangwa.'

Miles tapped the name into a computer tablet, then showed Winston the result. A French news headline which translated as, *"Karangwa – 'The Butcher of Butare' – arrested in Geneva."*

Winston explained, 'A Rwandan warlord arrested for genocide and war crimes.' He turned to Christie. 'Rwanda again.'

Christie agreed. 'Patrick Dembele at the Nairobi substation. Joseph carried that out personally.'

'Joseph's cleaning out old wounds.'

21

Randall's office was hidden away on the European Task floor at the end of a dimly lit corridor, where excess office furniture was stored.

The tranquil piano of Claude Debussy's *Clair de Lune* on Classic FM was playing on his wireless earbuds. His posture was perfect, everything at his desk adjusted to ergonomic perfection (a process that had taken weeks to optimise). He was studiously combing through more of Bogov's computer logs from the Death Clock memory stick. The more he looked, the more impressive he found the coding – like nothing he'd ever seen before. You don't infect over a million computers if your malware-coding is shoddy. Bogov's was airtight and bulletproof. The prime reason he had amassed such a fortune from the enterprise.

Randall picked away fussily at an avocado, feta, and couscous salad from Waitrose, scrunching his nose up as he removed any brown flaws from the overripe avocado. The Debussy track came to a gentle close, then the DJ reminded the listeners of the composer and track name. Randall let out a mocking chuckle at the slight mispronunciation. '*Day*bussy,' he complained to himself. 'It's *Duh*bussy.' He complained aloud, 'Honestly, it's national radio. Where do they get these troglodytes…'

His irritation expressed, he returned to the logs, pausing at an image file. It was easy to skip past, as it was merely a string of numbers followed by ".jpg". It didn't show the actual image that had been on Mercatone's computer hard drive, it was only a file name. Randall was about to move on when he noticed that the file name had been changed during the malware attack. And not by Mercatone. It could only have been altered by someone at the malware's end.

A few clicks away, Randall found that it hadn't been Bogov. All of his edits and keystrokes were identifiable under the same name. Someone else had changed the image file. Thanks to the boffins at GCHQ, Randall matched up the file name with an image log that Bogov's virus had extracted along with all the other information.

What Randall found made him freeze mid-chew. He dropped his plastic fork and picked up his mobile phone, frantically taking a picture of the screen. After scrambling out of his chair, his trailing leg pulled it over as he sprinted out of his office, knocking over a tall pile of stackable chairs in the hallway outside, creating an almighty crash that was heard on the next floor.

He charged towards the lifts outside the European Task Force control room – Winston and Grant's old working office – but the lift had just gone past.

Randall turned instead for the stairs, lunging up two, three stairs at a time with his gangly legs, all the way up to tenth floor. He hit the buzzer insistently outside the Tank's main door. He was gasping for breath, holding his phone up to the security camera that he knew everyone inside would be seeing. He pointed desperately to the screen.

Winston, vexed by the interruption when Grant's mission was at a crucial juncture, sent Miles to find out what was going on.

Randall burst through, his phone extended to them. He could barely get the words out.

'He hacked Mercatone's computer…to alter the official ICC record of the counsel for David Karangwa…He's replaced the lawyer's photo with his own…Mercatone isn't the target!'

Winston got straight on the radio to Grant and Gretchen, the point man and surveillance operative. 'Point and Survey…I've got something. Listen up…'

As the International Criminal Court was based in The Hague, the city needed somewhere to house the awaiting trial. Due to the sensitive nature of many of the trials, defendants couldn't be placed safely within existing Dutch prison facilities. A lot of the defendants had powerful enemies – these were warlords, arms dealers, and corrupt politicians – and there was a strong African contingent in the region from the Netherlands to Belgium and Northern France. The only way to protect defendants and make sure they went to trial was to keep them in a purpose-built facility, where they wouldn't have to mix with a random, public prisoner population, and anyone with a smuggled-in knife could get to them.

The United Nations Detention Unit was that place. Part of The Hague Penitentiary Institution, it was a solely UN-administered jail that was established during the International Criminal Tribunal for the former Yugoslavia. The penitentiary also housed the ICC Detention Centre, where those awaiting trial at the International Criminal Court were kept. Men like Slobodan Milošević and Radovan Karadžić had been inmates there while on trial for war crimes.

At the secure gateway at the front entrance, a middle-aged man pulled up in a plain family car with Dutch plates. He was wearing a brown tweed suit, the trousers slightly too short, the jacket slightly too big. Completing his outfit was a pair of wire-rimmed glasses.

He showed a passport-sized document and gave his name with a thick Congolese accent. 'Paul Kepchoge,' he said. 'I'm here to visit my client, David Karangwa.'

The guard checked his computer tablet for the day's list of approved visitors. He found the name "Paul Kepchoge" on the alphabetical list, along with a picture that matched the man he was looking at.

As the file had come directly that morning from the office of Robert Mercatone, there was no reason for the guard to doubt either the authenticity of the name or picture, or that Paul Kepchoge was anyone other than who he said he was.

He pointed the man towards the small car park, then gave instructions on how to enter the facility.

As "Paul Kepchoge" parked the car that had been stolen from Karangwa's genuine legal counsel – his body now dissolving in lime in a bathtub in an abandoned industrial estate on the edge of nearby Rotterdam – he thought about how long he had waited for this moment. Everything he had sacrificed and risked. Everything he had witnessed. And the terrible, terrible things that he had done, all just to arrive in that place at that moment. He felt no fear. Only determination to finish the job.

22

When the news about Charles Joseph filtered through to Grant, he knew that the time for games was over.

At such short notice, it was impossible to get Grant on the approved visitors' list. It would have taken hours, placing calls back and forth between the British embassy and ICC headquarters that were both painfully close across the city. By that time, Charles Joseph would be long gone.

Following closely behind, Gretchen got on the radio. 'Point, secure Mercatone and park up outside the prison. We'll take Joseph when he exits.'

Grant had to blow cover to answer. 'Negative,' he replied. 'I'm getting in there to stop whatever Joseph is about to do.'

Christie broke in. 'That's not our fight, Grant. And we have absolutely no authority to enter a United Nations facility.'

'I'll get permission,' he said, accelerating suddenly, and hard.

Mercatone struggled to lean forward against the car's inertia, wondering why his driver was talking to himself and driving like he was taking part in a rally. 'What is going on?' he asked, holding onto the back of the front passenger seat.

Grant relayed the situation as clearly as he could, navigating his way through the traffic. 'Mr Mercatone, I don't have long to explain this, so I need you to listen carefully. I'm a covert operative with the British Secret Intelligence Service. I have reason to believe that an assassin will attempt to gain access to the ICC detention centre this morning on false credentials. This assassin is very determined and very dangerous.'

Struggling to hold on to the seat in front, Mercatone spluttered, 'Assassin? Is this some kind of joke?'

'It's no joke, Mr Mercatone. Look at my face if you don't believe me.'

'An assassin couldn't possibly get inside the detention centre. It's heavily guarded and—'

'This assassin hacked your home computer. He's going to gain access by pretending to be David Karangwa's new lawyer.'

A look of horror crossed Mercatone's face.

Grant implored him, 'You have to get me inside.'

Mercatone was reeling. He couldn't decide if he was being tricked, or if he believed what Grant was saying was even possible.

Trying to shock him out of his stupor, Grant said, 'A man is going to assassinate a defendant in a United Nations facility, on your watch, on a case *you* are prosecuting. What are you going to do about it?'

Charles Joseph entered the prison, showing his credentials again. The front reception desk was like a bank from the eighties. A long glass screen extended all along the desk, with cheap and old desktop computers, and low-resolution black-and-white CCTV monitors set up for the staff.

The architecture was late seventies with the odd sprinkling of barely modern technology, including an X-ray machine to check luggage, and the most modern technology on display: a nude body scanner.

It was the same scanner that the American TSA who handled airport security had put into one hundred and sixty airports across the country. A scanner that the head of security at Israel's Ben Gurion airport had tested, and concluded that he could "overcome the body scanners with enough explosives to take down a Boeing 747". The Israelis passed. The Americans spent $1 billion on the scanners.

They looked fancy, but there was a terrible flaw in the technology. Search subjects in the scanner appear drawn with light colours, and placed on a black background. The problem was that metallic objects – as mundane as a keyring, or as threatening as a gun – appeared in black on the scans. All anyone had to do to avoid detection was smuggle in a weapon attached to their side and the metallic object showed up as black against the black background. Which meant it couldn't be seen at all.

It was a flaw that Charles Joseph had discovered, and had attached a .380 ACP pistol – a fully metal gun – under his shirt in a sewn-in pocket.

The guard waved him through, seeing nothing on his person. 'Mr Karangwa is this way, sir.'

Joseph felt his anticipation surge the closer he got to his target along an interminably long corridor. The guard showed him into a windowless room containing only a small wooden table and two chairs.

'Mr Karangwa will be brought in shortly,' the guard said, then left Joseph alone.

He reached calmly into the pocket sewn into his shirt, and put the gun into the more accessible inside pocket.

When the door opened, Joseph allowed himself a moment to smile, shutting his eyes for a moment.

This is it, he thought. I've waited *so* long for this...

A guard led Karangwa to his chair, then said, 'Thirty minutes, gentlemen.'

Karangwa wasn't handcuffed. He wore a plain navy suit and striped tie, which he loosened as he sat down. He snapped, 'Where is Kepchoge? Who are you?'

Joseph smiled. 'There is no reason you would remember.'

Karangwa looked over Joseph's shoulder, and called out, 'Guard.'

The guard opened the door.

But Karangwa's attention was centred on the gun that Joseph was flashing him inside his suit jacket.

'Sorry,' Karangwa stammered. 'It's nothing. My mistake.'

The guard, uninterested, closed the door again.

'As I say,' Joseph continued, 'there is no reason for you to remember me. Or any of the other thousands. But I remember you. The Butcher of Butare.'

'If you're here to kill me, get it over with,' said Karangwa. 'If you're looking for apologies, try elsewhere.'

Joseph had expected such stubbornness. When you had killed as many people as Karangwa had, it was the only way to escape your nightmares. With delusion or ignorance. 'You know,' said Joseph, 'most people know me as Congolese. They don't know that I was actually born in Rwanda. I don't call myself Rwandan, though. I don't call myself anything anymore. Countries...they don't matter anymore. I watch the Olympics, and I see these athletes traipsing through stadiums carrying their flags, and they all look dead to me. The people. The flags. Everything. I don't call myself anything, David, because the real me died in Rwanda.' He chuckled ironically. 'You know what the Western politicians and intelligence analysts said when the bodies started piling up? They said there was no reason to intervene in Rwanda. All they had there was people.' He laughed. 'All they had…was people! No natural resources to steal, no money to launder…Did you know that after the invasion of Iraq, over a billion U.S. dollars disappeared from banks and safes? They just put it all in bags and walked away with it.' Joseph pointed back and forth. 'That's what they think of people like you and I. Anyway, I was a small child. My mother and father had taken me to a church mission fifty miles outside of Kigali. There was nowhere we could go. The roads were ruled by the *Interahamwe* militia, their radios blasting speeches to seize us Tutsi cockroaches.'

Karangwa smiled, remembering the word. 'The *Inyenzi*.'

'You gave your gang maps and lists, so you could kill us more efficiently. The man my father had shaken hands with in church the week earlier was now standing over him with a machete, urging him to kill my mother or she would be raped by the group of men standing outside the church. He refused. The men dragged him inside the church. I heard my father's screams from outside as they chopped him apart. As you know, it is rare to be killed by a machete in the first blow. It takes at least four or five before you stop feeling anything. While the men did that, my mother and I ran away into the fields. That was when I worked out why I had seen so many piles of sandals and flip flops everywhere. It was people kicking them off so they could run away faster.' Joseph wagged his finger. 'But the real joke of it was when I found out years later: Tutsis and Hutus don't actually exist. The Belgians made them up out of some whacko anthropological theory. Whose nose looked like a Tutsi; who had a Hutu forehead. They would have been as well tossing a coin to decide who was what. And there we were, Rwandans, butchering each other over it.'

'If you ask me,' said Karangwa, 'Tutsis are very real. Cockroaches. *Inyenzi.*' He knew he was going to die. There was no point in recanting a lifetime of indoctrination now.

'You did it,' said Joseph. 'But the West made it possible in the first place. Now I'm going to hold up a mirror to them all. The politicians. The intelligence agencies. I'm going to make them all pay.' Joseph took out the gun. 'Starting with you.'

23

Mercatone was far too slow for Grant's liking, having to be pulled along into the detention centre's reception area. He couldn't keep up with Grant.

The guard behind the desk could barely make sense of Mercatone's ramble that was shot through with random Italian. Then a shot rang out from the bottom of the corridor.

A door to the room where Joseph and Karangwa had been sitting was thrown open, giving Grant his first glimpse of Charles Joseph in the flesh – as seen through the bulletproof window of a steel door.

Grant marched through the body scanner, Glock 17 pistol drawn. 'Open the bloody door,' he yelled insistently, then turned his rage at Mercatone. 'Get them to open it now! Open the bloody door!'

Mercatone shouted at the guard, 'I'm a United Nations Prosecutor! Open that door.'

The guard buzzed them in, and Grant charged through like he was possessed.

Gretchen was stuck outside the prison with no way of getting in. 'Point, I'm outside, ready to go. Tell me where you are when you need me.'

'Received,' Grant called, racing down the corridor, where he could see Karangwa's dead body. His chair had flipped backwards and there was a single bullet hole in his forehead. 'Where the hell is security...'

There was no one else in sight. Around the corner, he finally found someone.

It was the guard who had been outside the interview room. The moment he saw Grant, he fired.

Grant retreated behind the wall, bullets missing him by inches each time he stole a look around the corner. Armed prison guards ran towards Grant, yelling in a mixture of Dutch and English for him to put his weapon down.

The guard at reception hadn't got the message through to them that Mercatone had vouched for him. All they had seen was a man with determined eyes holding a pistol.

Grant didn't have a choice. He was hemmed in. The rogue guard was still firing away around the corner. If Grant made any move, it could be his last.

Grant dropped the gun and raised his hands. 'You can still stop him, he's outside...'

The rogue guard had finally turned and fled in the same direction as Charles Joseph, making for the car park via a series of doors that should have been locked but weren't.

The guards in pursuit ran out into the daylight, finding a car bearing the livery of the Dutch national gendarmerie *Koninklijke Marechaussee* – known by their informal abbreviation of KMar – speeding away.

Grant, having been freed from the other guards thanks to Mercatone, charged outside too. Anyone else would have given up. The car was too far away. When Grant saw the car in the distance, though, he didn't stop running. His arms pumping like mad, he radioed Gretchen, 'Survey! Joseph is in a KMar vehicle heading north out of the prison grounds. I don't have plates...' Grant looked to his left, and found Gretchen speeding over the landscaped gardens to join the road. She slowed down – barely enough – for Grant to jump in, then set off in pursuit.

Grant radioed Vauxhall Cross, 'This is Point. Survey and I are in pursuit of Joseph, heading north...' He held on to the guard rail for dear life, as Gretchen executed a sharp right-hand turn at speed, rejoining the busy main road. He craned his neck to see the road ahead. 'They're–'

Gretchen was yoga-calm and icily determined. 'I see him.'

Joseph might have been a ferocious warlord and ruthless arms dealer, but he was no getaway driver. He clattered into the sides of any car that got in his path, slamming his way through the centre of The Hague, and onto the A4 motorway.

The engine of the BMW gave a guttural roar as Gretchen floored the accelerator, taking advantage of a clear stretch of road ahead. It didn't last.

A double-decker car transporter swung into a different lane to avoid Joseph's manic driving, boxing the BMW in. Gretchen changed gear and threw the car into the hard shoulder to over-take the lorry, leaving just one car between them and the KMar Volkswagen Golf GT.

Gretchen told Grant, 'I'll pull up alongside. You take him.'

Grant had his gun in hand. 'Go.'

But as Gretchen bunted the car in front out of the way, Grant yelled in reaction to a gunshot going off inside Joseph's Volkswagen.

'What the hell was that?' he cried.

The rogue prison officer in the passenger seat was leaning to one side against the blood-spattered window, having been shot in the head. The Volkswagen lurched wildly to the left, as Joseph fumbled with the car door and pushed the officer out.

Gretchen had to take evasive action to avoid running over the body – not that anything could save him now.

Grant checked his side mirror, where a motorbike was fast approaching. Far too fast not to be related to their chase. 'We've got company.'

'I see them,' Gretchen replied, barging into Joseph in front.

Grant put down his window, letting in a torrent of wind as the car pushed well over seventy miles per hour. He took a few shots which missed Joseph, but shattered the rear window of the Volkswagen.

Joseph ducked below his headrest, trying to stay out of the way of Grant's gunfire while still watching the road ahead.

As Grant leaned out to take more shots, he heard something fizzle past his shoulder, which was followed almost instantly by the sound of automatic gunfire and the motorbike getting closer.

Joseph's back-up. One motorcyclist and a shooter on the back with an automatic submachine gun.

Grant pulled himself back into the car, as a barrage of bullets blew out their rear window. Then the car lunged to the right as the near-side tyre exploded.

Gretchen grimaced, trying to keep control, which was almost impossible at their speed. She had no option and hit the brakes hard. Then another tyre on the far side was hit, which dropped their speed further.

The motorbike was blocked from taking another shot by the car transporter, now suddenly Grant and Gretchen's saviour. The bike speared ahead to catch up with Joseph.

Helpless to do anything else in the situation, Gretchen pulled into a slower lane then banged the heel of her hand on the steering wheel. 'Damn it!'

Grant got on the radio. 'Control, it's over.' He exhaled. 'We lost him.'

24

In Christie's office, the mood was sombre following the Hague operation. Christie had had the British ambassador to the Netherlands burning her ear about the mess at the ICC Detention Centre. When Christie had suggested the ambassador was overreacting, he bellowed back, 'He broke three international treaties, Olivia!'

Christie was still seething about the conversation when Winston came to her office to plan their next line of attack.

'His attacks are becoming increasingly brazen,' said Winston. 'Marlow gave us a countdown of a week. To what? That timeframe brings us pretty much present.'

'What are you thinking?' asked Christie.

'I think he's going to hit us next. Here. In London.'

Christie wasn't buying it. She pushed her seat back and retreated to her window, looking out over the Thames.

Winston emphasised, 'We can't sit around and wait for him.'

That was all she needed to get the idea. 'What if we get Joseph to come to us?'

Winston looked at the ceiling. After they discussed it further, he knew that what she was suggesting was probably crazy. There was also a very good chance that it might work.

They called up Simeon who was surprisingly receptive about the idea. He had been working through Bogov's logs and thought he'd found something invaluable. He didn't have to convince Christie and Winston, though. It was Grant and Gretchen that needed to be persuaded.

Once the pair were on video link in a secure room at the British embassy in The Hague, Simeon came up to Christie's office to explain what he had found.

'It's Bogov's computer logs. Bogov said that he targeted by location, so I've been combing through the IP address locations, and there are five personal computers that had Bogov's Death-Weep virus on them. Computers belonging to Metropolitan Police officers in the Special Escort Group.'

There was silence. No one but Simeon knew where it was going.

'They've probably got compromised officers under their control now. The rogue Dutch prison officer had a malware attack two weeks ago. Bogov found child pornography on the hard drive. They blackmailed him, he cooperated, they killed him.'

Christie remarked, 'Nice to see terrorists with a moral compass.'

Gretchen asked, 'But why the SEG? They transport politicians and royalty.'

Winston replied, 'They also provide armed vehicle support for high-risk prisoners. They think we're going to transfer Marlow. It's overdue.' He looked down at his mobile which was ringing. 'Excuse me, I have to take this…' He took his phone out of the office.

Christie said, 'We've been fending off the Crown Prosecution Service for weeks now. We can't keep him locked up in Vauxhall Cross forever. Like it or not, our sense of security in having Marlow down in the basement is purely illusory. Charing Cross Police Station is far better equipped to hold someone like him. Or Belmarsh.'

Grant could see the angle now. 'You want to dangle Marlow to lure Joseph into an ambush. Then we can take him in open ground.'

Christie nodded. 'That's about the sum of it.'

'If we're going to do that, why take the chance in getting Marlow out in the open? We don't know what sort of manpower Joseph's packing at this point. What if, to anyone involved in the transfer, we make it look like Marlow's in there. Except he won't be. He'll still be tucked up here at Vauxhall Cross, and I'll be in the prisoner van.'

Simeon thought it through aloud as he stepped slowly around the room. 'Grant's the bait, Joseph appears. We take him down. The end.'

Winston came back in, his phone held to his chest. 'It's Randall,' he said. 'He's found something we need to take a look at.'

The air of momentum punctured, Christie asked, 'Can't it wait, Leo?'

'No, ma'am. Arkady Bogov was just shot and killed at our black site. That's not all. Randall has something that I think we all need to see.'

Randall was in the Tank – where he had spent the last three hours, checking and triple-checking his theory. He wanted so terribly to be wrong.

Now Winston, Christie, and Simeon had hurried down to the Tank, with Grant and Gretchen joining via video link.

Randall was pacing worriedly. 'We've all been trying to figure out what the next big play is for Charles Joseph. What does he want?'

Christie stopped him. 'Randall, we already know what Joseph's next target is.'

He paused in embarrassment. 'You have? You all seem to be taking it very well.'

'What do you mean?'

'Well, you don't look scared out of your minds, for one thing.' He chuckled nervously, then stopped when he realised no one else was feeling light-hearted.

Simeon said, 'The next target is the Met's Special Escort Group.'

'What?' asked Randall.

Winston interjected, 'That's not the play that Randall's found.' He said to him, 'Tell them what you told me.'

Randall said, 'I was checking the transcript of Bogov's interrogation at our black site. At one point he mentions "the great equaliser".' He hit the space bar on his laptop, which started a video. Randall shared his screen with Grant and Gretchen in The Hague embassy.

The video was shot from a tripod in a brightly lit interrogation room in an MI6 black site in Algiers, Morocco: the closest one they had to Andalusia. Bogov was in chains, locked to a desk. He was a lot more frightened than he'd been with Grant and Gretchen.

'Joseph wants to turn the lights off around the world,' Bogov explained. 'That's what he said. He called it "the Great Equaliser". I tried to talk him out of it. For someone like me, it would be like the loss of a parent or child. Online is my only reality. And when it's gone, it will take ten years to rebuild it all.'

The interrogator asked, 'Rebuild what, Arkady?'

Before Bogov could answer, a bullet ripped through the air past the interrogator, hitting Bogov in the chest, then another in the head.

The sound of the shots in such an enclosed space was deafening, even when relayed through video. Randall flinched internally at both shots, shuddering at the awful sight.

The MI6 officer responsible then edged into the camera lens field, turning his gun on the interrogator and his colleagues with wicked speed. The officer left the room, leaving the video running. He hadn't been seen since.

Randall hit the space bar again to stop the video, disconsolate at the scene he had witnessed. Even on rewatch, it didn't get any easier.

Christie and Simeon were a lot more weathered to such horrors. They took their time to react, thinking of the next steps.

In The Hague, Grant and Gretchen hung their heads.

Randall composed himself, a slight crack in his voice at the start. 'That phrase we heard Bogov use, the Great Equaliser, has been referred to in the past by game theorists: some sort of attack or act of terror that essentially levels the playing field on the international stage. The end of superpowers. Where, in the aftermath, nation states themselves cease to matter.'

Winston checked around the room. 'So, you all see the problem we have?'

Simeon replied, 'All I heard were more empty threats and vague posturing.'

Christie clarified, 'It means we can't just kill Charles Joseph when he comes to London.'

'But if we aren't killing him, what are we doing? The whole mission is to stop him.'

'If he's planning an attack on the scale that Bogov said he is, it's no good killing just Joseph. He has operatives everywhere, infecting every major intelligence agency around the world, and using compromised agents wherever he can. Killing him doesn't stop his and Marlow's plans. Islamic terrorism didn't stop the day bin Laden or al-Baghdadi were killed. Joseph's people can carry on without him. We need to destroy the network. We can only do that from the inside.'

Grant covered the computer microphone, whispering to Gretchen, 'Is she suggesting what I think she is?'

Christie said, 'We don't have any other choice but to infiltrate.'

'Only Gretchen has done that,' said Simeon.

Gretchen looked up to face her fate. She knew what had to happen now. 'I have to go back in,' she said.

'Wait,' said Grant, putting a hand out to interrupt. 'Let's just think about this a second...You can't go back in on deep cover. You've been AWOL for six months. Joseph will see right through it.'

Gretchen replied, 'As far as he's concerned, I'm still a disavowed agent. He's got no evidence to contradict that. My agent profile hasn't been reactivated. I'm still disavowed on the MI6 network. Even if Joseph has sources inside Vauxhall Cross, they'd never think for a moment that MI6 would take back a disavowed agent.'

'What about Svalbard?'

Christie said, 'All Joseph knows is that his men in Svalbard are dead. He knew Grant and Alex's team would be there, but Joseph has no way of knowing that Gretchen's been taken in by us.'

'Joseph's men were there to kill her too.'

'There's nothing that suggests that. Joseph's men only moved when they found out we would be there. Even we didn't know who we were going to find there, so Joseph had no way of knowing either.'

'The Chief's right,' said Gretchen. 'If Joseph knew I was already there, he would have killed me long before then.'

Winston checked, 'You really want to risk sending her back to him?'

'When he buys her story, he'll realise.' Christie raised her arms in impotence. 'We don't have a choice, Leo! We've got no other leads. We know that something is coming. That we don't have the specifics yet is irrelevant. When we find out their plan, it could be too late to respond if we don't already have eyes inside their network.'

Simeon said, 'You know, all of this is for nothing if Joseph doesn't come to London.'

'Oh, he'll come,' Grant assured him. 'A chance to hurt the agency that turned on him? He was last in the Netherlands. That's far too close to miss this. He'll want to get one over on MI6. He risked everything to hit Karangwa, the same as when he stabbed Patrick Dembele in the Nairobi substation. Dembele was in the Rwandan Patriotic Front. This is personal for him.'

Christie had heard enough. 'Leo. Get the word out that Henry Marlow will be transferred. Do it quietly but loudly, if you get my drift. Alex: leak a transfer request onto the system. Leave it STRAP One. We can put it on the mainframe where eyeballs will see it. We're going to smoke this lot out.'

25

Back in his office, Winston was packing up to go home for a few hours' sleep. Behind his venetian blinds, a deep orange sunset was glowing.

Christie knocked gently on his door. 'Leo. Do you have a minute?'

'Of course,' he said, offering her a seat, which she refused.

'I wanted to check that you're okay with our plan of action,' she said. 'Things moved quite quickly there. This is still your operation. You're Director of the Albion programme, after all. I didn't want you feeling like I'd pulled the rug out from under your feet.'

He put down the paperwork he was filing into his briefcase and sat down. 'What happens when Joseph's people realise it's Grant and not Marlow in the prisoner van?'

'That's when Gretchen comes into play,' Christie replied. 'It doesn't matter that they discover we tried to trick them. What matters is that they trust Gretchen and take her back.'

All of Winston's doubts were coming to the surface now. 'If

there's even a hint that Gretchen's betrayal isn't genuine, they'll kill her, and Grant too, *and* we'll lose Charles Joseph. Probably forever.'

Christie said, 'I'm still waiting for the point.'

'My point, ma'am,' he explained, 'is that Imogen Swann detonated Gretchen's life. She's been through hell and back because of her. She signed up for deep cover. She never signed up for what Imogen did to her.'

'She knew the risks, just like…' Christie broke off.

Winston paused, wondering if he should say it. 'Just like me?'

'That was completely different.'

Feeling brave, Winston ventured a more dangerous question. 'Ma'am, why was Imogen Swann burying Gretchen's deep-cover reports?'

'Alright, Leo,' she replied, showing a hint of shame. 'I told her to.'

'Why would you do that?'

'I was protecting our asset. Joseph. It was above Gretchen's pay grade and I couldn't have it coming out on the record.'

Winston's eyes narrowed as he joined the dots in his head. 'But Marlow…'

'I had no idea Marlow was even in play. All Imogen ever told me was about Joseph. She thought that Marlow could be contained. If he just disappeared that was fine by her. It was only once Grant started putting the pieces together about how Imogen tried to have Marlow killed that she knew she had to take action.'

Winston pondered his next question carefully. Although he and Christie went way back, and he liked to think of her as a friend, she was still C. The Chief of the agency. 'Ma'am, did you know that Imogen was abandoning Gretchen?'

She answered immediately. 'No.'

'But even if you did, you might not have stopped her.'

She paused. 'It was complicated.'

Winston went on, 'Because it wouldn't be the first time you left an agent behind.'

'Don't be a baby, Leo. It doesn't suit you. We don't do "no man left behind." If you want that, go back to the SAS. The only obligation we have is to the mission.' She could see that Winston was still struggling to get onboard. 'This might make you angry, but I want you to know that if I had to do it all over again – us and China – I would do the same thing. Because if I hadn't, we wouldn't be having this conversation. I would be talking to a director of barely half your ability.'

Winston didn't doubt her sincerity. That didn't mean it made it any easier to hear. He had the scars on his back and up the inside of his arm – not to mention the nightmares – to remind him.

He understood that Christie was under pressure like she'd never experienced before, but even for someone in her shoes, sending Gretchen back in to a high probability of death was a move that bordered on callous.

She said, 'Leo, I understand that it's in your nature to protect any operative you have in play. Even one like Gretchen who's never been in your stable. Believe me when I tell you that I'll do everything I can to get her back.'

'Like you did for me?' Winston asked.

Christie swallowed her pride. Deep down, she knew she deserved it. 'Get some rest, Leo. We've all got a big day tomorrow.'

In an agency SUV coming up through Kent at sunset, Grant and Gretchen were in the back seat.

Grant said, 'You know what will happen if Joseph doesn't buy your story?'

Gretchen replied, 'To sell it – to really sell it – will require one extra gear.' She turned to him.

After taking a moment to figure out her play, he sighed ruefully. 'The last piece required to make it convincing...Shit.'

'It will have to be airtight, though.'

Grant scoffed, then put his head in his hands at the mere thought. 'If we manage to pull this off, Christie will go nuts.'

'She'll understand when I get back with Joseph...'

'And I'm lying dead on a slab.'

She looked into his eyes, making sure he understood that she meant it. 'I wish there was any other way...but I don't see it.'

26

The Metropolitan Police's Special Escort Group most commonly provided mobile armed protection for members of the Royal family and government ministers. Occasionally, they also provided escorts for valuable, hazardous cargo, and for high-risk prisoners. A man like Henry Marlow was considered such a risk that he was named in the Prime Minister's classified security briefing that morning. But Olivia Christie had gone to great lengths to downplay the operation of moving Marlow to the category-A prison at Belmarsh. The last thing she needed was the Home Secretary sticking her oar in on operational matters or, worse, getting MI5 to handle the bulk of the legwork.

As Marlow was MI6's former agent, the Prime Minister had agreed with Christie that it would be best that they liaise with the Special Escort Group in handling the prisoner. The SEG would provide armed vehicle support, including the van that would be carrying Marlow. MI6 could have two operatives in the van with Marlow, but everything else would be on SEG's shoulders. There was simply no way of replacing SEG for any of MI6's own.

Christie had captured the landscape well when she explained to Winston, 'The Home Secretary will have a heart attack if she finds out we infiltrated the Met to execute a covert operation on British soil. The MI in our name doesn't stand for Mission bloody Impossible.'

Grant and Gretchen were in a windowless anteroom in the basement of Vauxhall Cross. An intelligence officer had a series of photographs laid out on a table, showing Marlow's fingernails and the colouring of his hands. Another officer applied different powders and make-up to match them exactly. Marlow had never had access to a nailbrush during shower time, so there was still slight discolouration under his fingernails that Grant wanted to be matched. As an added touch, it was probably overkill, but with Gretchen's life on the line, there wasn't a single detail that Grant would overlook.

The officers had been told that it was for a live test on a training op. They had no clue what Grant was about to do.

Once they had left the room, Grant got into a white jumpsuit of the same variety as Marlow's, along with white slip-on canvas shoes. Gretchen held the black hood in her hands.

'You sure you want to do this?' she asked.

'We said it's the only way, right?'

'Yeah.'

'Then nothing has changed.'

As she lifted the hood towards his head, Grant stopped her.

'Gretchen...If anything happens out there that...I'll get you. I'll find you. I won't let anyone leave you behind this time.'

'Same. Try not to break any international treaties out there, huh?'

He smiled.

'You ready?' she asked.

Grant nodded that he was.

The last part was attaching handcuffs that she didn't lock, then she knocked on the inside of the door, giving Winston in the next room the signal.

He'd been waiting with Marlow, who was hooded and handcuffed.

The next part of the process required absolute secrecy. With compromised agents around, anything other than total isolation from anyone but the true Albion inner circle could spell disaster.

Grant knew that all it took was one text message from a security guard doubting that the transfer was for real, and there would be a lot of dead bodies left behind.

In the other room, Marlow closed his eyes. It was already dark under the hood – the purpose was to enter a meditative state. He was on the cusp of something he'd been working towards for years now. If he was going to pull off the final stages, he couldn't allow adrenaline to get the better of him.

In Marlow's room, there was one window that looked out into the basement garage where the Special Escort Group convoy was waiting, engines running.

The driver, navigator, and the guard who would ride in the back of the prisoner transfer van along with Gretchen could see in.

As planned, Winston removed Marlow's hood and asked if he was ready. An unnecessary question, but for what was to follow, it was crucial that the police outside saw that it really was Marlow before they took possession of the prisoner.

To reach the garage required walking through the anteroom next door. Winston put Marlow's hood back on and guided him up out of his seat, and then walked him through to Grant's room. There, unseen by anyone else, Winston pushed Marlow down in the seat Grant had been sitting in, and seamlessly collected Grant dressed exactly as Marlow – down to the correctly coloured hands.

To the three men waiting outside the prisoner transfer van, nothing had changed. Grant had studied a video showing Marlow being walked in chains from his cell to the shower area days earlier, learning to copy the walk as closely as possible.

Marlow turned his head slightly, wondering why he was being sat down again, then he returned his head to centre. He began to chuckle when he realised he was being left behind. 'Clever boy, Grant,' he said. 'Clever, clever boy.'

Simeon stood next to him, taking over from Winston. 'Keep your mouth shut,' he said.

It was a massive convoy in the underground garage. Two prisoner vans: one carrying Grant-as-Marlow, along with Gretchen and an SEG guard; another to carry extra SEG armed support. Accompanying were outriders and two follow-on saloons that would be shared with each van.

None of the SEG officers looked nervous. Prisoner transfer was about as safe as it got in their line of work. Ordinarily. Most of them stood around making small talk with each other, confident that any action that happened would be in the prisoner van. On that assumption, they were only half right.

Winston handed Grant over to Gretchen, who spoke towards Grant's ear, 'Henry, my name is Gretchen. You mind your manners, and you'll be looked after just fine. We've got an ETA of one hour and twelve minutes, so when I lock you in get comfortable.'

The SEG guard put out his hand as if to take control of the prisoner.

Gretchen didn't jerk Grant away. They had prepared for, and expected it.

To keep suspicions low, Gretchen asked the guard, 'You don't mind?'

'No problem,' he replied, taking Grant by the arm.

Grant made sure to keep his upper arm muscles unflexed. Marlow was still in great shape for breaking over fifty years of age, but he had lost a lot of density in his arms in recent years.

The guard didn't check Grant's cuffs, the first indication to Gretchen that the guard might be their mole. He locked the cuffs into the metal ring attached to the bench that ran the length of the inside of the van wall. 'All good,' the guard told Gretchen.

The commanding officer marched down the line of vehicles, giving the circular hand signal that it was time to leave. 'Okay, people. Our revised ETA is one hour and fourteen. Keep it simple, make good clear calls. Let's move out…'

Christie joined Winston, hanging back at the garage window. 'They love all this,' she said.

Winston wasn't feeling nearly as comfortable. 'Let's hope that they all come back in one piece.'

'You'd better get upstairs,' said Christie. 'The chopper's waiting.'

27

Once the convoy got rolling out of the underground garage, out through the steel gates that led onto Albert Embankment, it formed a long snake of blistering blue lights and blaring sirens all slightly out of sync with one another. Traffic all around came to a standstill, with drivers wondering who on earth was being transported. The sight of the prisoner van and the length of convoy suggested a famous serial killer or terrorist. But the name Henry Marlow would have meant nothing to the people of London.

The convoy was almost too big. Unwieldy. The roads were single lane, which required a huge amount of cooperation between members of the public in their vehicles to make space. From front to back, it took almost a full minute to pass through, leaving a trail of confusion and traffic stopped at skewed angles.

When it reached the major roundabout of Elephant and Castle, however, the convoy became more manageable. One half continued east, the other heading southwest.

Overhead in the police helicopter, Winston confirmed in his radio headset, 'There's the split.'

Using decoy vehicles was standard practice for senior politicians, but not for prisoners. Olivia Christie had lobbied the Metropolitan Police Commissioner on the matter personally. With his sources inside MI6, Charles Joseph would have been expecting a decoy, but Winston had made sure it was leaked in advance which one contained the principal. The officers who had been targeted by Bogov's malware definitely knew what was going on. For the operation to be successful, MI6 *needed* Joseph to follow the convoy containing Grant. If Joseph and his team ended up guessing wrong and chased after the wrong half, then Gretchen wouldn't be able to re-infiltrate, and she might not get another chance.

Gretchen was in the van with Grant, the 'prisoner'. Sitting next to her was the SEG officer, who was texting on his phone. And being strangely mindful about Gretchen seeing the screen.

'Is that regulation?' she asked.

He put the phone away quickly. 'Personal.' he replied.

Gretchen held a finger to her ear, pretending to receive an incoming message. She paused, then radioed Winston for real, 'Affirmative, I'm strapped in here.'

Up in the air, Winston confirmed to Christie on the ground, 'That's the control phrase. Gretchen thinks that she has the mole in the van with her.'

In her office, Christie replied, 'That's good. If a rogue officer is in communication with Joseph, they must still think Marlow is really in there or they would have called them off already. Stay close, Leo. You're our eyes.'

. . .

Grant was in the dark wearing the hood. He could still hear information being relayed in his radio earpiece. He was waiting for the first signs of the convoy breaking up. It was the only viable way to attack. Break up the support vehicles, then attack.

The convoy was on Old Kent Road, a reasonably tight dual-carriageway with an additional bus lane. Traffic ahead meant that the convoy could never build up a strong head of steam, keeping the speed limited to thirty-five miles an hour. Navigating the many sets of traffic lights and pedestrian crossings didn't help, but it was the fastest route through central London.

Then it started behind. Unseen by the lead outriders and support vehicle. The driver of the prisoner van only caught the aftermath in his side mirror, seeing one of the support vehicles being wiped out from the side at a crossroads. It was no accident, as the driver of a black Range Rover made clear as it backed up, only to plough into the side a second time. The masked men inside brandished AK47s, but didn't fire them. The officers in the car were too dazed to go on the attack.

The Range Rover backed up again, and sped after the convoy.

The call came out over the radio that it looked like an attack was underway.

That was all the officers at the front needed to get their finger out and speed up. If they stayed at thirty-five miles per hour they would be sitting ducks. But speeding up meant a significant increase in risk to the public, many of whom seemed to be oblivious to the sirens and lights, walking off the pavement without looking. It was only the fast reflexes and advanced handling skills of the prisoner-van driver that avoided a civilian casualty.

.   .   .

Christie was frantic in her office, helpless to do anything but listen in as the attack unfolded. Leaning over her desk, she asked, 'What can you see, Leo?'

Shouting to be heard over the blades, he replied, 'They're coming from everywhere. They just knocked off four of the moto riders. Guys at the side of the road with baseball bats. They're stealing the bikes from them...'

Christie speed-dialled on her phone. 'Get the Met Commissioner on the line, now!'

A second Range Rover appeared at the next crossroads, taking out the second support vehicle.

The van driver blasted his horn at the traffic ahead, which was taking an age to clear. 'Where the hell is our back-up?'

The first Range Rover was all over the back of the prisoner van now that the other support vehicles had been taken out of the equation.

The van driver was starting to see daylight ahead, when an articulated lorry pulled out from the slow lane into the fast, then slammed on its brakes.

The driver hit his horn again, swerving in and out to remind the lorry that they were there.

The navigator told him, 'He must be with them.'

'Who's *them*? Who the bloody hell have we got back there? Hannibal Lector?'

The navigator radioed constantly, but he kept being told that back-up was en route. The decoy convoy had been sabotaged as well, being hit by retractable spike strips thrown out onto the road that punctured their tyres.

Trying to undertake, a double-decker bus pulling out from

the bus lane then knocked the prisoner van from the side. Now both lanes were blocked, leaving the prisoner van boxed in.

Overhead, Winston radioed to Grant and Gretchen, 'Okay, this is it, guys. Two black Range Rovers closing in behind you. All support vehicles are down. It's on you now…'

28

In the back of the prisoner van, Grant was being thrown around by the desperate attempt by the driver to escape the ambush. The driver mounted the central reservation, driving over row after row of plants, trying to force a way clear, but the traffic on the other side was solid. And every fifty feet was another lamppost, blocking any chance of speeding away down the centre.

There was nowhere to go. No escape.

Gretchen and the SEG officer held on to hand rails above their heads.

'What's going on out there?' shouted Gretchen.

The officer couldn't reply. His breathing was erratic, and he'd shut his eyes to try and compose himself. He knew what he had to do, and he knew that it would be the hardest thing he had ever done in his life. To try and make peace with it, he pictured his little girl who had been snatched on her way to school that morning. This was now the only way that he would ever see her again.

He was willing to do anything to get her back.

Anything…

. . .

The van driver glanced at the bus to his left. 'There are no passengers on that thing.'

'They're in on it too,' replied the navigator.

In the side mirrors, the driver could see the Range Rovers swarming them like hornets. 'We're going to get hit any second.'

The navigator braced himself for impact, holding onto his door and planting his other hand on the dash. The grim reality of their situation took hold of him. 'If this is organised crime, they'll shoot us, Matt. If I die, tell my wife—'

'Hey, cut that shit out! We're going to get out of this…'

In an effort to keep their plan on a strict need-to-know at director level, Randall and Miles Archer had been instructed to remain in the Tank, unaware of how spectacularly the operation had turned.

On Winston's orders, Miles was combing through photographs from Marlow's old hideout in Charles Joseph's compound, searching for clues about Joseph and Marlow's wider plan. Marlow had left reams of old official reports behind, and Winston had been convinced that, somewhere in that compound, was something that could connect where Joseph had been, with where he was going.

Randall was continuing his work on Arkady Bogov's memory stick, but he was finding it hard to concentrate. He drummed his pen anxiously on his desk. 'This is driving me crazy…Not knowing…' He dropped his pen with a frustrated sigh.

Miles was distracted, but not about the operation. He stopped on one particular photo, zooming in on his laptop screen for a closer look. 'That's weird,' he said.

'What is it?' asked Randall.

'Leo asked me to check these forensics photographs from Joseph's old Congolese compound. There was a ton of paper-work and Albion files that Marlow left there. But I didn't know that Marlow kept prisoners there.'

'Prisoners?' Randall leaned over to see the photograph in question.

'It looks like some kind of holding cell in the basement.'

Randall pulled back, confused. 'I've never seen that before.' While Miles kept thinking, Randall clarified, 'No, Miles. I mean, I was heavily involved in the forensics report. It was my analysis that led Grant there, and there was no mention of this place, and I've never seen that photograph.'

Miles said, 'It can't have been missed, because it was filed away downstairs in the record room.'

'Yeah, it's a scan of a hard copy. You can't just toss a hard copy in the bin. It would have been logged as missing. Who signed the final forensics report?'

Miles clicked to the accompanying document. 'It would have been a Hannibals report because it was dealing with Marlow. Everything relating to him went through internal affairs. But Imogen Swann was already dead by that point.' He scrolled down to find the name. 'It was Alex Simeon.'

'We can't ask him about it just now. The op is still live.'

Following his instincts, Miles tried to access the forensics report on Simeon's wife, but he was informed that he couldn't access the file. 'I'm going to the record room. Something weird is going on here.'

Downstairs, Simeon was alone in the windowless anteroom with

Marlow. He crouched down in front of him and removed Marlow's hood.

Simeon said, 'Are you ready? We have two minutes.'

'Probably less,' Marlow replied.

Simeon checked the path was clear, then led Marlow out of the anteroom to the empty control room next door, where agents and operatives checked in and out before and after assignments. Banks of computers that were wired into the MI6 mainframe were left unattended, the room cleared hours earlier in preparation for Marlow being transferred through the area.

Simeon left Marlow in the middle of the room, who shuffled around in his shackles.

Marlow gestured with a shrug. 'I'm a bit restrained here.'

Simeon took out the keys and unlocked Marlow's cuffs. With Marlow's hands and feet now free, Simeon stood over the keyboard of a computer terminal and dialled into the Hannibal mainframe using Imogen Swann's credentials. He knew them from his deep-dive into her hard drive, when he had, ironically, been thought of as the only man trustworthy enough for the job of investigating her crimes.

Simeon's heart stirred, both at the thought of what Marlow could do to him with his bare hands, and what he was about to do on Marlow's behalf. But there was no going back now. He reminded himself that he was doing this for a reason.

He felt Marlow looming behind him. Now that he was out of his glass box, Simeon had a moment to appreciate Marlow's incredible presence and intimidating aura. When Simeon turned around to offer him the keyboard, Marlow was much closer than he had expected.

Simeon gulped. 'Do you know where you're going?'

Marlow gave a tiny flick of his hand as a gesture to get out of the way. If time hadn't been a factor he would have savoured the moment. Instead, he focussed on the task at hand.

Simeon leaned closer as Marlow navigated to a part of the Hannibal network that Simeon had never seen before. It showed the fifteen flags of the countries that various intelligence agencies were from, all part of their vast, deniable network of black ops resources.

For the last piece of the puzzle, Marlow inserted a memory stick that had been prepared by Arkady Bogov and sent days earlier to Simeon.

An old-school 8-bit-animated skull with pixelated tears falling appeared briefly on the screen, along with the words "Time to cry, time to die". The calling-card slogan of Bogov's DeathWeep malware.

29

In the helicopter, there wasn't much they could do except detail what was going on, and it was getting uglier and more desperate by the second.

Winston directed the pilot to dip the left side so he could identify the number plates on the Range Rovers. He adjusted the focus on a pair of binoculars and asked for Miles's help on the radio.

After failing to get a response the second time, Randall cut in instead. 'Miles is gone, sir,' he said.

'Gone where?' asked Winston.

Randall explained as best he could.

As soon as he mentioned the photograph that seemed to have sparked Miles's curiosity, Winston asked what exactly Miles had seen.

'Something about Marlow keeping a prisoner,' Randall replied.

'Send me the picture.' When it arrived on his phone, an object on the ground piqued Winston's attention. He pinched the screen to zoom in. The moment he recognised Anna Simeon's necklace in the dirt, he told the pilot to take him back.

The pilot checked to make sure.

Winston aggressively repeated his demand, then told Randall to contact security. 'Tell them to issue a code two takedown of Alex Simeon.'

The code for a compromised agent on site. Deadly force authorised.

Winston said, 'Do it. Do it now, Randall! Miles's life depends on it. If you see Alex Simeon, or he comes to you, do *not* attempt to engage, do you hear me?'

Randall didn't need to be sold on the last part.

The articulated truck slowed down more, and the bus moved in closer still against the prisoner van. The SEG driver couldn't go right, or he'd plough into a lamppost; couldn't speed up because of the truck; couldn't go left because of the bus; and the two Range Rovers were blocking any escape through a sudden braking manoeuvre.

Their position now locked, the back doors of the truck opened, revealing a masked gang holding AK47s. They opened fire downwards across the road.

Warning fire.

A masked Charles Joseph emerged, waving his arm up and down, demanding they stop.

'This isn't bulletproof glass,' the navigator exclaimed. 'Slow down. They've got us!'

Joseph directed his men to open fire again, this time taking out the front tyres.

Pedestrians on both sides of the road scattered at the deafening cracks.

. . .

Inside the van, bullets pinged against the van's bodywork, ramping up the onslaught. Gretchen knew that the time was now. She pulled her gun on the rogue guard before he could react. He held his shoulders in a hunch, terrified of moving. Each second that followed didn't feel like getting closer to safety. It felt like death creeping nearer.

'Phone! Now!' Gretchen yelled, spreading her feet wide to balance herself against the rolling and yawing motion of the braking van.

The guard took out his phone, looking for a hint of a chance. And he got one.

The bus collided into the side of the van, knocking Gretchen off balance.

Taking advantage of the moment, the guard threw his phone as hard as he could at Gretchen, just as the bus collided again.

The impact made the van lurch to one side, throwing Gretchen into the side wall, causing her to dropping her gun in the process. She tried to rouse herself, but couldn't. The blow had been too hard.

Reacting to the sound of Gretchen's groans as she tried to reach her gun, Grant released his cuffs. He couldn't lash out until he knew what was in play, so he slid his feet across the corrugated flooring until his toes hit the officer's heels.

He's facing away from me, he thought.

The guard had kicked Gretchen's gun away and recovered his mobile. He shouted on a call to Joseph over the cacophony of bullets, 'I've got Marlow in here, ready for collection!' When he hung up, he drew his own weapon on Gretchen. The guard told Grant, 'They're coming, Henry. Hang tight. I've got this one covered.'

Gretchen shook her head, and held her hands up.

With the knowledge that the guard was facing away from him, Grant gently released his cuffs and whipped off his hood.

Gretchen gave the tiniest flick of her head at Grant. *Go.*

The guard saw it. But by the time he whipped around, Grant already had a hold of him.

The guard was still trying to make sense of the sight of anyone other than Marlow being under the hood. Grant whipped the guard around and got an elbow around his throat. He had a sudden flash of Martin Haslitt, the familiar feeling of cutting off someone's airway. It was a Lion's Kill choke. Grant's right arm wrapped around the guard's neck so that his windpipe was in the crook of Grant's elbow. Then, with his left hand, Grant reached across his torso and grabbed his right bicep, and put the back of his left hand behind the guard's head. If he had used his palm rather than the back of the hand, the guard might have pulled it free. This way – as Grant had been taught at Kill School – his forearm was flush against the back of the guard's head. All that was left to do was squeeze. Grant puffed out his chest and pulled his elbows together.

The guard lasted ten seconds before losing consciousness. The moment that he did, Grant lunged for Gretchen who was back on her feet, gun recovered.

The van slowed to a stop, and the sound of shooting was replaced by men shouting.

'You ready?' asked Grant.

'Yeah,' she told him.

Grant knelt on the floor and put his hood back on.

As Gretchen unlocked the back door, Joseph's men moved in.

Gretchen stood in their way, gun pointed at Grant. She shouted, 'It's not Marlow! Stay back!' She shot Grant in the chest. Twice in quick succession.

He catapulted backwards from the hips, arms splayed out on either side on the floor.

Joseph's men couldn't work out what Gretchen was doing and who she had just shot.

She dashed to Grant's side and removed his hood to show them. 'They swapped Marlow out. The bastards played us.' She made a show of checking his pulse. It was faster than normal, but healthy.

She shook her head. 'It's fine. The prick's dead,' she said, trying to lead them away. 'We've got to get out of here.'

But they didn't recognise her, and didn't know she was a rogue agent.

Charles Joseph appeared behind the men, wondering what was going on. 'Gretchen?' he said in surprise.

'There's no time to explain...We need to move!' She indicated the collective epilepsy of blue flashing lights speeding towards them.

'Come with us,' Joseph said, leading them away.

One of his crew set off a rigged explosion on the articulated truck, sending an orange plume one hundred feet into the air. Between the blown-out truck and bus, the road on that side was totally blocked. As planned, they took off on the stolen SEG motorbikes and left the carnage behind.

Christie was on her feet in her office, heart palpitating from the worst blowback of an op in her career. She could hear the sirens in the background through her window.

The Old Kent Road was on fire. The police radio had called out the loss of the bikes and how they'd been used to flee. Christie wanted a visual on them from the air.

But her helicopter was no longer in position, because

Winston had demanded to be brought back to Vauxhall Cross. And he wasn't responding to radio calls.

He was too busy running down the stairs, showing security his pass credentials as they hunted the building for Alex Simeon.

Winston's adrenaline hadn't been that high since he'd last been on a field op. He could sense the danger that Miles was in and he knew he simply had to do everything he could to get there in time. But there were so many stairs. So many corridors. So many swipe-card doors.

When he finally reached the basement anteroom where Grant had prepped for the op, Winston found Miles gunned down and Marlow gone.

An alarm was wailing, but he barely heard it.

Blood was rushing through his ears, through his heart, flooding his brain.

He checked vitals. Miles was gone.

Following the trail of open doors out to the control room that had been cleared of all staff in order to keep the op safe, Winston found a computer terminal blinking in the dim room.

On the screen it said, "Transfer complete". The amount of £3.4 billion.

Winston's world was collapsing around him, along with MI6.

He ran out to the underground garage, where Alex Simeon stood in the middle of the empty car park. Winston pulled his gun on him.

He ran up behind Simeon, yelling, 'I'll shoot you in the back, you piece of shit. On your knees! Now! NOW!'

Simeon didn't protest. He was too busy sobbing. Thinking about Anna. He interlocked his fingers behind his head.

Winston grabbed him, holding him while two security guards

came dashing out, having stumbled across Miles Archer's dead body.

'It was him, it was him,' Winston explained.

The guards were unsure, but Simeon didn't protest. They took control of him, placing him on his chest on the ground.

'I didn't know about the money, I swear...' Simeon cried. 'That was never the plan.' He craned his neck, trying to look upwards. 'Oh, Jesus...What have I done?'

Winston grabbed him by the neck. 'What is he driving, Alex? There's still time.'

Simeon shook his head. 'An agency car.'

Winston puffed in exasperation, releasing Simeon's neck. He ran to the control room to check the cameras that he knew must have been disconnected in advance. It would take an age to figure out what car he was in.

Marlow was gone.

Armed response vehicles swarmed around the stricken prisoner-transport van, its rear doors flapping open. There were two bodies inside. Only one of them was moving.

The rogue SEG guard.

The AR officers took aim and instructed him to get his hands on his head.

'I had to,' he wept. 'My little girl...' It was a refrain he would return to continually over the subsequent hours. He had indeed saved his young daughter's life. The question now was whether he would ever see her again outside of a prison.

When the van had been cleared of weapons, the senior officer approached the hooded prisoner on his back on the floor, ready to fire at the slightest hint of a threat. 'Lift your head if you can hear me!'

He got no response.

The officer crouched down as his colleagues covered him from behind. He checked the prisoner's pulse, getting the same healthy result that Gretchen had. 'No pulse! Get paramedics here *now*!'

30

THREE YEARS AGO

Widower.

The word didn't sound like something Alex Simeon should be. Not at his age. But that was what people could refer to him as now.

The funeral was as awful as he had expected. As his and Anna's marriage had progressed, he was hit with idle thoughts of what would happen when they got older. Would one of them get sick? If so, who would be first? He prayed that it wouldn't be debilitating. He would have done anything for Anna. What he wasn't sure that he had the strength for was watching her suffer. To be in pain every day and not be able to stop it. He had watched his mother die of a long and painful muscle-wasting disease, and the sight of her bed-stricken, with barely the energy to peel a satsuma or bring a glass of water to her lips, had crushed him.

Standing at the lectern in church, giving his eulogy, Alex felt the awesome power of what love could do to someone. How it could do the unthinkable. Like tell the most devious lie possible to all of his relatives. Anna's closest family and friends. To tell them she was dead. They all sat there in church, weeping for the loss of Anna, but also weeping for poor Alex, who was showing such fortitude and resilience in the face of grief.

As he said the words he had typed out the night before, he thought about how he would tell them 'all when it was over. Really over. Exactly what had happened, and how. Would they ever forgive him? Of course not. It was absurd to think otherwise.

And they would have been right, Alex thought.

Afterwards, at the function room, a buffet had been laid on. Alex didn't eat a thing. The idea of eating since travelling to Tijuana to identify his wife's body seemed ridiculous to him. Why would he want to fuel his body? To keep going on, now that everything had been taken from him?

That's what people on the outside thought. But Alex knew different.

It was with great relief that he arrived home, shaking off the most persistent relatives who wanted to stay the night with him. No one said it, but there was concern that he would kill himself.

He wasn't going to do that. Little did they know, now of all times, that it would have been unthinkable. There was work to be done. First, he had to wait.

Then the call came as promised.

He picked up before the first ring had finished. 'Hello?'

'Alex. How are you holding up?'

Simeon recognised the voice. 'I did exactly as you asked.'

'You did very well,' the man replied. 'You should be proud. Not many people could have managed what you have. To live with such a lie.'

'Who was she?' asked Simeon. 'The woman I identified in Tijuana?'

'No one of any real importance.'

'What happens now?'

'I'll call some day, Alex. A year from now. Maybe two. Maybe five. But waiting, in silence, is the only way you'll see Anna again.'

'How can I know she's really alive?'

'She's right here.'

Simeon paused. 'I want to see her, Marlow. I won't go any further until I know she's alive.'

A moment later, his phone pinged with a picture message.

As soon as Simeon laid eyes on his wife's face, his eyes began to fill. She was holding a copy of that day's *El Universal* – a Mexican newspaper – in front of her.

'You piece of shit,' Simeon cried.

'You'd probably do anything to find her, to see her again. Am I right?' asked Marlow.

Simeon was crying too hard to answer. He covered his mouth.

Marlow said, 'I knew when I caught her that she might prove useful to me someday. That remains the case now. She's alive and she'll stay that way, Alex. If you do your part, she'll be returned alive and well. If you don't, well…I think you of all people know what I'm capable of.'

31

The Angel of Independence – otherwise known as simply *El Ángel* – in downtown Mexico City was one of the most recognisable landmarks not just in the city, but in Mexico itself. A towering column at the centre of the Paseo de la Reforma roundabout, it featured a bronze statue of Enrique Alciati of Nike – the Greek goddess of victory – standing proudly on top. It was beloved by the locals, but as happens with all locals who live in or around beautiful places, to them, it was just another part of the decadent architecture of Mexico City – part of the background.

Anna Simeon, however, couldn't take her eyes off it. She had been drifting in and out of sleep as the sedative she had been injected with while locked in Henry Marlow's countryside safe house began to wear off. Her vision now clearing, she could also begin to hear the city's wonderful noise again. A great throb all around the SUV she was being transported in. The sound of laughter of young children playing on the steps of *El Ángel*; people ringing bells on their bicycles as they navigated the busy thoroughfare of Paseo de la Reforma; and

Mexican pop music streaming out of car radios through open windows.

She couldn't feel the heat yet, but she would. The driver and the guards travelling with her had turned the air conditioning way up. They were an international bunch, not used to the climate. Once Anna had been delivered, they would be on to another job elsewhere, back in Europe where they usually plied their black-market trade as hired guns.

Under her breath, Anna said, 'Alex…' She reached her hand out towards the driver.

The driver asked a guard, 'She okay?'

'She's hallucinating. It's the drugs wearing off. How long?'

'We're right there.'

The SUV pulled up outside the British embassy on Florencia, a six-lane one-way road with towering palm trees all down the centre.

A guard injected her again, and her whole brain lit up, every synapse firing. While she was still getting control of the sensation, the guard told her, 'Give your name at the embassy. They'll get you home.' Then he shoved her out onto the pavement.

She barely stayed on her feet. She swallowed hard and took a few steadying breaths. She knew where she was now, but her motor functions were still playing catch-up.

The guard at the front of the embassy watched her carefully as she approached. She had no bag, no possessions, and, unless she was carrying it in her underwear, no passport.

'Can I help you, señora?' he asked.

She replied, 'My name is Anna Simeon. I'm a British citizen.' She put a hand to her chest and looked around, overwhelmed at where she was standing. After three years, she really was free. It was over.

But she had no idea at what cost.

32

Grant regained consciousness in an ambulance bound for St Thomas' hospital on the banks of the River Thames. With him at all times to control access was the Met Commissioner's most trusted officer in Specialist Firearms Command. He knew nothing about Duncan Grant, or the truth about the prisoner that should have been wearing the hood. All he had been told was that the prisoner's identity was to be kept from as many people as possible until Grant could be handed over to agency personnel within the hospital. As far as the officer was concerned, the prisoner had been shot twice in the chest. A bulletproof vest underneath his white jumpsuit had saved his life, but a blow to the back of head had knocked him out hard.

The ambulance was received at a secluded underground entrance. The same one that would be used should the Prime Minister ever require emergency medical treatment. There was no reception area inside, no benches full of the injured or sick, or ringing telephones. The moment the stretcher was inside, a team of paramedics swarmed around, starting a whole array of tests and checks. They rushed down a bright corridor under the bowels of the regular building, taking the patient into an old, refurbished surgery.

Olivia Christie's personal body man – her most-trusted security guard – controlled access in and out of the room, strictly forbidding anyone not on a pre-approved list to come in.

The medical team weren't anxious. The patient's vest had absorbed the brunt of the bullets' impact, but painful swelling and bruising were already blossoming underneath Grant's skin.

Once the doctor in charge was satisfied that the patient was in the clear for concussion, the medical team left the room. It was now an intelligence operation. As stipulated by Olivia Christie, there were no Hannibal agents anywhere near Grant, and wouldn't be.

In the next room, MI6 doctors with classified clearance were in the final preparations with the body of a homeless ex-squaddie that had been found under a bridge a few days earlier. Official identification had proven impossible, and the man had been declared a John Doe. MI6 had got to him before the final paperwork had been filed. Now the man was theirs. The body wasn't perfect, but didn't need to be. He just needed to be a close enough match to be convincing if anyone in the hospital with links to Joseph did some digging.

Blood samples were taken from Grant. Fingerprinting done, using Grant's instead of the squaddie's. As far as the official record would go, the squaddie would be Duncan Grant – for as long as he needed to be.

The body would be held in a protected area of St Thomas' mortuary until the Joseph/Marlow op was over.

For anyone trying to check – even through the most inside of sources – Duncan Grant was dead. Shot by a rogue MI6 operative now working with the terrorists.

When all the procedures were complete, Winston was left alone with Grant in the private recovery room.

Grant sat up, wincing from the pain in his ribs.

'Not bad for a dead man,' said Winston.

'Yeah, I'll live.' Grant swung his feet down off the bed. He stared at the linoleum floor, fearing the worst. 'How many are dead back there?'

'We've counted five so far. Including one of our own.'

Grant looked up in horror. 'Gretchen?'

'Miles.'

'Miles? What was he doing there?'

Realising how much he had to explain about what had gone on at Vauxhall Cross in Grant's absence, Winston pulled him up to standing. 'Grant. Marlow's gone. He escaped.'

Grant's face turned to steel. 'Take me back.'

Winston brought him back to headquarters in the boot of his car. There was something low-tech and unsophisticated about it that reminded him of the old days. It wasn't so long ago, he thought, that he had been a junior operative thrown in at the deep end of the first Presidential election in Taiwan. He had been the one in the boot of a car then, ferried into Taipei City to smuggle out a dissident journalist with evidence of electoral fraud against the democratic victor.

Then he did the maths and shook his head at the disparity between his memory and reality. That had been twenty-five years ago. Princess Diana and Prince Charles were just getting divorced, and mad cow disease had broken out. Suddenly, he felt very old.

Traffic was at a standstill all around because of the events on Old Kent Road. Police helicopters swarmed the skies, sirens all around, but the vehicles associated with them always just out of sight. The city felt under siege.

Winston knew that those ten minutes alone in the car would be all he got to grieve for Miles. What had happened would be nothing compared to the aftermath. It would drag on for days, the intensity ramping up by the hour. He was sure of that. He had lived through enough of these crises to know how they played out.

He might have been a senior director at MI6, but he didn't have emergency 'blue light' credentials to escape traffic jams.

As traffic remained stalled ahead, he thought about Miles's final moments. Diligently running around, doing the job that Winston had taught him to do. Now he was gone. And Winston would have to be the one to call Miles's elderly mother to tell her what had happened. Now Grant was in the boot, and goodness only knew what he was about to get wrapped up in.

Winston knew that Grant would go after Marlow with everything he had. He had already proven that in the previous months.

Winston leaned forward, resting his head on the steering wheel. He felt tears escaping from his eyes, which he rubbed away quickly before they could fall. He thought he owed Miles that much. It wasn't a time to grieve. Not yet. It was a time to fight.

33

Vauxhall Cross was in what they called a 'quiet lockdown'. No alarms, no PA announcements. But access to any floor other than your own was off-limits. Everyone was assigned to their desk until further notice. No one to get in or out without the head of security's approval.

There weren't many people Christie trusted with her life. She would have thought Alex Simeon would be one of them. Now everything Christie thought she knew about safety and security within Vauxhall Cross had been turned upside down.

Now she didn't know who to trust.

Grant was brought to the Tank via back service lifts. The corridors eerily empty. All doors closed. Like a school at night-time.

Christie was in the Tank along with Randall, who was fielding phone calls at the far end of the room. Christie tossed down her phone on the table, showing breaking news online about the convoy attack. 'We are no longer a covert operation,' she said.

'It was always going to be a risk,' said Winston.

She paced across the room, frustrated at the lack of floor space. 'We did exactly what Marlow wanted. We walked right into it!'

Grant, clinging to whatever optimism was available to him, said, 'We might not have seen Marlow's escape coming, but we've got Gretchen back in Charles Joseph's network.'

Christie turned to Randall, who had finished his call. 'Speaking of which,' she said, 'where is she?'

Randall replied, 'Her tracker won't go live for at least another...' he checked his watch, 'twenty-one hours.'

Grant said, 'If they don't scan her in the first twenty-four, they never will.'

'I can't stand not knowing,' said Christie. 'But we risk her life if we switch it on any time before that.'

Winston agreed. 'Joseph could be based on the other side of the world. After hitting London and The Hague, he'll want to get as far away from western Europe as he can. We need to know where he is.'

Christie acquiesced. She let out a heavy breath. In her career, she had often found "waiting" to be a dangerously close cousin to "doing nothing".

While Christie had her back turned, Randall whispered something to Winston, who nodded in return.

Trying to be delicate, Winston ventured, 'Ma'am, about the money. We really need to know more about it in order to figure out where it's gone and how to get it back. It could be the key to locating Marlow too.'

She leaned against the short conference table in the middle of the room. 'The Fifteen Flags network wasn't just about better communication. If we were to defeat the sort of animals we were hunting, we had to have operations as well. That required money. Off-the-books. Only the Foreign Secretary, the Chancellor, and Prime Minister knew about it. We were funnelling more cash into Fifteen Flags than we could hide from the Treasury. As far as the Chancellor was aware, it was part of our standard covert operations budget. But it had to be quarantined somewhere safe. So it was kept within the Anticorruption department's budget somewhere only the director could access.'

'Alex Simeon knew about this?' asked Winston.

'No chance,' Christie replied. 'I knew he was a boy scout, but I wasn't prepared to open up Fifteen Flags to him until he had proven himself. But as the incoming director of Anticorruption, Alex had full access to Imogen Swann's computer in the aftermath of her murder. We didn't have a choice. We had to investigate her activities fully. None of us ever dreamed he could be compromised the way that he was.'

Winston said, 'Marlow wanted to be locked up in here. He knew every move we would make once he landed in that basement. Every countermove to our countermove. He gamed it all out. Like a chess player seeing an escape ten moves ahead. He knew we would never risk letting him out in the open after Joseph's attacks, and demonstrating that they had sources and moles within Vauxhall Cross.'

Grant couldn't help but admire the scope of it. Marlow's vision. One thing, though, remained troubling. 'He didn't go to all this trouble to steal money. It doesn't fit.'

'Even billions?' said Christie.

'Even billions, ma'am. What could he ever do with that amount of money that wouldn't go unnoticed? He kept Anna Simeon prisoner for three years just to create a source in Vauxhall Cross who could be extorted. The one source who, come the time, would be very much on the inside track. He wants to hurt us, but to steal that money? All of us in this room know that the agency's budget is ten times what it admits publicly.'

Christie and Winston exchanged a knowing and neutral glance.

Grant went on, 'So what does he do with it now?

Christie asked, 'Randall?'

He rearranged some windows on his laptop. 'The malware is blocking all of GCHQ's attempts to trace the cash transfer. I don't think there's any path that we could find that could be trusted, anyway. If this had been a simple smash-and-grab, it would be a different story. Bogov's DeathWeep malware changes everything.'

Christie asked Winston, 'What's Alex Simeon saying?'

He replied, 'He swears that he didn't know about the slush fund theft or escape. That Marlow's people told him it would be injecting a virus into our computers, nothing more. And no casualties.'

Christie approached the computer that Winston was standing over, about to play a video clip. 'Yes, well, trusting the word of a rogue agent is indicative of greater weaknesses.'

Winston started the clip, taken from the custody suite.

Simeon was sitting hunched in handcuffs, sobbing gently. He explained to the interrogator, 'If you really loved someone, you'd be willing to spend the rest of your life in jail if it meant that they could live. But I swear, I never knew about the money, or…' His voice cracked further. 'I didn't intend to kill anyone…but Miles got in the way…'

Winston stopped the clip. 'He doesn't know anything about how Marlow was going to flee, or to where, or what his plan was for getting out of the country.'

'So he says,' Christie remarked.

'I believe him,' said Grant. 'What does he have to gain now?

He's got blood on his hands. He knows he's not going anywhere but prison for the rest of his life. If he could give us so much as a sniff of Marlow, he'd do it.'

The others needed to be convinced.

Grant elaborated, 'He did all this for his wife. Saving her life is valiant in his eyes, but it's not worth as much if he never sees her again. If he could knock even a year off a prison sentence, he would do it.'

Christie told Winston, motioning at the computer screen, 'Get rid of that. I don't want to look at him.'

Winston shut the video player. 'We need to figure out what we can and cannot safely do. How's network security looking, Randall?'

He exhaled heavily at the direness of the situation. 'GCHQ is sending an emergency team over for analysis. What they've already looked at remotely isn't good. And it's the same that everyone else is seeing at Langley, Moscow, Tel Aviv. You name it, they're under.'

Christie asked, 'How much danger are our classified files in?'

'Well, Marlow can't open absolutely anything in the network that he wants. Each department is segmented using…' Randall rethought his original explanation for something plainer. 'Our most sensitive files are largely safe but not indefinitely. Undercover officers and operatives are not at risk. Ongoing operations haven't been compromised. From what GCHQ have seen so far, the malware is slowing us down, but not crippling us. Where it's hurting us most is interagency communication. Sharing intel.'

Christie said, 'To isolate us all.'

It made Grant think about Marlow's wider plan, and something Marlow had said. 'When we last spoke, Marlow mentioned this line…' He tried to remember it exactly. '"The part of you that you think makes you stronger, will be the very thing that destroys you." Bogov's malware infected the other agencies through the Fifteen Flags network because being connected on the same network was part of the design. The more connected the agencies became, the easier it was to hurt us all.'

Randall added, 'The problem now is, all the other agencies' funds have been frozen by the malware.'

Christie looked at the ceiling in frustration. 'How is this possible?'

'Have you ever had malware on your computer, ma'am?'

'How the hell would I even know?'

'You would know, ma'am. Believe me. You can't go anywhere. Do anything. Everything is locked. You can't run anti-virus software, shutting down and restarting does nothing, and you can't even go online to download a fix. Right now, every major intelligence agency in the world is locked in that nightmare.'

Winston suggested, 'Like an oligarch with frozen assets.'

Randall gestured towards him. 'Exactly.'

Grant asked, 'So if Marlow doesn't want money, what's he going to do with it?'

Randall pulled himself back towards his keyboard, setting off on a flurry of typing. 'Well, that's where it gets a little frightening.' He paused. 'If anyone wants a cup of tea, now would be a good time.'

34

Grant, Winston, and Christie huddled around Randall's computer while he navigated at lightning speed around various windows that were full of incomprehensible code to anyone but himself.

Randall explained, 'I have been combing through Bogov's computer logs from his memory stick whenever I could, and I found some rather troubling entries before the transfer op started. Events since then have now painted these in quite a different light.'

'What have you found, Randall?' asked Grant, eager to keep him on track. He trusted Randall, and didn't want to lose him in the room to some random analyst that Christie had worked with a dozen years ago. If he kept up too much technical talk, Grant knew that Christie would throw him overboard without a moment's hesitation.

Randall scrolled down through an interminable list of code. 'All of these lines refer to various attacks on domestic IP addresses. As Bogov said, there were thousands of them. What's most important are these thirteen lines here…' He highlighted them on the screen.

'What's so important about them?' asked Christie.

He didn't know how else to say it. 'They're probably the thirteen most important IP addresses in the world. They're the IP addresses of the thirteen root servers that make the internet work. Each identified by a single letter, A through to M.' His mind frazzled at how he was going to make what he had to say next understandable. 'How can I put this…Say you type a domain like Google dot com into your address bar. Those words get translated into a long number. An IP address. These thirteen servers are what translate domain names into numbers and back again. As you can imagine, hackers have tried to attack these servers in the past, because they're incredible important to the basic running of the internet. But a lot of people believe that the features of the system mean that if one or more parts fail, a whole host of advanced back-ups stop the system from collapsing. I am not one of those people.'

'You think it can be hacked?' asked Winston.

'It's humanity's nature to be imperfect,' replied Randall. 'It's what makes us capable of creating great art and music. It also means that anything we make can be undone. It's not a popular theory, but yes, Director, I believe the root servers can be hacked.'

Christie asked, 'Why are they so important?'

'Knock those thirteen servers offline, and typing Google dot com into your address bar won't do anything. You would have to type in the exact IP address. Imagine trying to send a text message, but instead of typing words you had to use binary code. You can imagine how hard it would be to write something as basic as an email.' He pointed at the screen. 'This here, is the first step to making the internet practically impossible to navigate.'

'That's it?' said Christie. 'That's their big plan? To *inconve-*

nience billions of people for a couple of days until the servers are fixed? They must be backed up hundreds of times over.'

'They are,' Randall conceded. 'But I don't think that's all they have planned.'

Winston folded his arms, wondering what Randall was seeing that no one else was. 'You said no one had successfully attacked these servers before.'

'They haven't,' Randall replied. 'Because of the dozens of failsafes and back-ups.'

Grant asked, 'What if someone attacked all thirteen at once?'

He raised his hands in acceptance. 'That's always been the fear. Until now, no one had the technology to beat them all at once. It's important to remember that it might be thirteen servers, but you shouldn't just be picturing thirteen different boxes sitting in secure locations somewhere. The root servers use a type of network that allows each server's IP address to share devices across multiple locations. So these thirteen servers actually share about a thousand different locations. They're located in everything from state-of-the-art secure warehouses like the kind Google and Facebook use, to small rooms on university campuses and research facilities. No attack or virus could penetrate them all before. The DeathWeep malware, however, is a different story. Bogov's logs show that over the last year, the virus has infiltrated all thirteen servers, on every device on the network. And no one has an idea it's there. It's lying dormant. Ready for the next phase.'

'What do you mean?' asked Winston.

'If the plan was to launch the malware into the root servers and make the internet very hard to use, it wouldn't be lying dormant today. It would have been activated already. Otherwise, what are they waiting for? But the malware's been lying dormant for weeks now. The only reason someone would do that...'

Randall exhaled, finally getting to the meat of it, 'is if they have something far bigger in mind. And by bigger, I mean terrifying.'

Christie asked, 'Why terrifying?'

Randall pushed his chair back from his desk to face them all. 'There's been a lot written by technology bloggers and writers over the years about how it might theoretically be possible to break, shut down, or even destroy, the internet.'

Winston said in confusion, 'Destroy the internet? How can that even be possible?'

Christie added, 'It's not like there's an on-off switch.'

'That's true,' said Randall. 'It's got about a thousand on-off switches. All with back-ups and failsafes and armed guards at dozens of data centres all around the globe, and exactly all of the endless measures you would expect to be in place to protect the internet.' He paused. 'But the fact is: there *is* a way of breaking it. I'm not talking about Facebook being offline for a few hours. I'm talking about turning on your computer or phone, and you can't do anything.'

'How would you do it?' asked Grant.

'Say that Joseph pulled off this server attack. The malware is sitting there, ready to be activated. If the server malware is activated, the next step would be to go after the intercontinental cables.'

'What are they?' asked Christie.

'We're all so used to wireless *everything* these days,' said Randall. 'But the internet exists because of hundreds of thousands of miles of cables. A lot of it underwater. Our so-called wireless world is only possible because it all has to be physically connected. We use cables.'

Winston said, 'There must be thousands of them.'

'About three hundred and eighty, actually.'

'Aren't they kept secret?'

'On the contrary, they're publicly listed. And most of them aren't hard to find. The American Federal Communications Commission publishes a list of them all. They're supposed to be buried underground, but a lot of them are brought to the surface on beaches because of ocean currents. There are about twelve major cable links that, if you cut them with an axe, would turn the internet into a series of islands that couldn't communicate with each other. With the cables cut, and root servers scrambled with malware, the internet is now landlocked. Emails and messages can't be sent around the world. Bank transfers; online orders of everything from clothes to medical equipment to online groceries; movie streaming; ebook downloads; accessing your cloud storage…all of these things and a hundred others just disappear. All web addresses are incomprehensible numbers.' He breathed in. 'Say you did *all* that, the final step would be blowing up the containers of what little remains.'

'What containers?' asked Christie.

'The data centres. The buildings that contain the actual servers that host the websites we all use every day. I'm talking vast warehouses that use up unimaginable amounts of electricity. Highly secure locations, policed like prisons…But not impenetrable. If those fell, it's not just about a slow, virtually inaccessible internet. We're talking about entire websites disappearing. Cloud storage. Every picture you ever uploaded for safe-keeping. Every post and picture on Facebook. Facebook itself ceases to exist. Amazon, gone. Google? Let's just say you had better have invested in a good set of encyclopaedias, because that just vanished too, along with every Wikipedia article ever written. All of those things we take for granted as being safe. All gone. Forever. All data *everywhere* is now frozen. Stuck with absolutely nowhere to go. Including trillions in cash and cryptocurrency, stuck in a digital purgatory, and no way of getting it back. It's an attack that's only ever been speculated on. I think it's the Great Equaliser Bogov talked about. A levelling of the playing field.'

'How so?' asked Winston.

'This isn't just about losing access to mildly diverting information and entertainment. It's about the fundamental functioning of normal society. All records of your bank accounts, taxes, mortgage payments, outstanding bills and debt – trillions in debt – all erased overnight.'

'But they can't be,' said Christie. 'They have to be backed-up—'

Randall was already nodding away. 'On the servers that have been rendered useless. Bricked. All of those records don't get stored on a memory stick and kept in a drawer for safe-keeping. They have to be on a network so they can be updated, and more files can be added to them. They're not air-gapped like a laptop that's never been connected to the internet. The second they go online for anything, they immediately become vulnerable. And with DeathWeep, everything is vulnerable.'

Grant shook his head at the play they were potentially looking at. 'If everything like that is destroyed, everyone starts over from zero.'

Trying to sum it up in a way that did it justice, Randall concluded, 'All told, it would be the greatest act of terrorism in history. A declaration of war on every sovereign country in the world. That would bankrupt entire countries, and cause casualties in…well, no one really knows.'

'Hang on,' said Christie. 'Why so many casualties?'

Randall cleared his throat as he tried to organise the full, real-world repercussions in a way that captured its true horror. His voice softened. 'I understand that people in your position in places like this fear the next terrorist atrocity. We've been saying around here for years that the next truly world-altering one will be chemical or nuclear.' He pointed to his screen. 'This might not be as obviously spectacular as a dirty bomb, or as nightmarish as a mushroom cloud over a major capital city, but it's ten times more effective if your goal is to cripple society and send it spiralling into anarchy. Entire economies will come to a standstill. There will be food shortages because supermarkets will have no ordering capability. That means shortages, and shortages mean riots at supermarkets over the last pack of toilet roll or pasta. We've seen it before, and under much milder conditions than this. Only this time, it would be a hundred times more intense. You're talking about bringing the world to a complete stop. It's not so much the casualties as it is—'

Grant cut in, 'Disorder. Chaos. Just like Marlow always wanted. Charles Joseph too. It's been their vision this whole time. What brought them together. Marlow saw that in Joseph when he first encountered him. Someone else who saw the world the way he did. Together, they've found a way to make it reality.'

Winston added, 'What Randall's saying fits with this Fifteen Flags attack. They're dismantling the entire system of society piece by piece.'

Christie found herself having to entertain the very worst of outcomes. 'Say they were to pull this off, Randall. How long to fix it all?'

'Ten years?' he replied. 'Maybe twenty to fully rebuild the infrastructure. To say nothing of the repairs required to society itself. Extreme poverty would be the norm. The economy would be reduced to a bartering system by the end of year one. Mass hunger and starvation by the end of year two as we reach the end of perishable resources. After that? All bets would be off.'

'Hang on,' said Grant, 'if this cripples the banking world too, what happens to the billions that Marlow stole?'

'That,' said Randall, 'remains an unknown.'

Winston asked, 'Do you have any idea when they might activate the malware?'

Randall clicked through to one last section. 'It's on a schedule to activate in forty-seven hours. And before anyone asks, no, it cannot be reversed, and it cannot be broken. It's not like picking a hair out of your salad. This is starting.'

Grant said, 'Marlow has been playing us for a very long time. We need to get on the front foot.'

Christie asked, 'How do you propose to do that?'

'I'm off-grid, and I need to stay that way. Gretchen is our only chance of stopping this. If word of my survival reaches Joseph, Gretchen could be in the firing line.'

Winston said, 'We've got almost a day before we can switch on Gretchen's tracker. That doesn't leave much time between finding out where she is, and finding a way to stop the rest of the attack.' He asked Grant, 'What are you thinking?'

'Gretchen is in with Joseph. But we could still get Marlow. And only one person potentially knows him better than I do.'

'Who?'

Christie answered, 'Anna Simeon.'

35

Ordinarily, professional negotiators would have been the only option in dealing with a long-time captive agent like Anna Simeon.

The psychiatrist assigned to her care since her flight from Mexico City touched down likened it to an 'almost unimaginable nightmare'. Never knowing if you'll ever go home again. Never being told why you're being held. The open-ended nature of the captivity was what drained resolve.

'Try not to linger on painful memories,' the psychiatrist advised Grant.

It's the painful memories we need, he thought.

He told her with sincerity, 'I'll do everything I can, doc.'

The reality was, MI6 needed information from anywhere they could get it. And no one had spent as much time in close proximity over the years to Charles Joseph and Henry Marlow as Anna Simeon had.

When Grant entered the 'softened' interview room – comfortable sofa rather than wooden desk and chairs; the microphone and recording equipment hidden away – he thought about how strong Anna must have been to survive those years of uncertain captivity. That person was still under her skin, in her bones. Of that he was sure. But that person wasn't what he saw on the exterior.

She was pale and weak from being kept out of direct sunlight for so long. Her entire body ached, her bones weakened by lack of vitamin D. The mood changes and fatigue she had suffered were symptoms indistinguishable from those triggered by the copious amounts of crystal meth she had been kept strung out on over the years, keeping her docile and compliant.

Grant had to get in and out as soon as possible before the meth withdrawals started kicking in. Which would be any hour now, depending on her tolerance.

Anna sat on the sofa, drinking a cup of tea, hands cradled around the mug for warmth. It wasn't cold in the room but she was shivery.

Judging by the exterior, it was hard to believe the woman Grant was in the company of had been a senior covert operative at one point. So good that she'd been trusted to go after the agency's most lethal assassin. Henry Marlow. As had become clear, the mission didn't go as planned.

Grant navigated his way through the conversation's opening with haste and compassion. Which was for both their benefit. Anna thought that she knew all about living hell. But the next seventy-two hours or so would be the very definition of that, as the last traces of meth left her body. Trying to get valuable information out of someone going through meth withdrawal would be nigh impossible. Certainly nothing that could be reliable, as memories and images became confused.

The groundwork sensitively laid, Grant asked about the mission to capture or kill Marlow.

'We had tracked down a former contact of his in Tijuana,' Anna explained, staring into her cold tea. 'Director Swann was desperate. She was jumping on any lead we ever had on him. So I was sent to check it out. I staked out the source for days, certain that my cover was solid. I never saw a tail, never had anyone on me. Still Marlow found me. I was walking back to my motel room one night, and I just felt this arm grab me from behind, and a mask went over my face. That was it. It went dark. When I woke up, it was daylight. Probably the next day. I was in this cage, this dog kennel…'

The psychiatrist scowled as Anna closed her eyes. She wasn't just remembering. She was reliving it.

'This is exactly what I said shouldn't happen,' she told Winston.

He said, 'Give him time.'

Anna continued, 'I could see out past the end of the property. We were in the middle of nowhere. Marlow was standing over me, the sun behind him which put me in the shade. I'll never forget that relief. It was *so* hot.'

Not wanting to get lost in details, Grant asked, 'What was he like?'

'He gave me water. He didn't say very much. Except to say that I wouldn't be mistreated and that I had nothing to fear.' She shrugged. 'I assumed he was going to kill me. Every day I thought that. For months. The only thing I didn't understand was why he would be keeping me alive. Torture and cruelty didn't really feature in his profile.' Realising she wasn't going to drink more tea now that it had gone cold, she put the mug down. 'I never did find out why he kept me alive. Then I was moved.'

Grant picked up the mug to make her a fresh tea. 'Do you remember where you were taken next?'

'To a new guy. He was the one who first drugged me. He did

it before we left. I barely even drank alcohol, so a hit of meth sent me to the moon. I don't know what happened. All I remember is being on a small plane. When we left Mexico it was morning, when we landed it was dark. Marlow wasn't there at the new place. The man in charge called himself Charles. I recognised him from Marlow's files. Charles Joseph. He'd been before my time, but I knew he was meant to be dead. And Marlow was the Albion who should have killed him.'

Grant placed down a fresh mug of tea, then showed Anna a picture of Joseph.

Anna nodded. 'That's him.'

'Do you know—'

Before he could get the question out, Anna interrupted, 'Where is Alex? I was told I would see him.'

Grant looked towards the two-way mirror beside the door, wondering how to handle the question. He was shocked that she hadn't been told.

She went on, 'I might look like a junkie to you, but I've still got an operative's guts. I've been kept too strung out for that shit to stay in my system long. If you want information from me, you should be deploying Alex to get it. The fact that you're not tells me something's wrong. Where is he?'

Grant said, 'Let me ask and find out.' In the corridor outside, he remonstrated with Winston, 'We haven't told her about her husband?'

'We can't,' he answered. 'She'll completely shut down.'

Grant looked optimistically at the psychiatrist.

She replied, 'Don't look at me. You two are running the show. I've told you what she needs.'

Winston said, 'Our assets have checked the old Joseph compound in the Congo. We know they're not there. If Anna was kept at a different location, that could be vital information.'

Grant exhaled in frustration, trying to keep his voice down. 'Gretchen needs our help. We don't have time for this. She doesn't need this bullshit. She needs the truth.' He went back in, any softness or gentility from his manner quickly dissipating. He crouched in front of her. 'Mrs Simeon. Anna. I'm going to level with you. One operative to another. My department, the whole agency is hurting. A lot. I don't know how much the agents told you on the plane, but Marlow has broken out of custody from Vauxhall Cross, and Charles Joseph is on the loose. We have an undercover operative in harm's way, and we need to find Marlow or Joseph as soon as possible.' He implored her, 'Is there anything you can remember that might help us find either of them? Anything?'

Anna got off the sofa, retreating towards the small kitchen area. 'What I remember is that all of Joseph's men were terrified of him. Almost every day there were murders. Random acts of brutal violence. Like they were in a video game. They would kill each other over the tiniest thing. Joseph encouraged it. Life meant nothing to them. It was all…meaningless. I was kept in a cell. In a basement. I hardly saw the light. One night, a gang of them opened up my cell and tried to undress me. They had spiked my food earlier on with something horrible. I couldn't move. I couldn't fight them off. They were all standing over me, some of them on their knees getting ready, when the ones at the back started falling away. I couldn't see what it was. Then the one who was ripping my clothes off, suddenly his hands went limp. I blinked hard and my vision cleared a little. It was Joseph. He had killed them all with a sword and chopped off the man's hands. They were sitting there in my lap. I heard weeks later that the ones who hadn't died were hung upside down by the feet until their heads filled with blood.'

Grant could picture the scene, having been in the middle of

something similar at Joseph's compound when hunting for Marlow.

Anna concluded, 'Through all of that, the only thing I could think was, I must survive this so I can see Alex again. So that I can see goodness again.'

Grant didn't have the heart to tell her. When she did find out, it was going to destroy her to see what had happened to all of Alex's "goodness". 'Anna, I'm going to get you what you want. I swear. When you look into my eyes, you can believe me – trust me – that I'll get Alex to you. I just need even one hint of another location. Please.'

She shook her head, unable to conjure anything. 'All I can remember is Mexico and the Congo.'

In the corridor, Winston mouthed to himself, 'That's no good. Come on, Grant…'

He knew that those locations had already been searched by local assets. Nothing found.

Grant asked, 'What about Marlow? Did you see him again?'

'Once,' Anna replied. 'He was angry at Joseph for loading me on the meth. They argued about it outside my cell. It turned into this whole other thing about Saudi Arabia–'

Grant didn't know what it was yet, but his instincts told him something was coming. 'Saudi Arabia? What about it?'

'Joseph kept yelling that "we can't risk it, we can't risk it, Henry." Marlow said that he wouldn't stop until he was in a grave.'

His heart quickening, Grant asked, 'What "he", Anna? A man from Saudi Arabia that Marlow wanted to kill?'

'I don't know who it was.'

'When do you think this conversation happened?'

She paused to think, feeling at her temples as a wicked

tension headache came on. 'Probably six months ago. Not long before they moved me back to Mexico.'

Grant prepared to leave. Before he did so, he crouched down in front of her again. 'Mrs Simeon. I'm going to get you your husband. You have my word on that. I can only hope that I've got a fraction of your strength. No matter what happens with your Alex, I want you to remember that you're alive. That's the most important thing. That's the only thing that matters.'

Wondering about the cryptic comment, Anna didn't have time to ask him to elaborate.

Grant was straight out the door, passing the psychiatrist on her way in. He told her, 'She sees her husband within the hour.'

The psychiatrist protested, 'I really think—'

'The *hour*,' he insisted.

Grant told Winston, 'It's Mohammad bin Abdul. The Crown Prince. Marlow will go back for him.'

'Wait…The argument that Anna described happened long before Lyon, everything with Imogen Swann…'

'Marlow was already hunting him back then, planning how to strike. The Crown Prince is a hard man to get to. Marlow tried in Paris and failed. He didn't fail often in his career, but Abdul played him. He has ferocious security everywhere he goes. Marlow knew that Abdul was behind the hit on him years earlier after the Kadir Rashid hit. Marlow's tying off loose ends. He's on his final plans. And he won't go down without Mohammad bin Abdul.'

Winston got straight on the phone to Christie. 'Ma'am, Grant thinks Marlow will go after Crown Prince Abdul.' When they were done, Winston waved for Grant to come with him. Striding ahead, he told Grant, 'It's on.'

36

Christie's car pulled up outside Clive Steps on Horse Guard's Road, which was the quieter entrance to the Foreign and Commonwealth Office building. Foreign Secretary the Right Honourable John Wark MP had his umbrella over his head, tiptoeing through puddles to get to the open back door of Christie's armoured, chauffeur-driven Jaguar XJ, having excused himself from his Chief of Staff and the conference call he should have been taking with the Indian Defence Minister.

'Thanks for finding time, John,' Christie said. 'Or should I be calling you Sir John now?'

He chuckled with faux-modesty. 'That's months away from being confirmed.'

'Of course. As if we don't know these things months in advance.'

'I didn't find time, Olivia. I *made* it. Let's press on, shall we.'

As the driver set them moving again, Christie raised the soundproof barrier between them. 'I thought I should let you know about an operation.'

Wark turned his back on the window as the car sped along Horse Guard's Road, past the back entrance to 10 Downing Street, towards the Victoria Memorial roundabout at Buckingham Palace. They would perform the loop along the Mall until they were done. Wark said, 'Would that be the massive covert operation you executed earlier today without so much as a sodding email to the Home Secretary?'

'You put me in this job for a reason, John. Because you trust me to make the difficult decisions. It was my judgement that MI5 and the Home Office couldn't be trusted with what we were doing with Henry Marlow. It's also my judgement that I'm trusting you with this.'

'And what is "this"?' he asked.

'I'm sending our Albion to Dubai to stop Henry Marlow murdering Crown Prince Mohammad bin Abdul.'

Wark put his hand to his head in disconsolation. 'There are about four things about that sentence that send a shiver up my spine. Is it Grant? Of course it is. Another maladjusted young man looking for mothers or fathers in all the wrong places. Ten-a-penny, and what do they ever get us?'

Christie retorted, 'Duncan Grant got us Henry Marlow and saved your bloody life!'

'And now he's going after him. Again.'

'It wasn't Grant's fault that Marlow escaped.'

'Oh, yes. He was out trying to capture another of your failed assets. Charles Joseph. Tell me, Olivia. When exactly do we get on top of this thing once and for all?'

'Grant will stop it,' said Christie. 'He knows Marlow. He's caught him before.'

'It's my understanding that Marlow wanted to be caught last time.'

'I think Grant's overstated that particular theory. It might well have been a back-up, but Grant had Marlow bang to rights.'

Wark repositioned himself so he could look Christie directly in the eye. 'Olivia, we were terrified of Marlow killing the Crown Prince before, and that's as true today as it was then. Maybe more so. Do you *really* trust Grant to stop Marlow?'

Unwavering, she answered, 'I do.'

He pushed his lips out, thinking it over. 'I trust that you believe that, really I do. I just don't know that I trust Grant as much not to fail. We should notify the Saudis to be on the safe side.'

'No,' said Christie. 'John, speaking frankly. We need Abdul in plain sight, in public as planned. If he goes into hiding, so does Marlow, and Grant loses him.'

'And I suppose this great internet bomb that your analyst is so obsessed about will go off.'

'It's a very real threat, John.'

'One that you're prepared to risk the Crown Prince's life over?'

She paused. 'I wish there was some other way.'

He knocked on the divider to the driver and the car slowed halfway along the Mall. Wark smiled as the car came to a stop. 'I forget sometimes,' he said. 'How ruthless you can be in the right circumstances.' He paused. 'I don't want to know about it. This meeting never happened. But whatever you do, keep it off the bloody PM's desk. I've got a knighthood in the post, you know.'

37

Only fifty years ago, Dubai in the United Arab Emirates was just
another small, unknown town in the middle of the unforgiving
Arabian peninsula on the coast of the Persian Gulf. The
discovery of oil in the region changed everything. Transforming
Dubai from a desert backwater port into a booming metropolis,
as petrodollars flooded the area, along with gargantuan mega-
projects like the Burj Khalifa, and the soon-to-be tallest structure
in the world, the Dubai Creek tower. In what seemed like no time
at all, it had turned itself into a hub for tourism and business the
likes of which had never been seen before.

Grant looked out of his first-class cabin on the Emirates 777
jet from London to Dubai. They were currently flying over
southern Iraq, after years of being routed over Iran during the
Iraq war. The luxury on offer was baffling to Grant. He had
insisted on an economy seat, but Christie overruled him. In his
current off-grid situation, she wanted him hidden away from as
many people as possible. The cabin on the Emirates flight
certainly provided that, with its own floor-to-ceiling sliding door

for total privacy. Not that privacy was at the forefront of Grant's mind. He was too busy worrying about Gretchen and where she might be.

After a sleepless night, Grant opened his blind to find plentiful evidence of the grand building projects that the Emirates had taken on. There were man-made islands and skyscrapers. From the air, it all looked so temporary. Like a child who spends all day building an intricate, sprawling sand castle, only to watch the tide come in and wash it all away.

It hadn't taken much work for MI6's Middle East desk to find out where Crown Prince Abdul was going to be. That weekend, there was only one event to be seen at. The Dubai World Cup – the world's richest horse race.

The Emirates airline laid on complimentary transfers from Dubai International Airport from a fleet of Mercedes and BMW cars. A steady stream of which went back and forth from the city to the airport all day. They weren't the only vehicles grabbing Grant's attention.

On the far side of the road was a queue of red tankers, lined up nose to tail for over a mile.

'What are all the petrol tankers for?' Grant asked.

'They're not for petrol, sir,' the driver informed him. 'It's sewage from the Burj Khalifa. The building isn't connected to a sewage system, so every day these tankers queue up to collect all the waste and take it out of the city.'

Grant said, 'Maybe they should have knocked a few floors off and laid some pipes instead.'

The driver tried not to chuckle.

Grant's hotel was at the centre of Dubai, close to a highway that had four lanes too many for the traffic that was travelling on it.

The Armani Hotel Dubai was – to Grant's amusement – in the Burj. The tallest building in the world, it housed an array of corporate suites and residences, as well as the hotel.

The interior took Grant's breath away – a vast tubular-constructed archway framed the lobby, which was coloured in warm browns and muted neutrals. Modelled on Armani's sleek, understated style, it was every bit as minimalist as their couture stores.

At the check-in desk – signing in as Mr David Webb – Grant was suddenly aware of a smiling young woman approaching, dressed in, of course, Armani.

'Hello, Mr Webb,' she said in some pan-national accent. 'My name is Lucille, I will be your personal Lifestyle Manager during your stay.'

Grant did a double-take. 'I'm sorry?'

'I will handle everything for you, from restaurant bookings to personal shopper experiences at the nearby Galleria Mall, if you so desire.'

Everyone at the hotel got one.

Grant picked up his small carry-on luggage. 'I'm more of a room service kind of guy, but thank you.' He reached into his jacket pocket for his phone and showed Lucille a picture of Henry Marlow, taken from his personnel file that was used to build legends on covert ops. When operatives asked for people to identify faces from plain passport photos, it looked like they were working for law enforcement. In each operative's personnel file was a library of assorted photographs. The photo showed Marlow with a group of supposed friends, whose faces had been computer-generated. Grant had been added in by field-op support, making him and Marlow out to be best buds.

Grant explained, 'I got separated from my friend at the airport, and I was expecting him here…Do you happen to know if he's checked in yet?'

Lucille was happy to oblige, taking control of a check-in computer. 'Of course, Mr Webb. What is your friend's name?'

'Harrington,' said Grant. 'John Harrington.'

Another of Marlow's old legends.

MI6 had tracked Marlow by facial recognition to a storage warehouse in Fulham where he kept his old passports. They dispatched agents to the scene soon after. Of the set that were issued together many years ago, the one missing from the stack was for John Harrington.

And according to Lucille the Lifestyle Manager, John Harrington had checked in three hours ago.

Grant knocked his knuckles appreciatively on the marble countertop. 'Thank you, Lucille.' Before he left, he added, 'If he asks for me, keep it quiet. I'd like to surprise him later.'

38

The corridors upstairs were like something out of a science-fiction catwalk. LED cove lights at the base of the walls, and doors that blended in with the surrounding walls, creating an illusion of one continuous wall. The only indication of there being rooms behind were elegant white numbers attached to the doors.

Grant was in the Fountain Suite, which brought yet more minimalist decadence. Floor-to-ceiling windows gave spectacular views of the Dubai skyline, and a man-made lake where the Dubai Fountain played out a vast, intricately choreographed fountain show throughout the day.

Although the hotel had no less than five world-class restaurants inside, Grant didn't want to risk running into Marlow. He was confident Marlow wouldn't try to ambush him. Someone with his experience could have easily pulled a similar trick to Grant's with the photo of Mr Harrington, but Grant trusted that Marlow's task there was to hit Crown Prince Abdul. Not that Grant had an inflated sense of his own abilities, but Marlow would have been risking his entire endeavour by ambushing

Grant. Even if Marlow got away, he risked an injury that made getting to Abdul impossible. With that in mind, Grant retired to his balcony with a room service steak and some vegetables, following a rigorous yoga session on the carpet. His focus was on being mission-ready when the time came. That meant having fresh muscles that weren't burned out from excessive bodyweight exercises. Delayed onset muscle soreness (DOMS) often affected Grant more following a long plane flight, and DOMS hit hardest not immediately after exercise, but from twelve hours after. Yoga ensured that he would be nimble, and his mind settled.

After dinner, there was a heavy knock on his door. A leather box had been left on his doorstep without any note. The young MI6 operative who had left it – stationed at the British embassy – didn't look back as he heard Grant's door open. His heart fluttered as he hit the button for the lift.

Grant took the box inside and opened it. The delivery had gone as planned. Inside the box was a Glock 17 pistol.

The hotel was quite the city's social hotspot. From eight p.m. onwards, the drive-through portico outside the lobby played host to an endless series of supercars, limousines, and chauffeur-driven SUVs. Grant looked down at it all with grim fascination. The two-tier system at play as the elites left their cars for the immigrant valets to park, and the casual tourists stood gawping at their phones as they recorded video clips of the gleaming cars for their Instagram feeds.

Grant couldn't understand the modern fascination for crass consumerism, of always searching for something fancier, newer, better. When he was a child, Grant's mum and dad had splashed out on a three-day holiday to a Spanish resort so his dad could play golf, and Grant and his mum could sit by the pool. Three

days in the cheapest villa was all the Grants could afford, but one
night they had visited the resort's five-star Felipe Hotel. Duncan
found it all bewildering, as his mum and dad spent most of the
dinner staring at the fancy outfits of the hotel guests, and specu-
lating about how much money they had and what they did.

Grant's mum and dad wanted better for their boy. But it was
much more than that. After one comment too far, Grant asked,
'What does it matter how much money they have? Aren't we
good people?'

'Of course we are, sweetheart,' his mum replied.

His dad then added, 'The only people who say money can't
buy you happiness, son, are folk that have never been without it.'

Standing on the Armani Hotel balcony, he still felt like that
little boy in the Felipe restaurant so many years ago. Looking
down at the mass of phone screens being held in the air to record
the illuminated fountain show, the air dense with bewildered awe
from the masses at what the ingenious rich people had done in
the middle of the desert. The idea that if you kept throwing
money into projects, sheer scope and scale would triumph over
creativity or beauty. Dubai was about neither, as far as Grant
could tell. It was simply about being the 'biggest, the 'tallest'.

Grant felt sorry for all the people down on the ground. They
had no idea what was coming their way. The way of life they had
become so accustomed to – where everything was focussed on
making everything easy, fast, or convenient – how quickly it could
all go away, and what would be left then? Nothing but the thing
that Grant knew most about: survival. Everything that so many
people had constructed their lives around – their social media;
the wardrobes they had spent a fortune building up; the techno-
logical gadgets they craved and constantly updated – wouldn't be
any use to them if Marlow and Joseph succeeded in their attack.

A year from present, Grant knew that there could be riots in the streets over food. Mass protests. Civilian disorder. When that happened, life would revert to what had always mattered: staying alive, and helping as many others as possible survive as well.

Grant didn't need any of their branded luxury items. Sure, they were nice. There was nothing wrong with striving to improve your lot in life. But Dubai had nothing to do with that. It was about envy and lust. Grant didn't 'need' anything to survive. If he were to ask any of those people on the ground to name five things they couldn't live without, they would be able to rhyme off five pretty quickly – then beg for another five on top.

There was nothing that Grant 'couldn't' live without. As long as his heart was beating, he was satisfied.

39

The Dubai World Cup race night at Meydan Racecourse was the culmination of the two-month-long Dubai Carnival – where thousands of fans would pack into a grandstand a mile long. It being Dubai, it was, of course, the world's richest horse race, with a purse of $12 million up for grabs.

Over $1 billion had been spent building the racecourse, and all the attendant five-star luxuries that one would expect, but what gave Meydan its distinctive atmosphere was that it was a place where the ultra-rich mixed openly with the working-class of Dubai. With a betting slip in your hand, yelling at a horse that you've never met, everyone is the same.

Mohammad bin Abdul – the Crown Prince of Saudi Arabia, Deputy Prime Minister, and Saudi Minister of Defence, to give him his full titles – was in one of the executive boxes high up in the grandstand with one of his distant cousins. Both were in immaculate white *thobes* and red-and-white-check headdresses. An entire army of servers and personal assistants were on hand to attend to every whim or desire. Champagne and expensive

Scottish whisky flowed freely. Abdul favoured Macallan 1979 Gran Reserva. A bargain, as he saw it, at a mere £6000 a bottle.

Abdul watched the horses parading around the paddock, the place where racegoers could get a proper close look at the horses. Abdul's horse, Nihil, wasn't expected to be up there with the biggest favourites, but he still got a chill in his stomach in anticipation.

'Do you know why I love horses?' Abdul asked rhetorically. 'It's not like buying a European football club. With them, you can basically buy any old shit hole, throw five hundred million euros at it and you'll likely get some success. If you're persistent like Roman Abramovich and keep throwing money at it, you might even win the Champions League. But horses? There is no throwing money at the problem. Of course, money helps. For example, the horses in my breeding operation eat the finest mince, and quails' eggs. These are very good for their strength. And did you know how much swimming helps? All of my horses swim, you know why?'

It wasn't uncommon for Abdul to ask twenty questions of someone and wait not once for an answer. He wasn't interested. He would always tell you the right way to do something. His way.

'Race horses have very fragile legs. The daily impact of training on different surfaces can cause injuries. That's why I had a swimming pool lane built for my stables in England. The trainer walks them through and the horse gets a good workout against the resistance of the water without the impact on its joints.' He took a long sip of Macallan, his wandering eye caught by a young woman in the executive box next to his. She had flowing blonde hair. His favourite.

She might have been with one of the most famous pop stars in the world, but their riches, property portfolio, and list of obscene luxuries weren't in the same league as Abdul's.

Pop stars. Formula One drivers. Such people didn't impress
Abdul. He barely noticed them. The only ones who were even
close to his level were the other emirs and the Russian oligarchs.
As far as elites went, Abdul was the one per cent of the one per
cent.

He explained to his cousin, 'You have to work and breed your
way to the top in horse racing. This fucking city…it's so boring.
Such a joke. Money is the enemy of creativity, my friend. You
stop working to find solutions to problems. Here, you just throw
money at all of your problems.' Distracted by the lingering nervy
presence of a young male PA, almost indistinguishable from
Abdul in terms of dress, Abdul snapped, 'Approach and speak, or
leave me in peace, *inshallah*.' He didn't budge an inch as the PA
leaned down towards his ear to whisper:

'You have a phone call, Your Royal Highness.'

Abdul made eyes at the blonde on his way to the private bar
area, where he took the phone from Ghazi, his head of security.

The moment Abdul appeared, the staff behind the bar
scattered.

He held the phone to his chest until the room had cleared –
except for Ghazi. There was nothing Abdul didn't trust his body
man to hear. God only knew the things he had seen, and heard,
in the Crown Prince's company.

A male English voice at the other end declared, 'Your Royal
Highness.'

'John,' said Abdul. 'You sound stressed.'

'Not stressed. Perhaps concerned.'

'I take it that means you have something that should concern
me?'

'I thought I should give you fair warning about a couple of
our guys who have gone off the reservation. Nothing you can't
handle.'

'Who?'

'Henry Marlow and Duncan Grant.'

'Together?'

'Heavens, no. Marlow is coming for you. Grant's only there for Marlow, but you and I have a long history and I thought it only right to warn you to keep your security tight.'

'I appreciate that, John. Tell me, if my men encounter these two, where would you like them returned?'

Wark paused. 'No return necessary. This is just one old friend looking out for another.'

Abdul hung up and said to Ghazi, 'It never ceases to amaze me, John Wark's lack of loyalty.'

Ghazi was a mountain of a man. Thick and wide. Always ready to act, he never wore something as impractical as a thobe. Always in a bespoke, crisp suit. 'A problem, Your Royal Highness?'

Abdul handed him the phone. 'The same British agents as before. Marlow and Grant. Tell the others to be on the lookout. They might try to hit tonight while we're among a crowd.'

When he returned to his cousin's side, he sat down with a sigh.

His cousin asked, 'Is everything alright?'

Abdul forced a brief smile. 'Like I was saying about horses: there are some problems in my life I cannot throw money at.'

40

Grant had chosen the most grey-man outfit he could think of, to best blend into the many thousands in the crowd. He wore an anonymous navy suit, and a white shirt with no tie. If Grant could ever avoid wearing a tie on an op, he did so. No other piece of clothing provided such good leverage to an attacker.

Once he was inside the grounds, in front of the grandstand, he passed a queue for the entrance to the exclusive boxes, which weren't in short supply given the extraordinary length of the grandstand. They had been cleverly priced and positioned. Offering the opportunity to be within a few levels of the most important emirs and sheikhs. It made those with tickets for them feel like they were royalty, and a lot of them tried to dress for the occasion.

Grant couldn't help but smile as he noticed their bespoke suits in all manner of garish colours, and mismatched patterns; loafers with no socks, and oversized fedoras as if they were hip Italian men stepping out for the famous Pitti Uomo fashion festival in Florence.

I should have dressed like a total pillock, Grant thought. *I would have blended right in.*

Back at GCHQ in Cheltenham, England, the racecourse CCTV was relaying through their state-of-the-art facial recognition technology. The analysts had access to MI6's multi-angle mugshots that had been taken of Marlow when he arrived at Vauxhall Cross, giving the best possible chance of a successful match in the crowd.

Randall was in the Tank, providing a communication link between Grant and GCHQ. 'Nothing yet, Grant,' he informed him, scanning the crowd as if his own life depended on it.

Grant waited patiently among the crowd near the finish line, halfway along the length of the grandstand to cut down on the potential travel time once Marlow was located. There was no point in making a show of himself, haring around trying to find a needle in a haystack. Knowing Marlow was on the property had kicked his heart rate up. This wasn't Lyon. Or Paris. This time, there was so much more at stake. In a country like the UAE, if the mission went south and he was captured by local security services, extracting him – if at all – would be a lengthy process. And likely a painful one. The British government couldn't possibly accept that Grant was one of theirs. Not officially.

But all of that paled in comparison to the true nightmare scenario: the Saudi Crown Prince murdered at Dubai's premier social event, Grant captured by a foreign power, and Marlow still free.

The tension in the crowd had been rising since the horses were called for the final race.

Then a possible match came through from GCHQ, which Randall immediately relayed. Grant could barely hear the description through his earpiece, and he didn't want to be seen pressing it. He crouched down to tie his laces, using the moment he was hidden among a forest of legs to press the earpiece in a little harder.

'Say again,' Grant said.

Randall was watching the live feed come through, a white square locked on to a man wearing an outfit that would have seemed right at home at Henley Regatta, wearing cream trousers, a navy linen jacket with gold buttons, and a cream panama hat. Looking every bit the English expat.

Randall repeated, 'I think we have him...'

The crowd around the main standing area swelled as the last calls went out over the PA.

The gates opened for the start of the race, and an enormous roar went up from all around.

There was plenty of noise for Grant to speak into his radio without drawing too much heat now. He worked his way out of the throng.

'Hang on, Grant,' Randall told him. 'He's wearing a hat and we're waiting for final confirmation.'

Grant scoured the area for signs of a cream hat. Although there were a lot of Englishmen in the crowd, there weren't a lot of panama hats. Something that Marlow knew, as well as that without it, facial recognition would pick him up within a few minutes. Grant picking out a single cream hat in the crowd would likely take far longer.

The race itself would last only a few minutes. The crowd's energy kicked up as the horses galloped down the back straight. The anticipation and volume kept growing with each furlong, each length, each stride.

In the camera feed, the man in the hat made a sudden move towards the grandstand, giving a more optimal angle on his face from one side. The camera locked in for a hard zoom.

Randall recognised him instantly. 'Grant, we've got him. He's going into Stand B.'

After receiving a full description, Grant had to fight his way through the crowd, everyone facing the other direction.

The horses made the final turn for the home straight, the crowd's cheers and shouts of encouragement reaching fever pitch.

What no one saw was an Indian man in ordinary clothes duck under the guard rail that bordered the race track itself. He was carrying a sign that was written in Arabic.

The translation: *"RIGHTS FOR WORKERS NOW!"*

It was easy to forget that in a country of such opulence and wealth, so much of it was built by cheap labour from India, Pakistan, and Bangladesh, who were lured in by work agencies promising steady pay. The main hurdle to getting there, though, was the extortionate costs the agencies charged in advance, citing work- and travel visas and employment contracts. Costs of up to $3000, despite Emirati law stating that it was employers who had to cover such costs. But the government was always in such a rush to complete some new construction project that it turned a blind eye. Upon arrival, construction workers like the Indian man had their passports confiscated by their employers, even though the practice had been made illegal twenty years ago. Essentially turning them into prisoners. Slave labour, open to constant abuse until their 'debts' were settled with the agencies. Such horrific practices had led to an epidemic of suicides among immigrant workers.

The Indian man planned to be another one. He had broken through the racecourse barrier, ready to die in order to be heard.

The horses were bearing down on him as he held his sign aloft. Some of the horses pulled up themselves, or their jockeys stopped them. For the leaders out front, there was nowhere to go.

The man careered straight into their path, mouthing to God to make his death mercifully quick.

It was.

He was knocked over between two horses, sending him spiralling to the ground where a stray hoof delivered a fatal blow to his head.

The man's sign fell from his hand, catching Nihil's rear legs.

The on-course announcer on the PA paused and stumbled with his words. Instinct told him to carry on calling the race as three horses broke through cleanly.

Some boos and jeers rang out across the crowd. Most were in quiet shock.

Abdul got to his feet with a cry of, 'No! Nihil!'

His horse tumbled to the ground, spilling his jockey out of the saddle.

Abdul roared, 'That peasant *mutt*! He'd better be dead or I'll kill him myself...' He stormed out of the box, heading for the racetrack.

Grant followed Randall's directions towards Marlow, struggling to make up any ground. The atmosphere around the grandstand was muted as an ambulance pulled onto the track to try and revive the Indian man. The track manager was quick to insist that they erect a screen around the body while they performed CPR.

'I need Abdul,' Grant radioed.

Randall replied, 'We had him on the screen in his box...The stables,' he exclaimed, catching sight of Abdul accompanied by Ghazi. 'They're going to the stables, Grant.'

Grant paused in a crowded bar area inside the grandstand. 'What about Marlow?' he asked.

'We're trying to pin him down but there aren't as many cameras inside.'

'Keep scanning, Randall. If he went out of sight he might have changed clothes.'

Grant went back in the direction he had come from, making his way towards the paddock. He didn't have long to find a mark. It would need to be someone in the trainer circle. He fought his way through the crowd, speed his only concern now. If he didn't act fast, Marlow might get to Abdul before him.

The paddock was full of trainers and their vast entourages. There were so many men in *thobes*, and none of them were any good to Grant: their class-1 passes were hanging around their necks and would be impossible to remove unnoticed. He needed a Westerner. And he found one.

With so much attention still on the track long before the finish, Grant was able to gently tug a trainer's assistant's pass dangling from his trouser pocket. When the man reacted to the slight vibration, Grant was already out of sight.

Grant pushed and shoved his way through the scandalised crowd. 'I'm close to the stables, Randall. I need Marlow. Now!'

Randall could see Grant's tracker on the screen charging through the satellite map of the racecourse.

The second Grant was clear of the crowd, he ran down the tunnel that ran underneath the grandstand and led toward the stables.

Marlow was still ahead of Grant at the pre-parade ring, having dropped his jacket and hat on the stairs a few minutes earlier to take advantage of a CCTV blind spot. If Grant was on site, Marlow knew that GCHQ's cameras would have picked him up by now. He was banking on Grant continuing to hunt for someone in his previous outfit rather than getting GCHQ to continue scanning faces. He banked wrong.

Marlow spotted a steward's white bib that had been left at the pre-parade ring. He picked it up quickly on the move and slung it over his shirt. Now he looked like any one of dozens of official helpers buzzing around. He upped his pace, eyeing the stables ahead. In near-perfect Arabic, he asked one of the other stewards, 'Where is Nihil's stable, my friend?'

The steward gave him directions. Then warned him that the Crown Prince was around there and he didn't look happy.

Marlow smiled.

41

At the stables, Abdul was consulting with the vet about Nihil's condition. Nothing was broken, but Abdul was still on the war path. After dismissing the vet, he told Ghazi, 'Get someone to make enquiries about the Indian. I want to be sure he's definitely dead.' Abdul patted his beloved horse. He said, 'No one damages my property.'

Ghazi did as he was told, telling Abdul, 'I'll be right outside, sir.'

When Ghazi left, he expected to find his two henchmen close by on the lookout for Marlow, as he had instructed. But they weren't there.

The other horses and trainers were returning from the track, bringing a hum of conversation, and whinnying and nickering horses with them, on top of the brass-band music playing from the grandstand speakers. Following two horses' withdrawals pre-race, Nihil's stable had ended up isolated from the others, on its own at the end of the row.

As Ghazi opened one of the doors to the empty stables, he found his two men lying in a heap. He shut his eyes as he felt the point of a knife press into his lower back.

'Nice and easy,' Marlow told him. 'Or I'll put you in a wheel-chair for the rest of your life.'

Next door, Abdul was petting the horse when he heard the stable door sliding shut. Abdul stopped. He spoke without turning around, 'I was expecting you.' He turned around slowly, keeping his hands raised.

Marlow stepped forward, holding an all-black Gerber Gear Ghoststrike knife to Ghazi's back, and a sure grip around Ghazi's neck as he slid the stable door closed.

'You should have left me alone,' Marlow said.

'Probably,' admitted Abdul. 'But you interfered, Henry.'

'No, I just wouldn't do your dirty work.'

'My dirty work was also your government's dirty work.'

'Oh, I won't spare them either.'

The door slid open again. This time it was Grant. 'Stop, Henry,' he said. He had his Glock by his side. 'I can't let you do this.'

Marlow squinted. 'Do you ever get déjà vu?' He smiled to himself. 'Well, isn't this cosy...' As Ghazi tried to pull free, Marlow strengthened his grip. 'Now, now,' he said, snarling into his ear. 'Any further moves like that, Ghazi, and I'll gut you like a fish. I'm not here for you.'

'You'll die before you take him,' Ghazi snarled.

Abdul kept his hands up. 'Calm, Ghazi. Calm. These men are obviously confused.'

Grant kept his gun trained on Marlow. 'Drop it, Henry. It's too late. You can't get to him. Drop the knife or I drop you.'

Marlow edged further into the room. 'You really don't understand who your enemies are, do you, Duncan? Abdul sent two of his best men after us, yet here you are trying to save his life.'

'Henry, we can talk about this,' Grant said, beginning to circle to keep his distance. 'But I can't do anything for you if you kill Abdul or Ghazi.'

'I tried to disappear,' he retorted, pulling tighter around Ghazi's neck. 'But you're never out. Not all the way. They won't let you. When are you going to understand that?'

Abdul backed up, trying to calm the horse that was exhausted from the race and adversely reacting to the tension in the confined space. 'Take it easy, Henry. No one's going to harm you...'

Grant knew that he had little time to act. The only way for Marlow to get to Abdul – the one he really wanted – was to drop Ghazi. He was too strong to merely disarm. Killing Ghazi was the only way.

Marlow said, 'Why don't you just walk out of here? You could always say you got here too late.'

'Last warning,' Grant said, still circling.

Abdul, thinking only of himself, quickly pulled his hand back and struck the horse on its hind as hard as he could, letting out a loud yell as he did so.

The horse cried out in pain, springing its front legs high into the air.

Ghazi tried to use the sudden distraction to break free, spinning around to face Marlow who plunged his knife into Ghazi's stomach.

Ghazi staggered back, covering his gaping wound with one hand, reaching out for Abdul with the other.

Abdul only had eyes for the stable door.

Grant felt at the trigger, thinking about squeezing it. He knew that he could end Marlow then and there. But as Christie had said, killing him wasn't enough. Still, the temptation was overwhelming. Grant held his pose, then grimaced, taking his finger off the trigger. He couldn't do it.

Abdul scrambled to the stable door, slipping on the hay as he went. He threw the door open and escaped, leaving Ghazi bleeding to death on the ground, while his horse whinnied and neighed in fear and aggravation.

Grant and Marlow faced one another.

'You can't do it, can you,' said Marlow. 'You don't realise that you still need me. What about the decryption code to access the stolen slush funds?'

Grant paused.

'Oh yes,' said Marlow, holding the bloodied knife to his temple. 'It's all in here. Kill me, and there's not another soul on this planet who can access that money.'

'Killing you might be worth a few billion, Henry. MI6 might look at it as an investment.'

'Maybe so.' Marlow explained, 'But in twenty-four hours, if I don't enter a key number into the detonation device that's linked to every internet data centre around the world, they all go up in smoke. And I'll bet your boffins at MI6 have already told you what that will mean.' He shrugged. 'Levelling the playing field, Duncan. It's only fair.'

'That's the Great Equaliser.' Grant exhaled in horror.

Marlow said, 'You can't kill me, Duncan. Unless you want to personally light the fuse on the biggest terror attack since…' Impressed at the scale of his own enterprise, he concluded, 'Well, ever.'

Grant shook his head in confusion. 'It's not you. This plan… it's indiscriminate. You don't blow up an entire market. You stake the market out for three days, then take out your target with a sniper rifle. This plan is Charles Joseph up and down, but it's not you…'

His energies focussed on Marlow and the impossible choice he'd been given, Grant didn't notice Ghazi pulling out a concealed boot knife from under his trousers.

The moment Grant lowered his gun a fraction, Ghazi slashed at his ankle.

Grant cried out in agony as the blade cut deep into his flesh, barely missing his Achilles. He crouched down, grasping at the wound as blood poured between his fingers.

Seizing the opportunity, Marlow hightailed out of the stable, finding one end covered by Abdul's men who were tentatively closing in for a counterattack.

Grant tried to set off in pursuit, but Ghazi took his legs out from under him with a devastating sweep-kick.

Abdul's other men charged into the stables to regain control of the situation. Grant was surrounded, and wounded.

Ghazi somehow got to his feet, indicating to the others to stand Grant up.

Hobbling as they did, Ghazi pulled back a fist and smashed it across Grant's cheek.

It felt like a meteor had landed on him.

The overwhelming power of the strike sent Grant to the ground once more. Abdul's men pulled him up and the lights went out.

A hood went over Grant's head and his hands were cuffed behind his back, as he was carried out of the stables towards an unmarked van outside.

Grant's mouth was full of much blood that he had to spit some out. 'What are you going to do?' he wheezed as they bundled him into the back of the van. 'Kill a British secret service agent?'

Unseen by Grant, Abdul crouched down and lightly slapped Grant on the face.

He said, 'I didn't rate Scottish assassins last time, and my opinion hasn't changed. In case you're wondering who's to blame, your good friend the Foreign Secretary John Wark gave you up.' He chuckled. 'He'd rather save me than kill Henry Marlow. That's what your government thinks of you, Mr Grant.'

Grant pulled and struggled, but he couldn't break free.

Abdul said, 'I tried to deal with you before. I won't make the same mistake twice. This time, you'll be on my turf. No abandoned train tunnels. No games. No chance. John Wark might trust you to never reveal the details of our property deal, but I'm not really the trusting kind. When he told me you were coming here, I couldn't believe my luck. Duncan Grant, walking straight into my arms. You're going to find out what happens to enemies of the Crown Prince, in a country where no one can hear you scream. After all, Mr Grant, you can't scream if you don't have a head.'

Running through the crowd, Marlow pickpocketed a drunk Russian who had his arms around two young women. He had picked the man because of his regular-fit trousers, which made it easier to steal his car key.

The women spluttered laughter as the man told them a joke. All three too drunk to realise what had happened.

When Marlow got to the car park, he pointed and pressed the key button constantly across one hundred and eighty degrees until he saw a set of headlights illuminate − a Lamborghini Aventador.

When the Russian and his two women reached the car park, they found a white steward's bib lying on the ground next to the empty space where his £230,000 car had been just thirty seconds earlier.

In the distance, if the Russian had listened closely, he could have heard the engine revving, the exhaust spluttering, as Marlow made his escape.

42

The Cessna turboprop plane had been in the air for two hours since leaving a private airstrip outside Lahore, Pakistan, and Gretchen still didn't know where they were going. There was room for a dozen of Charles Joseph's best operatives in the main cabin, plus a Pakistani pilot with a currently revoked licence earning the biggest payday of his life.

Gretchen checked her watch, counting down the time until her tracker went live and beamed her location back to Vauxhall Cross. It would be any minute now.

The atmosphere onboard had been tense. Joseph had assembled a fearsome collection of agents and operatives from around the world. Germans. Swedes. Russians. Spaniards. Americans. They came from all over, all with one thing in common: they had all been disavowed by their native countries' intelligence agencies. To a woman and man, they were animals. Mercenaries who cared about nothing more than getting paid. And anyone who stood in the way of that had best have skills, be fast, or be good at hiding. Because working with Joseph wasn't about idealism. A lot of them couldn't have cared less about what Joseph wanted. It was a job. And for operatives with their histories, the black market was their only option.

There had been some discontent among Joseph's crew about the idea of bringing Gretchen along. Two of them had known her only tangentially from the past and spoke highly of her abilities. Joseph also argued that she had been a loyal servant in the past – but many questions remained about what had happened in London. Eventually, somewhere over the northern tip of Afghanistan, a few of Joseph's closest allies wore him down. They had been with him from the start, going all the way back to the Congolese Civil War. Men who had grown rich with him, and they didn't want their meal ticket being taken away by some – potential – British double-agent.

Gretchen knew what was coming long before it happened. Then, finally, Joseph came to the back of the plane, sitting in the opposite row to hers.

He said, 'I thought we should talk, Gretchen.'

She had grown to be repulsed by how he said her name. The slight roll of the "r". 'What about?' she asked.

'London,' he replied. 'This MI6 man Duncan Grant. You shot him in the chest. Why not the head?'

Gretchen answered calmly. 'A chest shot is the percentage play. The biggest target. You don't mess around with head shots when someone's running at you.' Deflecting a little too eagerly, she asked, 'What about Marlow? How are we going to get him out now?'

Joseph turned his crew with a chuckle, telling them, 'Guys... Gretchen wants to know how we'll get Henry out of MI6 headquarters.'

They chuckled among themselves.

Joseph explained, 'Henry escaped. He's out!'

Gretchen looked enthralled rather than horrified. Her additional confusion was genuine. 'What? How?'

'Henry has his ways. It was lucky we had you in there: where have you been?' He edged closer. 'I was worried you'd been turned, my friend.'

Gretchen knew her cover inside out. The challenge now was having it come out as part of a conversation rather than reciting rote information. 'When you sent me to Istanbul, I got a tail. I couldn't shake it.'

'MI6?'

The answer to that was crucial to Gretchen's chances of survival. 'No. Someone else. Private contractors. I didn't know what they wanted, and I didn't want to lead them back to you. I could handle whatever came my way, but the mission was bigger than that. Bigger than one person. I couldn't jeopardise that. So I ran. And waited.'

'Waited for what?'

'For MI6 to find me.'

'Why did you want them to find you?' he asked. 'You were a disavowed agent.'

Gretchen had been thinking at length about how to answer such a question and wasn't thrown. 'I *was* disavowed,' she said. 'Then I found out that my old handler Imogen Swann had been killed. Before she died, she had found out that I had turned, but had tried to cover it up. She was the only person in MI6 who knew I had gone rogue. With her out of the way...' She trailed off intentionally, allowing Joseph to fill in the rest.

He smiled at the audacity of the move. 'You were in the clear to go back to MI6 and work them from the inside.'

She tilted her head as if to say, yes, now you get it. She explained, 'I knew eventually MI6 would find my old transmissions to Imogen Swann, and they would trace my location. So I hid far away from your operations.'

'That was you,' said Joseph. 'In Svalbard. *You* killed my men.'

Her answer to that question would be something of a gamble. There was a chance that he would simply throw her out of the plane then and there. But Gretchen was betting on Joseph admiring her willingness to do anything that pulled the wool over MI6's eyes.

'I had to,' Gretchen said. 'It was the only way for me to convince MI6 I was for real. To get them to believe my cover story. I thought having a mole inside MI6 would be worth far more than a couple of half-witted assassins. Trust me, you're better off without those morons, Charles.'

He couldn't help but be taken in by the moves she had apparently made.

Gretchen concluded, 'Once MI6 swallowed that, I was completely in the clear to act as a double-agent. I got back inside the agency and made sure I was part of the prisoner transfer. If I hadn't been there, you and your men would all be dead.' She flashed a wicked smile. 'You're welcome, by the way.'

'I don't normally rely on luck,' said Joseph, his demeanour stiffening. 'I find it hard to accept.'

Still to convince him, Gretchen looked into his eyes, communicating her deep belief in what she was saying. 'It wasn't luck that put me in that prisoner transport. It was MI6's arrogance. They willingness to use me to cover up their lies. Your life is less than nothing to them. I saw that with how they treated you. How quickly they discard you. There's nothing they wouldn't do, no one they wouldn't sacrifice to maintain their weakening grip on the world. That's what people like you and I see so clearly: the old world order is crumbling. They built nations on a lie: that in time everyone would be free.

Everyone would be safe. They would hand power back to the people. Now we have totalitarianism by stealth. The biggest lie of all: democracy. Freedom. Where did they ever get us? Extremist governments led by television personalities. Wars fought for nothing more than oil and private contracts. A global financial elite rigging the game to keep all the chips on their side of the table. And they talk about avoiding tyranny and corruption? They invented it!'

Joseph delivered his final question on the matter. Looking for the answer that would make him believe her. 'What do you want to do to them?' he asked.

'That's easy,' she replied. 'I want to destroy the entire system.'

Joseph looked towards the others and sniffed dismissively. He lowered his voice. 'These guys, they just want money. For me…it's not about money, Gretchen. They took everything from me. You understand? When my mother and I escaped Rwanda for the Congo, we lived in a refugee camp. The UN soldiers raped my mother in front of me. They beat her. They beat her so badly that she bled internally. They dumped her body in a river.' By his expression, he was picturing it as clearly as the day it happened. 'I was eight years old. They were supposed to be protecting us. I ran away after that and joined the Congolese army. A kind man – a fearsome warrior – took me in. He showed me what the world's true meaning is: there is none. There is no hope. When I agreed to help MI6, I thought I could see one last way out. To stop the carnage. But they played me the way they played you, Gretchen. They sent Henry to kill me, and it was the biggest mistake of their lives. He saw what I was doing. The loyalty that I had engrained in my men. He understood that the only answer to violence and brutality was to give back the same in kind to the world. To punish everyone. There will be no discrimination when we are done. When our plans are complete. Everyone will suffer equally. If our enemies are to pay for their crimes, then everyone must pay the price. It all has to be destroyed. Every country broken; every flag ripped apart.'

Joseph's unwavering belief chilled Gretchen to the bone. 'Let chaos decide,' she said.

He got to his feet. 'It won't be long now until Bogov's malware activates. Then there will be no going back.'

'What comes after that?' asked Gretchen.

'That's what we're going to discuss with Tagan,' he replied, laying a hand on her thigh. Creeping upwards.

Gretchen had to fight every impulse in her body to not recoil. 'What now?' she asked. 'Where are we going?'

'Somewhere no one will find us. Somewhere cut off from the world. Where we can carry out the last stages far from prying eyes.'

Gretchen peered down at the scorched landscape below. 'Afghanistan? Iran?'

'You'll see. We'll be landing shortly.'

'What do you need from me?'

'Protection,' he replied. 'This part was set up by Henry. He's meeting us there, but—'

'Henry will be there?' Gretchen felt suddenly robbed of breath. She was confident that she had convinced Joseph she was for real. But if Marlow had encountered Grant anywhere since London, it wouldn't take long before he told Joseph that Grant wasn't really dead. Being on deep cover required a certain set of skills. Gretchen had always found this one the hardest: acting like your cover isn't about to be a blown.

Joseph said, 'Henry has set us up with a man I haven't dealt with before. They say this man cannot be trusted. I need someone I can trust by my side.' He said *sotto voce*, not wanting the others to hear, 'These men and women are loyal, but I want someone with tactical nous by my side. Until I get a read on this strange man.'

'What's so strange about him?' she asked.

He turned his head away in amusement. 'You'll see.'

In the Tank, Randall had fallen asleep at his desk. After nearly thirty-six hours straight, his body had given in and taken the sleep it was so desperate for.

Then a location icon appeared over Central Asia, and gradually zoomed in on a final position. It beeped quietly in sync with each further zoom inwards.

Randall shot up from the desk like a firework had gone off in the room. His eyes bleary from sleep, his brain still registered that the icon he'd been waiting for so eagerly had gone live. He fumbled with his glasses, then announced quietly, 'We've got her.' He then shouted, 'We've got her!'

At the other end of the Tank, Winston abandoned his paperwork and bounded over. 'Where is she?'

Randall shook his head in surprise. 'Turkmenistan? What is she doing in Turkmenistan?'

43

The battered Toyota Land Cruiser arrived at the rear of a decrepit apartment block in southern Riyadh. Five men got out in white *thobes*, silent, determined, focussed. An old Saudi man smoking a cigarette and sitting on a rickety chair at the back entrance waited for Marlow and the men to go inside, after exchanging solemn nods.

The old man unfurled a fabric blind that covered the door-way, hiding it from view.

The men hurried up the stairs. They had established a base there over the previous months, but they could never feel truly safe in the city. There were eyes and ears everywhere. The old man had been a trusted ally to them; a believer in their cause that was as old as the stray grains of sand beneath their feet.

The apartment was cool in the afternoon, facing away from the raging sun that brought almost unbearable heat on a daily basis. The lunchtime smell of *kabsa* – richly spiced rice with fish and chilli salsa – and *mugalgal* lamb drifted up from the streets below. It had been many hours since the men had last eaten, but that would have to wait. There were final preparations to carry out. Work to do.

The leader peeked through the shutter on the open window, looking out onto a busy market street full of fabric and spice sellers. At the end of the street was a large brick yard, dominated by Imam Turki bin Abdullah Mosque that ran around three of the square's sides: Deera Square. At that time of day, it looked pale and anonymous. But when the sun set, the building would light up, turning it golden – one of the most beautiful sights to be had in the Saudi capital.

The leader surveyed the wall that was covered in research notes and maps with various routes drawn around the nearby streets in different colours. Escape routes. Photos placed on the map around Deera Square showed Crown Prince Abdul accompanied by Ghazi, along with lists of the various times that Abdul had attended the square.

It was sometimes called Al-Safaa Square.

But many knew it by its more colloquial name, so-given for the gruesome ceremonies that were carried out there.

Chop Chop Square.

Two of the men set up prayer mats for everyone, aligning them according to *qibla* – the direction towards the *Kabba* in the Sacred Mosque in Mecca. They would be prayers for strength and courage. For what was to follow, they knew they could be seeing Paradise very soon.

The leader then placed one final photo on the wall. At the centre of the map of Deera Square.

A copy of Duncan Grant's official MI6 personnel photograph.

44

When they landed and Gretchen realised they were in Turkmenistan's almost completely empty airport, she got a sinking
feeling. Joseph's quip about a 'strange man' now made a lot of
sense. She had heard a lot of things about the President's son,
Tagan. Ranging from "loose cannon", to "total psychopath". No
one in MI6 really knew how much of it was true. What they
knew was only half the story. Now Gretchen was about to find
out the other half.

When they disembarked the plane into a private hangar
owned by Tagan, Joseph held back to take a phone call.

Gretchen tried to stay close to get some sense of what was
being discussed, but Joseph waved her on. Her eyes were everywhere, searching for any sign of Marlow. She didn't know how
long she might survive before news of Grant's survival came out.
As soon as it did, she knew she was dead.

Then she heard Joseph say the only thing that could comfort
her.

'Henry, where are you?' he asked.

Gretchen turned away to sigh in relief, out of sight of the others.

Marlow said, 'There's been a change of plan. Once you're done, meet me at the final rendezvous. We could have a problem.'

'What sort of problem?' asked Joseph.

'I picked up a tail in Dubai.'

'What were you doing there?'

'Trying to take care of one last piece of personal business.'

Joseph shook his head in anger. 'Abdul...You're risking everything, Henry!'

'I managed to escape,' he assured him. 'But we're going to have to bring our plans forward by twelve hours.'

'Twelve hours?' Joseph exclaimed. 'Henry, there's not time...'

Gretchen joined the others, pretending to pay little attention to the time frame just mentioned.

'We have to make time,' Marlow insisted. 'Tell me, is Gretchen with you?'

Joseph stopped walking, then took a step back into the shade. He turned away from the others so that he couldn't be heard. 'How do you know about that?'

'I overheard some things at Vauxhall Cross before my escape.'

Joseph's eyes shot towards Gretchen. 'Tell me, friend...Did you hear anything about Duncan Grant?'

'Yes. The bastards swapped me out for him. I'm sorry, Charles, there was nothing I could do.'

Still staring at Gretchen, Joseph asked, 'Is it true he's really dead?'

Marlow replied, 'Yes. He's gone.'

'You're sure.'

'Yes, I'm sure.'

'How do you know?' asked Joseph.

'The same source who helped me escape,' said Marlow. 'He confirmed it to me. Grant is dead. Gretchen killed him.'

Joseph nodded slowly, turning away again. 'Good. Then Gretchen is definitely on our side.'

'Is she with you?'

'Yes. We're about to meet Tagan.'

'Keep her close, Charles. I need her with us at the rendezvous.'

'What is this, Henry? What's going on?'

'I can't explain it yet. Just make sure she's there.'

Joseph paused, confused as to why Gretchen was suddenly such an important part of their plans. 'I'll bring her.'

When the other operatives boarded a pair of shuttle vans, Gretchen ask Joseph if everything was alright.

'Everything's fine,' he replied. 'But when we're done here, we meet Marlow at the final rendezvous.'

'Final?' she said.

'We're bringing our plans forward. We'll meet Marlow there.'

She hadn't expected this. She thought there was still time. Now she had to somehow find a way to delay things, and get to Marlow as well. If for any reason Grant had failed at his end, it would all come down to her.

'Did he say why?' asked Gretchen.

'All he said besides was that Duncan Grant is dead. Henry confirmed that you killed him.'

'How did he confirm it?'

Joseph paused. 'You seem surprised.'

'No,' she lied. 'Relieved the prick didn't get away.' Her mind was racing. Was Marlow mistaken? But Gretchen knew that Marlow would never confirm something that wasn't certain. She knew she hadn't killed Grant.

Which left one question tugging away at the back of her mind: *why the hell had Marlow lied?*

45

In a region with a lot of competition when it came to crazy, personality-cult dictatorships, Turkmenistan had a good case for being the wildest of the lot.

At first glance from the outside, the capital of Ashgabat was gleaming, covered in pristine white marble buildings, manicured gardens, huge boulevards, elegant fountains, and towering monuments. It would have been a beautiful, if beguiling, place to visit if not for one creepy aspect: the city, like its airport, was almost completely empty. The whole totalitarian checklist was on display. Statues of the President riding a horse. Bookshops full of nothing but poetry titles written by the President. Gretchen could have been forgiven for thinking that they had actually landed in North Korea.

Like there, the internet was completely censored by the government, blocking all social media apps and news. And it was almost impossible to obtain a travel visa.

What had made it all possible were the fourth-biggest natural gas reserves in the world. Reserves that were estimated to last for another 300 years. There was a lot of money to be made with such reserves, and not many people outside of the President's immediate family would ever see any of it.

The pair of white shuttle buses took Joseph and the others through the centre of the capital. The roads were deserted, but their host had insisted on laying on a full police escort to speed them towards him. There seemed to be more police than there were civilians on the road. In Turkmenistan, criminal activity was largely the preserve of the President's family. Most specifically, his son. Tagan.

Gretchen found it puzzling that Tagan would use the police to help ferry around a black-market of mercenaries to an official Presidential palace, but she was about to learn that there was little that Tagan couldn't get away with.

Tagan's personal aide, Bashim, greeted the crew at the front steps of an enormous white palace, crowned with an ostentatious white-pearl horse statue. The police didn't stop, driving back down the mile-long driveway.

Everywhere Gretchen looked there were armed guards wearing sunglasses, dressed in full combat gear. They were clearly not just for decoration.

Bashim wore a three-piece tailored suit and mirror-like shined shoes. His English was as polished as his shoes, cultivated in the private schools of Switzerland where he had accompanied Tagan in his studies.

Joseph and Gretchen followed closely, while the others trailed behind, awestruck by the lavish surroundings.

They were taken to a sprawling room that was full of price-less antiquities, like something that belonged in the Romanov dynasty. Huge oil paintings depicting historical scenes of their political and military might during the nineteenth century, when

Turkmenistan was known and feared for its involvement in the Central Asian slave trade.

Tagan sat at the end of a long banqueting table, tearing into a whole roast chicken with his bare hands, while a set of speakers fit for a concert venue blasted The Doors 'Break on Through (To the Other Side)' at a deafeningly high volume.

With a mouthful of chicken, Tagan sprang to his feet in excitement and shouted, 'Welcome, my friends! Sit down!' He was wearing a sports tracksuit and white trainers that were brand new out of the box – he never wore trainers or shoes longer than a day.

A Magnum .44 cal revolver sat next to his chicken platter, along with a mirror dusted with cocaine remnants.

Joseph ushered his crew out to the hall – everyone except for Gretchen, whom he held back by the arm. She and Joseph sat a few seats away from Tagan. Gretchen eyed the gun, and the gun-range target on a wooden stand off to one side.

Tagan asked, 'Are your men hungry or what?'

Joseph replied, 'They're fine.'

Tagan took his seat again, and handed the chicken to Bashim, muttering something dismissive in Turkmen. 'I had a workout…' Tagan said, beating his chest like a gorilla, 'I had my protein. I am invincible.' Then he suddenly grabbed the revolver and fired a single shot at the target. The bullet landed close to several others in the head zone.

Gretchen didn't move, but she was surprised to see Joseph's hands flicker with fright ever so subtly. He's nervous, she thought.

Tagan fist pumped and yelled, 'Yeah! Just like Dirty Harry.' He asked Joseph, 'You know this film?'

'I know it,' said Joseph. No stranger to excess, even he was caught off guard by the bizarre scene.

Tagan put the revolver back on the table. 'So,' he sniffed. 'We do business?'

'If you have what we need.'

'If I have what you need?' He directed his confused chuckle in Gretchen's direction. 'What *you* need, man? What I need is my money.'

Joseph gestured towards the laptop case that Gretchen was holding for him. 'It's all right here...' he said.

Tagan held his hand up while he switched tracks. For a few seconds, the room turned silent. He kept his hand raised, eyes shut tight, begging for no interruptions. He didn't want to miss a note.

The track wasn't immediately obvious to anyone other than Tagan. All that could be heard was a few stray plucks of an exotic-sounding guitar and a few light cymbal rolls.

Then the more familiar guitar picks of The Doors 'The End' began. The room filled with Robby Krieger's iconic, creepy guitar line, and Jim Morrison's haunting vocals.

Tagan mouthed along to the opening words, eyes still closed as tight as he could. He made a fist and held it to his heart. When he opened his eyes, it became clear that he had been moved to tears. It wasn't just the music and drugs doing their work. He had dusted off far more than just the cocaine on the mirror. He had drunk a good chunk of a bottle of Louis XIII de Remy Martin Rare Cask Grande Champagne Cognac. There were fewer than twenty bottles of it in the world. Tagan had wiped out over half of it before lunchtime.

He wiped away the tears from his eyes. 'I'm sorry, friends. But this song moves me like no other. You ever see *Apocalypse Now?*' He made a chef's kiss in the air. 'It's so *real*, man.' He took a long slug of the brandy. 'You know...I have access to the best coke in the world. Totally pure, man. There is nothing I can't get that isn't the best of the best. But you know…' He gazed admiringly at the bottle of Remy Martin. 'There is absolutely nothing better than drinking during the day.' He broke into a mad cackle of laughter. 'Whisky? That is a drink for boys. Port is the real drink for men. But, any man who aspires to be a hero?' He held the brandy aloft. 'This is it, my friends.'

He took out a silver box from his tracksuit pocket and tapped out a long line of cocaine on the mirror. Once he had hoovered it up, he grabbed the gun and fired another round into the target. Another direct head shot. He put the gun down and clapped his hands. 'Okay! Money. Let's do this…' He motioned for Bashim to bring over a laptop. Tagan swore at him in his native tongue, then told him, 'Come on! Let's go! As soon as that money lands, it's—' he made a mushroom-cloud sound and motion – 'the count-down begins, and there's no going back!'

46

Tagan and Joseph set up their laptops side by side. Tagan's was set up on a page to receive bank account information. The amount to be transferred was listed as $400 million.

Joseph typed in the account number.

Gretchen's heart pounded so hard she was worried that Joseph would hear it or feel the vibration. She now faced an impossible dilemma: if the transfer went ahead, Tagan had said from his own mouth that there would be no going back. But she didn't stand a chance of killing Joseph and Tagan and getting out of the palace alive. There was not only Joseph's crew outside in the hall. The palace and its surrounding grounds were swarming with Tagan's private army.

She couldn't see any other way. She had to act immediately or it might not matter what Duncan did. Wherever he was.

She was out of time. Joseph was already typing in the account information. If the transfer started, she wouldn't have longer than ten seconds to stop the transfer and get off all the shots she needed. It would be suicide. But doing nothing wasn't an option. She knew how much was at stake if those data centres were blown up.

Gretchen reached inside her suit jacket, ready to draw.

Joseph finished typing the account number, then hit the *Enter* button.

Gretchen took a final calming breath as Tagan returned to his chair.

Joseph hit *Enter* again.

And again. Getting the same error message.

Gretchen asked him, 'What's wrong?'

'The account isn't recognised,' replied Joseph.

Tagan's eyebrows lifted. 'You need to check the number?'

'I know the number inside out,' he snapped.

Tagan picked up his gun again. 'No money, no bang.' He fired at the target, this time missing the head by a few inches. He examined his hand, inspecting it carefully. It was trembling from too much cocaine and booze.

Joseph leaned back away from the table. He had tried a half dozen times. He was out of ideas.

Tagan slouched in his chair. Eyes wide, nose red. He stared at Joseph, trying to get a read on him as the transfer continued to stall. 'What's taking so long?'

Joseph replied, 'The transfer's not going through.' He shook his head helplessly at the laptop screen.

Tagan laughed. Quietly at first. Then built to a sudden, manic guffaw. He struggled to calm himself down, then asked, 'Am I...am I in my bed right now?'

Joseph didn't know how to respond.

Tagan repeated the question. 'Because, my friend, when I'm being fucked...I like to be in bed.'

Gretchen watched him fidgeting with the gun. If this kept up, she wondered whether Tagan would just shoot Joseph. If he did, though, he would probably kill everyone else in the room.

Tagan had nothing to fear. He had the police dropping off arms dealers at his palace in the middle of the day. He could do whatever he wanted.

He lifted his hand in defeat. 'Looks like those oil wells live to fight another day…'

Joseph paused. 'Oil wells?'

Tagan was no longer smiling. He was as baffled as Joseph was.

'What about the data centres?' asked Joseph.

'What the hell is a data centre?' Tagan replied. There was no longer any humour in his tone.

Gretchen could see his eyes shifting from drunken pleasure to anger. A red mist descending.

The Doors song was building in tension through its long middle section, about to unleash its chaotic climax.

Tagan closed his eyes and took up his gun once more. Allowing himself to be swayed by the momentum of the music, he took aim at Bashim, who was standing innocently to one side.

As the music peaked, Tagan pulled the trigger, shooting Bashim directly in the chest. The force of the shot sent Bashim flying back off his feet against the wall, before sliding down into a collapsed heap.

Tagan said, 'I loved him like a brother. He always looked after me. He would die for me.' He took aim at Joseph. 'You? I don't really like you. Now imagine what I'll do to you if I don't get my money.'

Joseph showed him the laptop screen. 'You saw yourself what is happening. It's Marlow! He's screwing us both.'

'Or you're screwing *me*. Either way, I've spent a lot of my own money setting this job up. I want my money, Charles.'

Trying to mollify him, Joseph said, 'I'll get it. I'll get it from Marlow.'

Tagan got to his feet. 'You think I'm going to just let you walk out of here? You have everything you wanted from me, and I don't get paid?' He slapped himself on the forehead. 'Are you crazy?' His attention was diverted by the sight of Gretchen reaching into her jacket for her gun. 'Don't,' Tagan warned, turning the gun on her.

Joseph said, 'Gretchen, what are you doing?'

She couldn't allow Tagan to kill Joseph. Even if she somehow survived the ambush, Joseph was likely the only one who knew the final rendezvous.

Trying to give a reason he would understand, Gretchen said, 'He'll kill us all. We can't let him risk the bigger mission. We're too close to the end.'

Joseph seemed to agree.

Tagan warned her one last time.

Unseen, slumped against the wall, Bashim took out a gun of his own, and with his dying breath fired off a single round at Joseph.

It pierced his shoulder and sent him spinning a half-turn off his chair.

Gretchen pulled her weapon and fired at Tagan, who ducked under the table for cover. The sound of multiple gunshots didn't go unnoticed outside by Joseph's crew. The doors to the banqueting room burst open, and the mercenaries opened fire with everything they had at Tagan and Bashim.

Bullets pierced the speakers, the paintings, everywhere. It was a reckless return of fire to intimidate and keep Tagan in hiding until they could close in.

The music cut off, leaving nothing but the sound of automatic gunfire.

Gretchen pulled Joseph clear of the table, as shards of wood from the table sprayed up over them: Tagan's troops were firing back from a balcony overhead.

'I've got you!' Gretchen told Joseph, hauling him away by dragging him backwards.

Tagan emerged from his hiding spot under the table, letting off the last rounds of his Magnum until the chamber clicked over, empty. One of Joseph's team caught him with a bullet to the stomach, which pierced him with an agony that Tagan didn't know could be possible.

Gretchen covered the others by firing at the banqueting hall doors, yelling for them to make for the vans outside.

But they were met with immediate resistance, coming from the entrance to the Palace.

Marble was shattering all around, bullets coming from every direction.

Tagan's men might have had the numbers, but they were dealing with battle-scarred professionals who had been down and dirty in combat all their lives. The only fighting Tagan's troops had seen was during target practice at the gun range. They had all the desire and heart, but none of the ability.

They were falling from every position, clearing the way for Gretchen and Joseph's escape. The rest of the crew covered them, as Gretchen's eyes landed on the two shuttle vans parked at the front.

Reinforcements soon arrived on the exterior balconies, wiping out most of Joseph's guys who had been running towards the vans.

Now only Gretchen, Joseph, and four more operatives remained.

Joseph grimaced in pain, holding the wound at his shoulder to stem the flow of blood. 'Get us out of here...' he cried.

Gretchen pulled him around to the far side of the bus where there was more shelter, and piled him into the middle seats. One of the others took control of the driving, setting off the second they could.

Hardly any of the windows on the shuttle van survived, sending glass flying inside. Everyone was bleeding or wounded in some way, including Gretchen who had caught a face-full of glass on one side.

As the driver raced them off along the driveway, Gretchen knelt over Joseph in the back seat.

The driver, an American, called back, 'Is he going to be alright?'

Gretchen told him to concentrate on the road ahead. Which was blocked.

The guards at the driveway entrance had lowered the security barrier and were firing their pistols straight at the windscreen, aiming for the driver.

Everyone inside kept their heads low. There was nothing else for it other than brute force.

The guards, accepting that they weren't going to stop them in time, bailed to either side of the driveway, barely escaping the front wings of the van which crashed through the wooden barrier.

They had escaped the Palace grounds, but only seconds later they met a cavalcade of police cars, all with their lights and sirens going. Every officer knew that if they failed to stop the people who had attacked the President's son, there would be hell to pay.

Two mercenaries in the seats furthest back in the van had FN-SCAR assault rifles, and were putting them to good use against the Turkmen police.

With consummate skill, they took out front tyres and shot out windows, intimidating the others to back off. They didn't have the firepower to compete.

Only two police cars remained up for the challenge. A young constable firing ably from the passenger side, hanging out the window.

The American driving the van yelled out that there was a roundabout ahead, and to hang on.

He pulled off an expert power slide, taking them at speed around an enormous fountain with a marble horse at the centre.

The police car attempted to follow, but it spun out, unable to handle the turn at such speed. They crashed into the wall surrounding the fountain, then pinged back into the path of the police car following.

The shooters at the back confirmed. 'We're clear!'

Gretchen held Joseph's wound, telling him to hang on. Worried that she would lose him before he could tell, Gretchen asked, 'Where's the rendezvous, Charles?'

He groaned, struggling to enunciate.

Gretchen leaned closer, encouraging him. 'Come on, we made it. We got out. You've just got to hold on. Now, where is the rendezvous? It's our only chance, Charles…'

The others were conferring angrily.

'Marlow fucked us…'

'It's game time…'

Gretchen told them to shut up.

Joseph lifted his head to whisper in her ear. It was all he could manage.

The American eyed her in the rear-view mirror. 'Where is it? Where are we going?'

Gretchen blinked heavily. 'The Empty Quarter. Saudi Arabia.'

47

Grant could tell from the angle of the sun, and roughly how long they had been on the road in the Mabahith armoured van, that he was likely being taken to either the Al-Haa'ir or Ulaysha prison.

He had been flown by private cargo plane to Saudi Arabia along with three terror suspects who had been awaiting extradition back to their homeland. Now Grant was on his own, arms cuffed behind his back on a metal bench, in a locked cage in the back of the van.

He asked no questions. Made no pleas. Yelled nothing. There was no point. He figured he was in for a rough ride. It would be better to keep his strength for later. When it mattered.

He knew from the British embassy briefings on the area that the nightmare scenario would have been Al-Haa'ir: a maximum-security Mabahith prison twenty-five miles outside Riyadh. Far from prying eyes.

It housed all kinds of offenders, from Al Qaeda operatives, to out-of-favour Royal family members – normally for failing to bribe the correct official or, indeed, bribing the wrong one. There were journalists, political activists, businessmen. Many of them held on spurious charges, awaiting a trial that defied the traditional meaning of the word. What distinguished Al-Haa'ir was what went on in the various cells. There were isolation and torture rooms. Rooms dedicated to sexual abuse. Noise torture. The list of degrading methods was endless. The Mabahith's imaginations cruelly inventive and sadistically creative.

It was with great relief that Grant saw a sign on the edge of the grounds that declared he was entering Ulaysha. He knew from his reading that Ulaysha was mostly used for arbitrary detention. A holding jail before decisions were made about what to do with someone. As far as prisons in Saudi Arabia went, it could have been so much worse.

His optimism was to be short-lived.

When the rear door of the van opened, intense white light and heat poured in. Grant turned away from the light, unable to take the brightness.

He was hauled outside and held upright by four guards who took it in turns to beat his legs with their batons. They were amazed at the pounding he could withstand. They actually had to switch hands to continue their blows. Eventually, everyone has a physical limit. Even Grant.

He wilted and fell to the ground, leaving the guards exhausted and out of breath.

Now that he was 'softened', the guards dragged him inside, still puffing from the effort.

Grant tried to stay focussed, taking in any environmental clues he could. But there was nothing specific he could make out, other than the clanging of iron doors. There was no shouting. No televisions. Just eerie quiet.

The guards dragged Grant to an anonymous, empty, windowless room. Before he could orient himself, a guard shoved a dirty rag into Grant's face.

He knew from the smell that it wasn't chloroform. Which made sense, as it took at least a minute of cooperative breathing for chloroform to take effect.

The rag in his mouth had a slightly sweet smell and was taking effect within a few seconds.

It was sevoflurane. Used as a powerful inhalational general anaesthetic. Grant kicked and fought with everything he had, lasting several seconds longer than the guards had ever experienced before.

Finally, he was knocked out.

He was woken up by hard slaps to the face, and a Mabahith guard in a black beret yelling at him in Arabic.

Grant's vision was cloudy, like he'd been swimming in an over-chlorinated pool. No amount of blinking could totally clear it, but he could make out that he had moved to a significantly bigger room than a jail cell.

To his left were dark figures across the room, around twenty metres away, sitting at separate desks. Directly in front of Grant was a large table on a riser or dais. A man in a white *thobe* sat behind it. Behind the man was what Grant came to recognise as the bright green of the Saudi flag.

He blinked hard a few more times, as he heard the internationally familiar sound of a gavel landing on wood. There was a constant back and forth in rapid Arabic from the judge and a man behind Grant. Grant looked down at his hands. They were handcuffed in front of him. He was able to stand. Painfully. But he could do it.

Grant turned to the man nearest him. 'Are you my lawyer?' he asked.

The man didn't reply.

Grant repeated the question.

The man told him, 'It's better for you not to talk.'

'Better for you, or better for me?'

Crown Prince Abdul had autonomy to do basically whatever he wanted in the Kingdom, but his father still insisted that if he must arrest opponents that he at least go through the sham of officially charging them with a crime.

After a perfunctory back and forth between the judge and Grant's court-assigned lawyer, the judge began to address Grant in an emotionless drone.

Grant said, 'I want to know the charges...'

The judge droned on.

Grant called out, angrier this time, 'I demand to know the charges!' He knew he wasn't going to get any due process. It was fear, from knowing what would likely happen next.

The judge barely altered his tone to tell Grant to sit down and be quiet, to show some respect.

An officer in an all-brown uniform strode over and punched Grant hard in the face.

Grant shook his head at one side, then his eyes twinkled as he said, 'I'm sorry, I didn't catch that. Could you repeat it?'

The officer hit him again, this time drawing blood.

Ironically, the blows cleared his vision a little further. Looking around the room, everyone was involved with paperwork, scribbling frantically while the judge addressed Grant. At the back of the court was Ghazi, sporting fresh bruises on his face. Under his shirt and suit, he was heavily bandaged from the knife wound inflicted by Marlow.

The judge broke for a moment, then gestured at Grant's lawyer.

The lawyer told him, 'You are charged.'

Grant replied, 'Charged? With what?'

'Terrorism.'

The judge spoke again, then banged his gavel.

'You are guilty,' the lawyer informed him.

The judge stared at his paperwork while he banged the gavel again like an afterthought. '*Euqubat al'iiedam,*' he said.

Grant looked in dismay at the lawyer. 'What did he say?'

The lawyer quickly gathered up his things and shuffled them into his briefcase. 'Death penalty,' he said.

When Ghazi left the court with everyone else, he met his boss outside. 'It's confirmed, Your Royal Highness.'

Abdul patted him on the arm with a grin.

48

The stainless-steel door of Grant's cell crashed shut.

He was curled up on the ground in the foetal position, a wave of crippling nausea flooding his stomach – a side-effect of the sevoflurane.

His mind was a black fog. A whirl of images from throughout his life faded in and out of focus – the opposite of his life flashing before his eyes. He was seeing a slow replay:

His mother making tea on their stove, humming the tune to 'Peggy Gordon' to herself...

A young Duncan bounding down enormous sand dunes on South Uist in the Hebrides, calling out for the attention of his parents, who were sitting out on a tartan rug eating homemade jam sandwiches...

Duncan's eleven-year-old hand in his dad's rough, calloused hand. Both wearing black suits. Standing at a graveside at a windswept cemetery on the Isle of Skye. Waves crashing on the beach nearby...

Duncan as a teenager in his childhood cottage home, having

dinner in the kitchen by himself. Duncan saying hi to his dad arriving home from work and getting a tired response...

The image repeated. Next time, his father slurred, then dropped his briefcase on the floor...

Then again. This time his father didn't reply. His shirt was untucked. His footsteps wavering. When Duncan lifted himself from his chair to see out of the kitchen window, he saw the car was parked lopsided in the gravel driveway...

Then Duncan was older. Late teens. Rummaging through all the kitchen cupboards and drawers and cabinets. Eventually, he found a bottle of whisky hidden away, rolled up in a tartan kitchen towel. Duncan poured the whisky down the sink. When his dad caught him, he threw Duncan aside like a rag doll. His rage was incandescent. When Duncan protested, his dad lashed out at him, screaming insults...

Then Duncan was by his dad's hospital bed. His dad's eyes were open and he looked terrified. Duncan realised it was because he knew he was going to die. Any hour. Any minute. And his dad couldn't handle it. The enormity of life being over, beckoning in the darkness, and uncertainty of death.

Such images played on an agonising loop in his head. Unable to stop them, all he could do was wait it out.

Then, magically, new images appeared.

Duncan was on the brutal hill climb of Jacob's Ladder in the Brecon Beacons, the rain being driven into his face by gale-force winds. The other SAS recruits could barely stay on their feet, but Duncan kept his head down, marching on at twice their speed.

His only thought was: *One foot in front of the other. One foot in front of the other.* He hadn't noticed the other recruits dropping out, until he looked over his shoulder and realised that it was just him on the side of the mountain. Everyone else had quit...

Then Grant saw his family at Christmas, sitting around the

living room fire. His dad was singing The Corries' 'Peggy Gordon'. He always sang it to Duncan's mum. The lyrics expressing his love in ways that he never could. It was only after Duncan's dad was in the ground that Duncan understood what it can do to you. To lose someone you love that much. To love them with your entire body. To lose them is to lose everything.

He lifted his head. He was on the ground again. How long had it been? Hours? Days? They had drugged him again, that was for sure, but it was wearing off.

Enough to see a figure dressed immaculately in white, sitting in a chair in front of him.

Grant was shackled to the floor. Even if he had been capable of movement, he couldn't have reached the man.

Grant blinked hard like before in the courtroom, but nothing would shift the cloudiness. They'd dosed him heavily this time.

The figure came closer, and Grant could make out the Crown Prince's *thobe* and the familiar red-and-white-check of his headdress.

'You British never fail to amaze me,' Abdul said. 'Blundering into business that has nothing to do with you.'

All Grant could produce was a long string of drool spilling over his bottom lip.

Abdul continued, 'They told me that they gave you a dose that would have stopped a large horse. Yet here you are. Still fighting. It would be admirable if it wasn't all so futile.'

Grant started to laugh. A low chuckle at first, growing in volume.

Abdul said, 'You are in terribly good humour for a man who is going to have his head cut off in under,' he checked his diamond-encrusted watch, 'an hour and a half.'

As the effects of the sevoflurane started to wear off, Grant murmured, 'I...feel...sorry...for you...'

Abdul did the only thing he could in the circumstances. He laughed. 'You pity *me*?'

'You might wear the clothes of Islam...but you'll never know what it's like to believe in something.'

'And you, Mr Grant. What do you have that's worth so much in this moment? Face it: you fought for nothing. Gave up your life for nothing. To protect the shameful secrets of MI6. And now you're going to die. They'll stitch your head back onto your body, and bury you in an unmarked grave as a non-believer. You'll die alone. And you'll rot alone.'

'I'm not...alone,' Grant stammered, half-delirious. 'Peggy Gordon. I'll always have Peggy Gordon.'

When two guards entered, Abdul stood up, preparing to leave. 'You can be as brave as you want, Mr Grant. I know what will really be in that head of yours when the sword is above it.'

Grant had to fight just to lift his head, summoning all his energy to call out, 'Abdul...'

He stopped in the doorway in silhouette.

'My head's killing me. You don't happen to have an aspirin, do you?'

Abdul hated that Grant was still fighting. Still defiant. He said, 'Goodbye, Mr Grant.'

49

Deera Square had long since cleared after *Jum'ah*, the Friday congregational prayers earlier that afternoon. The streets had quietened with the setting sun. All the shops and businesses had closed up. The roads were deserted, too.

Executions were never advertised in advance. Friday was the most common day for them, shortly after *Jum'ah*. An execution on a Friday evening was uncommon, but Riyadh had been known to execute as late as nine o'clock at night.

When locals on their balconies on the nearby streets saw the Mabahith arrive in several vans, setting up a perimeter at the centre of the square, calls soon cascaded along the streets from balcony to balcony.

An execution! was the cry.

The prevalence of mobile phones in Riyadh and the tight-knit communities meant that the word quickly spread, and Deera Square began to fill.

Speculation was rife on who was being brought to receive the Kingdom's – and, by extension, God's – justice. That was how most of the locals thought of the callous act about to take place there, giving the square its other namesake: Al-Safaa Square.

Justice Square.

The *sayyaf*, or swordsman, Faisal bin Nayef Aziz, was the first of the officials to arrive, pulling up in his own car to gentle applause and some cheers. The arrangements had been hasty, rushed through by the Crown Prince himself. When the *sayyaf* received the call after *Jum'ah* he wasted no time, packing up his sword in its leather scabbard. There had been no need to check the blade for imperfections before leaving: his children, as they often did, had helped him clean it the previous evening.

If anyone had made plans for that evening, they were immediately forgotten about. Outside of Riyadh, watching Aziz in action was considered a gift, seeing an artisan at work. None of the Kingdom's other executioners operated with such flair and smoothness of motion as Aziz. For the capital's locals, there were increasing opportunities to see him in action: the rate of executions had skyrocketed in recent years – the vast majority political activists.

While Aziz strode to the cleared area at the centre of the square, murmurs broke out about who the offender was. Word had leaked from Ulaysha Prison that the condemned was a Westerner. An unheard-of event.

It was illegal to record executions in the Kingdom, but the fervour with which the police checked and re-checked the gathered onlookers for illicitly recording mobiles suggested that something unique was on the schedule.

The Crown Prince exited his black Mercedes to applause and cheers from the people assembling. He gave agreeable waves to them, keeping close to Ghazi. Abdul greeted Aziz by shaking his right hand. '*Assalaam 'alaikum,*' he said.

May peace be upon you.

Aziz replied in kind. '*Wa 'alaikum assalaam.*'

And peace be upon you.

A white van pulled up outside the square, pointing its headlights into the square to aid visibility.

Grant was pulled from the back of the vehicle. He had a black hood over his head, and couldn't see anything through it other than the faintest hint of the Mabahith's vehicles' headlights.

In the gathering darkness and with a hood on, Grant's other senses lit up. He could hear hushed conversation from the hundred or so that had gathered. He could feel sand on the bricks underfoot. He could smell cooked lamb in the air.

These were the things he thought of as being his final memories.

And then from nowhere, he found the tune of 'Peggy Gordon' appearing in his head. Like a mantra to comfort him in his last minutes.

The fascination with getting a closer look at the condemned Westerner forced the Mabahith officers to assert themselves in restraining the crowd.

Grant was able to walk, but the guards kept a forceful grip of his forearms to lead him to the clearing. There was a good twenty-metre gap between the execution spot and the public. Although they were an intrinsic part of the proceedings, the authorities still insisted on a certain level of decorum and respect from the public. The Mabahith were vicious in their retribution for any inappropriate behaviour.

Aziz prowled the cleared area, like a caged lion having to make do with insufficient space. This was his favourite part: the anticipation. Relishing the sombre energy of the public. He loved feeling their adoring eyes on him. Basking in his pure, unrestrained masculinity.

He rolled out a black fabric mat where Grant would be brought to kneel, smoothing it with his hand, almost caressing the material. His reverence for what was about to happen was no act. He saw his job as a great responsibility. Every execution required a diligent attitude. No one wanted to see a *sayyaf* require several hacks at someone's neck in order to behead them. The people wanted clean quick kills.

After all, they weren't savages.

Grant tried to focus only on the tune of 'Peggy Gordon'.

He had often wondered how he would stack up when his time came around. Would he take it like his dad, or would he find some strength? Some people questioned why it mattered how a man conducts himself in his final moments. To which Grant would have said, when your final moments are all that's left, it matters a great deal.

He felt a hand on his shoulder pressing him down.

It was Aziz's.

Grant didn't know how quickly it would happen once he was on his knees. Would they say a prayer? Would they say nothing? How would he even know it was about to happen? Would he feel the blade on the back of his neck first? Some kind of collective intake of breath from the crowd as the *sayyaf* raised his sword high above his head? Or would everything turn black before he even realised the blade was about to land?

Grant didn't feel fear. He was just acutely aware of an imaginary timer counting down. What happened when the timer stopped, he didn't know. But he didn't fear it. To him, it made no sense to fear death. In his experience, people fear death more than pain. Which Grant had always found odd. Life hurts a lot more than death. When the blade landed on his neck, the pain would be over. Then death, as Jim Morrison once said, became a friend.

ANDREW RAYMOND

Aziz explained in Arabic, 'Stay very still and it will be over quickly. Move, and it will be extremely painful.'

He adjusted Grant's neck angle, tilting it lower for a thicker, fuller target. He looked at the sky, wishing there was more light. Once the sun fell below the horizon, night-time came on fast in the Kingdom.

Grant was aware of the guards that had been standing at his side now retreating. He was in Aziz's hands now.

As Aziz removed the blade, it made a harsh, high-pitched slicing sound against the grain of his leather scabbard.

Grant braced himself. Would it be agony? A white-hot instant of searing agony? Or just blackness. As fast as putting out a light?

Abdul took half a step forward, his eyes hungry for the sight of the blade making contact.

Then he whipped around at the sound of two sharp – and loud – snaps in quick succession from the edge of the square. None of the crowd could say for sure what they were. But when they saw Aziz peer into the gloom, his arms held up at his shoulders in shock, a number of cries rang out. They had better eyesight than the others, and saw the blood seeping through Aziz's *thobe* at the chest. The stains grew. Unmistakably blood.

50

Ghazi grabbed Abdul, pushing him low to the ground as chaos broke out all around. People running in every direction as the five gunmen advanced into the square. They were armed with powerful high-capacity assault rifles. It would be a long time before they ran out of bullets.

Grant's shoulders involuntarily shot up towards his ears, then he felt the crushing weight of Aziz's body land in his lap. Grant sprang himself back, losing balance in the process. With his hands still cuffed, he lay helpless on the ground on his side.

The police and Mabahith all turned on their heels to fire at the shooters. Before they could even reach their weapons, another three near-simultaneous shots rang out.

The Riyadh locals might not have understood the sound, but Grant did. They were the sounds of suppressed gunfire from M4 carbine assault rifles.

Within a few seconds, there were five more bodies on the ground. The crowd scattered in terror. Riyadh was normally as safe as you would expect from a city ruled with an iron fist. The locals – many of whom were too young to even have a memory of a terror attack – had softened since the early years following nine eleven, when Al Qaeda had made inroads to the Kingdom. Everyone thought that those days were long gone, but apparently not.

From the corner of Al Thumairi Street, the gunmen emerged wearing brown *thobes*, and making light work of their opponents.

Ghazi hustled Abdul into his Mercedes and sped away, clipping a number of pedestrians as he drove with reckless abandon through the square.

The police and Mabahith retreated to take cover, relinquishing the square to the attackers. They couldn't have cared less about leaving Grant on his own. They weren't going to risk their lives for a condemned man.

Unable to reach his hood, Grant was an open target for the shooters. Then a hand grabbed the back of his shirt collar, hauling him to his feet.

'Let's go,' one of the gunmen told him, hauling him along and keeping him low. 'Keep moving, Grant,' the man said.

He pulled Grant's hood off on the move, while some of the Mabahith officers decided to actually try firing their guns, if for nothing other than the appearance to the public of having put up some defence.

Absorbing themselves into the fleeing crowd, three of the gunmen dropped their weapons and ran at full speed towards a waiting van on the corner of the square under a palm tree, the engine running. Grant was thrown into the back seat, and had to duck down as the bodywork was struck by several Mabahith bullets.

All five of the gunmen were safely inside, the van speeding away, racing through the crowded streets against the flow of traffic.

The driver had no other option but to mount the pavement, blasting his horn and flashing his headlights to clear some space to get through.

'What's happening?' Grant spluttered, overcome and disoriented.

The man who had grabbed him said, 'Leo Winston had a message he wanted to give you. He said you would know what it meant.'

'Leo?' said Grant. 'What have you done with Leo?'

The gunman shook his head. 'He said, "no man left behind." We're Fifteen Flags, brother.' He held out his hand. 'Not every Saudi is with men like the Crown Prince or the Mabahith.'

Grant shook it slowly at first, then with increasing force. He pulled the man into an embrace. 'Bloody Nora, am I glad to see you...' The enormity of what had just happened hit him like a truck. He tilted his head back and let out a visceral howl of relief. 'Shit...!'

'My friend,' the leader explained, 'we don't have much time.' He showed Grant a tablet that had a map of the country on it. 'Vauxhall Cross received a communication from Henry Marlow four hours ago. He's set a location. He wants you.'

'I don't understand,' said Grant.

'He has Gretchen. We have to get you to Marlow or he's going to blow the data centres. Marlow wants you and you alone.'

51

The highways were empty on a Friday night, allowing the Fifteen Flags operatives to make quick progress south out of Riyadh, heading deep into the Rub' al Khali desert. It wasn't called the Empty Quarter for nothing. As far as the horizon, there was nothing but increasingly mountainous sand dunes, electricity pylons, and the faint glow of oil well flares.

The highway cut a path through the dunes, promising only a greater, deeper emptiness the further it went.

The driver had killed the headlights. They could be seen from too far away. He flinched whenever anything appeared even half a mile back in his rear-view mirror.

The sky was completely clear, the last traces of sunset to the west making way for an abundance of stars.

Grant's only thoughts were on Gretchen and stopping Marlow. He was still coming to terms with his near-execution, humming away like a phone app analysing data in the background while the screen's off.

It wasn't long ago that only camels could traverse such a

harsh and unforgiving landscape. The construction of roads through the Empty Quarter oil fields was testament to the almost limitless resources of the Arabco Oil Company – Abdul's family company.

The road still showed evidence of the tail end of the most recent *shamal* – a season from spring to summer where wind speeds could reach up to thirty miles per hour, dry winds capable of shifting huge amounts of sand. Keeping the roads clear during *shamals* was a constant task. It wasn't unheard of for entire mile-long sections of road to disappear under the sand.

The driver said something in Arabic to the team leader.

'We're here,' he told Grant. 'This is as far as it's safe to go. Marlow has threatened your agent if we come any closer.' He handed Grant a radio earpiece.

After a quick check, Grant heard Winston coming through from Vauxhall Cross.

'Grant,' Winston said, his voice grave, 'it's good to have you with us.'

'Thanks, boss. For–'

'We don't have much time, Grant,' Winston said. 'He's got Gretchen. She should be there with Charles Joseph already.'

'Leo,' said Grant, 'I can't kill him. I can't kill Marlow. He's–'

'We know, Grant. He told us about the decryption code. You've got to get it out of him. Somehow…'

'Sounds like a great plan, Leo,' Grant muttered.

'I'm going to be right here with you, okay?'

As Grant prepared to go, the leader offered him a gun.

'I can't shoot him,' said Grant. 'And I can't risk antagonising him. There's no way he won't search me.'

'Okay,' he replied, taking out a small bottle instead. 'You should try.' He demonstrated holding the bottle up to his nose. 'To clear the drugs in your system. It will help, my friend.'

Grant took the bottle, recoiling from the stench of ammonia before he had even opened it.

Smelling salts.

It only took the briefest waft near Grant's face to give him a jolt – the ammonia gas rocking Grant's nasal and lung membranes, triggering a violent respiration that sent a rapid hit of oxygen to his brain. Grant gave a quick shake of his head, feeling sharper already.

He made his final thanks to the Fifteen Flags operatives. '*Alf shokr*,' he said.

A thousand thank yous.

The leader replied, '*Yeayishak.*'

Wishing you long life.

'Yeah,' said Grant. 'I'm not so sure about that right now...'

52

The Fifteen Flags van left him at a turn-off from the main road to a dirt track that was mostly covered by sand. The air was sharp and chilly – it only took a few hours for the temperature to drop massively in the Empty Quarter. A brisk wind had kicked up as well.

The winding track led towards a group of bright orange flares on top of tall metal towers, burning off excess gasses to maintain safe pressures in the oil field. The refinery was another ten miles away. Far out of sight.

There was no time to hang about. Gretchen could already have been in harm's way. He caught little glimpses of her in his mind as he ran. How she had looked at him on the *cueva* dance floor. Heat in both their eyes.

Grant slowed as he saw a brick hut up ahead that was surrounded by a perimeter razor-wire fence. The end of the road. To go anywhere beyond towards the wells required off-road vehicles, or a heck of a lot of leg power to stomp through the soft, deep sand.

Marlow was waiting for him, standing on his own in front of the brick hut. He was holding a pistol. He called for Grant to stop, and show if he was carrying.

Grant lifted his light linen shirt, showing nothing held in his waistband, or holstered at the ankle.

When he got within fifty feet, Marlow called out, 'Even if I told you checkmate was coming soon, it wouldn't help you see how it was going to happen. You have to look at the whole board to see it, Duncan. You can't see it all. Not yet. But you will.'

'Where's Gretchen?' he demanded.

'All in good time, Duncan.'

'Whatever you want with her, take me instead. She was never in this with us. It was me who sent you into Vauxhall Cross. Me who stopped you.'

Marlow sighed. 'Oh Duncan…can't you see yet? You didn't stop me. I gave myself to you. Do you really think I would have left myself with no escape in that underground tunnel? That I didn't know you would stop me shooting myself when I was cornered? It was all leading to this. This moment between us.'

'Then keep it that way,' said Grant. 'Why involve Gretchen?'

Marlow shook his head. He sounded disappointed. 'You're still not seeing the whole board, Duncan. But you will soon enough.' He pointed the gun at Grant, getting him to back up.

In the distance, from the direction Grant had just come from, was the faint silhouette of an SUV with its headlights off.

'This is one of his fields,' Marlow said, checking the magazine of his gun. 'The great Crown Prince Abdul. Seems as appropriate a place as any to end it.' He didn't take his eyes off the approaching car snaking its way through the dunes. 'When this is over, Duncan. I really hope you can understand what I've done. When I was a boy, I would visit my grandfather and we would play chess. Sometimes there would be months between visits, but we kept our game going the whole time. It went on for two years. Each time I went back, I looked at the board to check where all the pieces were. I never forgot. Of course, my grandfather wasn't the cheating type. He died before we got to finish our game. To this day, I still remember where all the pieces were on his board. Just like you will remember all the moves that led to our game here. It's your final puzzle, Duncan.' His eyebrows lifted at the thought. 'I wish I could go back to where you are now. So many choices to make.'

Grant didn't know what to believe. His thoughts returned to the scenes at Joseph's Congolese compound, and the scenes of depravity and violent anarchy Grant had found there. Marlow's psyche had broken long ago.

In the Tank, Christie conferred with Winston, as they and Randall listened in to the satellite feed.

'What do you think he's playing at?' asked Christie.

Winston replied, 'Whatever's coming, Marlow has thought it through logically.'

Christie said, 'That doesn't really do much to drain the feeling of dread in my stomach.'

Winston stared in pure fear at the drone thermal-imaging of the scene on Randall's screen. Winston said, 'Imagine how Grant's feeling right now...'

The SUV trundled to a halt, stopping a stone's throw away from Marlow and Grant.

Grant tried to prepare himself for whatever might happen. If the Devil himself emerged from the car, Grant wanted to have anticipated it.

As it turned out, it wasn't far away from the Devil.

Charles Joseph stepped down off the running board at the passenger side, holding his wounded shoulder, a gun in his free hand. He paused at the sight of Grant, giving a dismayed chuckle. 'Henry,' he announced. 'Call me crazy, but this is no longer feeling like an equal partnership.'

'Whatever do you mean, Charles?' Marlow asked.

Gretchen stayed back, letting the three others help Joseph forward.

Joseph groaned from the effort of walking. 'I'm lucky that the bullet in me didn't kill me. It might yet...'

'Shame,' said Marlow. 'I had rather been banking on Tagan finishing you off.'

Joseph swung around to take aim at Gretchen's head, despite the pain it caused him. He called out to Marlow, 'You said that Grant was dead.'

'How about that,' said Gretchen. Knowing there were no moves she could make, she allowed the American agent to disarm her.

'You knew about this?' Joseph asked Marlow.

'I knew that if MI6 were *really* swapping me for one of their operatives in that transfer, they would have vested him at the front. That's what they do to actual prisoners in those transfers.'

Joseph said, 'You knew that Grant wasn't dead. You let me take in a mole.'

'I was hoping it would be Gretchen. Anyone else would have worked too. But Gretchen is better.'

'You wanted Tagan to kill me.'

'Let me guess...too much brandy?'

'You should never get drunks to do your work for you, Henry.' Joseph turned his gun on Marlow.

'Ah, ah, easy now,' Marlow warned him. 'Kill me, and three

point four billion is gone forever. Frozen in cryptocurrency. If you kill me–' he looked around Joseph's men, so they understood what was at stake, '–if anyone kills me, the decryption code dies with me. It's a very long number, Charles. If you feel lucky, you could always guess. Wouldn't recommend that, though.'

Joseph shook his head in confusion. 'Why would you hide it in cryptocurrency–'

Marlow interrupted, 'If we're destroying the internet? Surely you can work that out for yourself now.'

Grant snorted as the reality hit him. 'He was never going to do that.'

Marlow said, 'I'm glad someone's paying attention. Thank you, Duncan.'

Joseph looked beyond Marlow at the oil well flares. 'This is what you're blowing up? A couple of oil wells?'

'I thought you of all people would understand – that anyone, like the Crown Prince, who tries to kill me? I make sure they bleed. His wells are just an added bonus. Like an extra unrequested olive in a martini.'

Joseph no longer cared about anything else. He shouted, 'I want the money, Henry! After everything we have done together. You want to throw it all away. For what?'

'Don't be so ungrateful, Charles,' said Marlow. 'I helped you get your revenge. I got you inside with every target you wanted to hit…'

While everyone's attention was focussed on Marlow's gun and whether he would fire or not, only Grant and Gretchen saw the subtle move Marlow made towards his trouser pocket. He reached inside for a small radio detonator and pressed the fire button.

53

All along the dunes behind him, a wave of orange fire erupted from the ground, sending tonnes of sand into the air as the ten different explosions went off from left to right, covering a mile across.

The force of the blasts reached Marlow and everyone else a second later, causing the distraction necessary to allow him to fire off single rounds into Joseph's remaining operatives, dropping them all before they could return fire.

A wall of flames mushroomed hundreds of feet into the air, followed by a cloud of bilious black smoke as the oil wells burned.

In shock, Grant quickly dropped to the ground, expecting a shootout.

Vauxhall Cross went haywire in Grant's ear, reacting to the sight of an enormous heat cloud on Randall's screen, accompanied by the roar of the explosion and gunshots.

Joseph made a move towards the back of his trousers.

Marlow took aim at Joseph. 'Don't, Charles. You know you'll never get off a round before me.'

'Why?' Joseph asked, fighting through the pain.

Marlow replied, 'When I came to your compound all those years ago to kill you, Charles, you know what I saw? God's work. I saw it so clearly. This is what He does with the universe. Acting with chaotic randomness, striking down the innocent. You and I, Charles…we've seen too much to believe in anything anymore. But he…' Marlow pointed at Grant. 'Duncan still believes in something. And I find that inspiring.'

Grant backed up against the chain-link fence, nodding at Gretchen as she looked to him for reassurance.

Marlow continued, 'Your problem, Charles, is that you make decisions based on emotion. You're indiscriminate. You want to burn the whole world down. That's just…' He paused to think of the right words. 'Not me.' Marlow took aim at Joseph's head and pulled the trigger.

Grant turned away, telling Vauxhall Cross. 'Joseph's down. It's just Marlow, Gretchen and I.'

Marlow turned witheringly to Grant with his hand held out. 'Duncan, I can't have this commentary in the background. It's really distracting.'

Grant slowly reached towards his ear and pulled the radio out.

Gretchen was still reeling in shock from Joseph's murder. She kept staring at his body.

Marlow took up a position between Grant and Gretchen, alternating between aiming at them. 'And then there were three…' he said.

Oil began to fall like rain in a mixture of fat globules and a fine mist.

Grant got back to his feet. 'What do you want, Henry? As far as I can see, it's over. You've got the money all to yourself.'

Marlow retorted, 'I think we both know that I'm not interested in the money.'

Grant held his hands out. He didn't attempt to get close to Marlow. 'Henry,' he said, 'in half an hour this whole place is going to be crawling with the Mabahith. Is that part of your grand plan, too?'

'No. I want to talk to you about what you believe.'

Gretchen glanced at a pistol lying next to one of the dead operatives.

When Grant shook his head to say 'no', Marlow whipped around to aim at her again.

Marlow said, 'See, Charles was a guy who saw more horror than anyone I've ever known. Cannibalism, genocide, routine dismembering of limbs and torture: these were all normal for him. The guy never stood a chance!' He wagged his finger at Grant. 'But you...' He walked towards him. 'You, Duncan, have every chance. What I want, is for Grant to prove me wrong...'

As soon as Grant saw Marlow's shooting arm stiffen, he charged at him.

Gretchen could tell what was going to happen. Her face was a picture of acceptance.

'I'm sorry, Gretchen,' Marlow said, taking aim at her. 'But everyone who comes after me dies. Eventually.'

Grant was still a distance away when he screamed, 'No!'

Gretchen closed her eyes, knowing that Marlow had already decided, and there was nowhere to run. 'It's okay, Duncan,' she told him. 'Try not to–'

Marlow squeezed the trigger, letting off a gunshot that was louder than anything Grant had ever heard. It stopped him in his tracks. After stumbling a few steps while Gretchen hit the ground, he ran to her.

Crouching beside her, the edges of his vision went black. His mouth hung open, trying in vain to produce any kind of sound. Even though he knew in his heart that she was dead, he still tried to pump life into her heart, and air into her lungs.

Marlow tossed his gun on the ground without so much as a glimmer of emotion at what he had done. It meant nothing to him. Nothing at all.

'It won't help, Duncan,' he said, falling to his knees at the centre of all the dead bodies. He knelt down, like a man awaiting an executioner. 'What you need in a game of chess, above all, Duncan,' Marlow explained, 'is to be exceptionally good at attacking your opponent's weakness.'

Grant pulled back from Gretchen's mouth. She looked like any other dead body he had ever seen. The chilling stillness. The frozen expression.

Marlow elaborated, 'In your case, Duncan, it's your moral superiority. Your steadfast refusal to kill someone not because you have to. But because you *want* to. That's what MI6 wants you to be. That's what they *need* you to be.'

Grant finally met Marlow's eyes. 'What have you done?' he said under his breath.

'You believe you're on the side of good,' said Marlow. 'So I had to destroy everything you believe in. Only then can you fully understand what I am. How they take all that idealism, and turn you into a killer. Then they take that killer, and turn you into a butcher. Into a savage…'

Grant wiped the oil from her face, from her hair, that was turning from red to black.

Grant stood up and faced him, staring at the gun on the ground.

Marlow bowed his head. 'It's time to do what you never could before. To overcome that last weakness. Become like me. Take your revenge, Duncan…'

In the Tank, Winston and the others looked on in horror as the scene unfolded almost silently now – Grant's radio only picking up the faintest trace of Marlow's voice.

Randall played with the equaliser to get a better reception.

Christie held her hands to her face in dismay.

Winston's heart was pounding, his fingers trembling as he told Grant on the radio, 'Duncan, listen to me. This is what he wants you to do…'

Christie could barely watch as the screen showed a scattering of bodies appearing as white on the thermal-imaging.

Grant was walking slowly towards Marlow.

54

Grant could hear Winston's voice emanating distantly from the earpiece dangling around his neck. But he wasn't listening.

He picked up the gun and held it against Marlow's forehead. 'You want me to be just like you. Lost. Alone. Vengeance your only fuel.'

'It *is* a choice,' Marlow admitted. 'That much is true.'

Grant's knuckles were white. He had never held onto a gun so tightly in his life. 'You think if I shoot you that it proves how corrupt the world is? Huh? Is that it? That the world will somehow make more sense if you can turn me into a killer like you?' In his peripheral vision, he could see Gretchen's body on the ground. He forced himself not to look at it, because he knew what would happen if he did. 'You want me to shoot you. To put you out of your misery.' Fighting back tears, he croaked, 'That's not what she would want...' He pulled the gun away, leaving behind an indentation on Marlow's forehead from the pressure. 'I want the decryption code, Henry.'

'Then you want something you can never have, Duncan. It

dies with me.' He glanced at him, checking his emotional temperature. 'Don't think about what Olivia Christie and the Foreign Secretary will do if they find out. Think about how much Gretchen's life was really worth to you.'

Grant stepped back, shaking his head at Marlow's mind games. He knew that Marlow would never give up the decryption code either way. He just wanted to give Grant reason to doubt the path he wanted to take.

The oil was stinging his eyes. He tried to wipe it away with the back of his hand, but that was covered in oil as well.

Marlow's face and body were illuminated orange from the vast flames over the dunes behind. Giving him a demonic glow.

Marlow told him, 'See the whole board, Duncan. It's your move.'

Grant looked past him at Gretchen. Crumpled on the ground.

All it took was a fraction of a glance for him to decide.

'She wouldn't want me to...' Grant took two more steps away.

Marlow knew what was coming, though. He closed his eyes in relief. He was going to win.

When Winston saw Grant retreat, he puffed in relief. Then the white body on the screen turned back towards Marlow with his arm out.

Winston cried out, 'No...!'

Marlow's body shot backwards in sync with a burst of white light from the end of Grant's outstretched arm.

Randall asked, 'Were those gunshots? Those looked like gunshots.'

Christie exhaled as she turned her back on the screen. 'They were gunshots,' she confirmed.

Grant kept the gun held out. He said, '...but I have to.'

The loss of Gretchen hit him in an instant, as further explosions rocked the oil wells behind.

In his earpiece, Winston was shouting, 'Grant! I'm sending Fifteen Flags to get you. Hold on, son...I'm not leaving you there. Just hold on...'

At the inner doors of the Tank, Christie was on her phone. She said, 'I need the next free minute that the Foreign Secretary has got.'

Grant dropped the gun by Marlow's side. He looked to the sky, his eyes closed. He wiped his hands down his face. Oil dropped from his fingertips like blood. Staining the sand.

The Fifteen Flags operatives were speeding their way back to him at breakneck speed.

For Grant, there was only one thing left to do now.

Run.

ONE MONTH LATER

Winston waited until nearer closing time before heading to the King's Arms. It was Friday night, and the place was full of ageing politicos from Westminster, lawyers, and anyone else who wanted to watch the football on big screen TVs while chart music played at obnoxious levels that made conversation impossible.

As soon as Winston made it to the bar, having to push his way through the throng to get there, he remembered why he never usually came in on a Friday night. The atmosphere was different. Few regulars. The music was different too. Most of all, everyone was much worse for wear. Winston couldn't work out if he had rose-tinted glasses on about 'the good old days', but the atmosphere in the city around weekends was less jovial. The drinking was harder, like people were trying to get away from something, rather than purely celebrating or having a good time with friends.

Ordinarily, he would have turned at first sight of the crowd and gone home. But it hadn't been an ordinary day.

Winston ordered his pint from a barmaid he didn't recognise, and who certainly knew nothing about his ritual. 'Barry not in?' he asked.

The barmaid made a pained expression and held her ear out.

'Barry not in?' he repeated, louder this time.

'Night off,' she replied.

He brought the pint closer, receiving a shove from someone from behind. He shot them an irritated glance.

The offender raised his hands in apology, his eyes narrow, speech slurred. 'Sorry, mate, sorry, mate…'

'You're alright,' Winston told him with the barest thread of patience.

He stared into his pint as he always did, thinking about how far he had come. Four years sober. It was supposed to feel good – like a victory. He just couldn't figure out what he'd won.

He looked around the pub, taking the scene in again with fresh eyes. Was this what he had sacrificed his life for? The freedom to do all of this? To protect this?

He thought about Grant. Lost and alone out there. He hadn't called in as expected since the Fifteen Flags had aided his escape from Saudi Arabia. He wondered if Grant was even still alive. Whether one day soon a call would come through from some small Scottish police department when Grant's fingerprints, matched up with those kept on file for him, were flagged by the Ministry of Defence, and Winston was called on to make the twelve-hour journey to identify a body.

He knew that there had been something between Grant and Gretchen. But he'd had no idea of the impact it was having on Grant.

Winston felt as awful as the day before his last drink. And he didn't think it got much worse than that. It had been a feeling far beyond displacement. It was a feeling of being completely unmoored. To anything. To anyone. He had piled his life's worth into MI6. Without that, what was he really for?

That he didn't have an answer to that scared the hell out of him. It also made him question his routine in the pub. What was the point of going through all of the temptation and pain of sobriety if he was still going to feel the same at the end of a day. At least when he was drinking it gave him a few hours of respite from the grind.

That was the scariest thing of all to Winston: all the things that he thought he believed about his life were falling away, and he didn't know how to stop it.

He turned to leave, his pint still standing there.

The barmaid watched him through the window, expecting him to stop outside for a cigarette. But he didn't. He kept walking. Winston had had enough.

The barmaid picked up his glass, wondering to herself why someone would have two sips of a pint and then leave?

It wasn't just the change to his usual routines that made Winston feel off. Before he left for the night, the Foreign Office had received confirmation that Gretchen, Marlow, and Charles Joseph's bodies had been found near the scene of the oil well explosion. It was going to take days to cap the wells, after which their capacity would take months to recover.

It wasn't about oil, though. Or destroying the internet. That much was clear. What MI6 did know from the analysed drone footage was that Grant had killed Marlow with multiple gunshots. And now he was off-grid with absolutely no safety net or extraction team in a country whose second-in-command had just tried to have him beheaded. There weren't many people who had experienced the kind of isolation and loneliness that Duncan

Grant would be feeling right now. But Leo Winston was one of them.

A few minutes later during his walk home, Winston's phone rang.

Number withheld.

'Leo,' he answered.

'Can you talk?'

Winston stopped walking. It was Grant's voice.

'Where are you?' asked Winston.

He paused. 'Back home. Skye.'

'You need to come in, Duncan.'

'I'm not coming in.'

Winston sighed disconsolately. 'Grant, listen to me. You have to. Olivia told me today that there's going to be an enquiry.'

'About Marlow?' asked Grant.

Winston snapped, 'About Marlow, about the money – everything, Grant! Everything!' He closed his eyes and tried to take a calming breath. 'They're going to suspend me.'

'Of course they are,' said Grant. 'It's never the ones at fault who pay.'

'Randall got the money back.'

'How did he manage that?'

Winston laughed darkly. 'He figured out the decryption code. Six figures. Guess what it was.'

'I couldn't begin to.'

'One two three four five six.'

Grant said nothing. It was Marlow's last laugh. One last laugh into the abyss.

Winston went on, 'The Foreign Sec doesn't care. He wants your head, Grant. The money was still in play when you shot Henry Marlow.'

'That was the job I was given,' replied Grant.

'Yeah, well…you and me both, sunshine.'

Grant said, 'I was in my car tonight, driving around the island. It was pitch black, and I realised after five minutes that I'd been driving without my lights on. I pressed the accelerator, speeding up and speeding up. I couldn't see a thing. The only thing keeping me on the road was my memory. I didn't care anymore. I just wanted…to feel something. Something other than this. That was when I realised what has to happen now. Who's to blame for all of this. For Kadir Rashid. Marlow. And now Gretchen. I'm going to find them. I won't stop until they're in the ground.'

Winston paused. 'Duncan, I know you must be very upset right now. Why don't I come up to see you?'

'By the time you get here I'll be gone.'

'Duncan–'

'Do you think I'm broken, Leo? Is that it? I am not broken. I've never seen things so clearly in my life. They're going to pay.'

Grant hung up.

Winston held on, until eventually the line went dead.

In his living room, Grant surveyed the pictures and photos and maps that he had assembled ahead of his next mission. He had itineraries, timetables, and the photos he had taken of Gretchen Winter outside the restaurant in Granada. Taken on a burner phone as part of their cover.

He had printed out a copy of it and pinned it to the wall. As a reminder to himself of what it was all about. The mission that could very well be his last.

He took down the pictures of Crown Prince Mohammad bin

Abdul and Foreign Secretary John Wark. But he left Gretchen's attached. It seemed somehow appropriate.

All that was left to do was pick up the holdall he had packed, slip on his navy baseball cap and brave the weather outside. It had turned sharply from clear skies to rain and thunder.

It could do that on Skye.

As well as in the heart of a covert operative with revenge on his mind, and nothing left to lose.

* * *

THE END

Duncan Grant will return in 2022.

ACKNOWLEDGMENTS

Without the incredible editing, support, and love of my wife Emma, this book wouldn't be half of what it is. I couldn't do this without you.

There were a few resources that were invaluable in the writing of *Dead Flags*.

I started considering how a terrorist might try to destroy the internet after reading Sam Biddle's brilliant article about it in Gizmodo.

Tubes by Andrew Blum (Penguin Books). This is an immensely interesting book about the internet, and what parts it's really made of.

Paul R. Spickard's book from 2005 *Race and Nation: Ethnic Systems in the Modern World* provided some helpful tidbits of the history of the Turkmen people. And Drew Binsky's YouTube travelogue series was very helpful on some background information on the country itself in the modern age.

* * *

Finally, to all of you, dear readers, thank you for all of your lovely emails, Facebook comments and messages, and anything else. They are truly appreciated. As I always say, a writer is nothing without readers, and you lot are the best out there.

Your good humour and encouragement really keep me going.

- Andrew

Printed in Great Britain
by Amazon